CW01500502

CRUSHING SNAILS

CRUSHING SNAILS

Emma E. Murray

Published by Apocalypse Party

Book Design by Mike Corrao
Cover Design by Matthew Revert

Paperback: 978-1-954899-15-5

To the love of my life, Martin,
and my sisters Tara and Hannah.

Thank you for the love, support,
and hours of conversation about serial killers.

WINNIE CAMPBELL

AGE 11

The drill rattles the wall, pausing only long enough for Mom's hands to pick at the bits of plaster and peer inside before starting again. I know that's what she's doing because I've watched her from the cracked kitchen door night after night. It's always the same. Pulling my pillow over my head, I try to ignore it, but this is the fourth night in a row. I just want to sleep. Anger slithers up my throat and my face burns red, the rage simmering just below the skin.

Dad's in the hall, waiting for me. He must've known the lack of sleep has been getting to me.

"Honey, you know she can't help it. I'm gonna try to get her to come to bed again in just a bit."

"Do it now." I stamp my foot but make sure my voice doesn't rise above a harsh whisper.

"I tried." He runs his hands through his hair, avoiding my eyes. Still, without looking at me, he reaches out, rubs my shoulder. His hand feels heavy with guilt. The color drips from his face, leaving it the ghostly pale of shame. Nausea clenches my stomach and the world tumbles around me. I love him, pity him, despise him, need his comfort all at once. Dad clicks his tongue. It's not his fault, but I hate how he's always apologizing for her. "You know how she is. Let's let her search a little longer and I'll try again."

Back in my room, the sounds of demolition have stopped, but Mom's muffled ravings carry through the weakened walls.

"How dumb do they think I am? Of course, I noticed. How could I not? I know you're listening. Goddamn spies!"

Her fingers poke and scratch inside the holes, pulling out chunks of drywall, trying to find anything to prove it isn't all in her head. As her voice fluctuates between anger and pitiful wailing, a tight feeling catches in my throat, painful and phlegmy.

I cover my head again and pray she'll tire herself out quickly, that her renovations won't go too far into the night. I need some sleep. There's a math test and the first round of eliminations for the spelling bee tomorrow, and I can barely spell my own name after so many sleepless nights. But my prayers are unanswered as the minutes, then hours, pass by.

At one point, I hear Dad talking to her again, but it quickly grows into a furious shouting match, followed by his footsteps stomping away. The drilling begins again. I glance at the clock on my nightstand, the numbers glowing red and angry: 1:00 am.

When I open the kitchen door, it's exactly what I expect to see. Mom in her nightgown, bare feet covered in chalky dust and paint chips, her hands white with plaster except for the cuts where drops of blood bloom out through the cakey mess. The drill is on the counter next to her. The wall is more holes than wall at this point, wooden studs showing through them like gaping wounds. Mom's peering into one of the smaller, higher holes that she'd just started on last night. Her lips move as she talks to herself, an unintelligible murmur from across the room. She's so engrossed, she doesn't notice me until I speak.

"Mom, you've gotta stop. It's so late and there's school tomorrow." The words are loud and firm, but I don't yell. I know better than to yell. It'd just rile her up more.

She stops, stares, her eyes looking not at me but straight through.

"Honey, lower your voice. The mice are recording us. We don't want to give them any more fodder than they already have." As she finishes, she casts a sneer at the ruined kitchen wall.

The anger bubbles and boils over. I can't contain it anymore. I want to stop myself, but I snap.

"No, they're not. I'm sick of playing along. Just look! Believe me, I've looked. We've *all* looked in the holes, hoping to see that you're not just losing your mind and torturing us, but there's nothing there! The government isn't spying on you. Why would they be? You don't have any secrets. You don't have anything worth knowing at all."

I regret it all the second it leaves my lips, but there's no taking back what I've said. Mom's face flashes with sharp hatred but then it breaks into a muddled, confused mess, the boundaries blurred like a drowned watercolor.

"You don't know what you're talking about."

"There's nothing there, Mom. No mechanical mice. No recording devices or cameras. It's not real. Please." I can't stop the tears that rush forth in a wave of quavering sobs. "Please, just stop. Believe me."

"I—" she pauses, her hands falling to her sides and dangling like dead fish. She tries to start but the words are gone with a sigh and a shake of her head. She tries again, but the words still fail her, and she finally closes her mouth, swallows, not looking at me. Slowly, tentatively, she raises her eyes to meet mine.

"I don't know if you're right or if you're wrong, but I agree, I'm tired too. That's true. You must be so very tired, sweetheart."

"I am." I collapse in the kitchen chair, its wooden feet screeching against the linoleum. I can hardly keep my eyes open as the adrenaline dissipates from my veins.

"Oh, goodness. Maybe I just need to sleep. But first, I think I need a little tea and maybe a snack to settle my nerves. Won't you stay with me, have a little? Please?" The way her voice breaks, meek as a child's, washes pity and a kind of anxiety over me, like I have to be the adult in the room. I hate that, but I accept it. I nod then place my face in my open palms, eyes against the hot skin.

"Okay, Mom. Okay."

The whoosh of water into the kettle, clicking of the burner then the roar of the blue flame coming to life, the tinkle of the matronly porcelain teacups that had once been her own mother's as she sets them out.

"Chamomile. Yes, a little of that will calm my nerves." I listen to her prattle to herself, but she doesn't sound deranged and confused. She sounds like my mom again and the lull of sleep nearly overtakes me.

The sizzle of oil in a pan. She's whispering about a bit of food. My stomach growls. Maybe she does still know best. I am a little hungry. I think back to all the times, years before when I was little and often scared, when I'd have a nightmare and she'd whip up a midnight snack to go with the lullaby and extra hugs that cast the spell of sleep on me again.

I pry my eyes open and look at Mom. So pale, she could be a ghost in her wispy, shapeless nightgown. When she turns to grab the plates, I'm taken aback by how drained she looks, all color gone except for the blue veins pulsing in her temples and the searing green of her irises. The way she moves, something just slightly off, wooden and ominous. I watch those eyes, glazed and empty, and my heart pounds in my throat. A tinge of fright shoots through my mind but I hush it away.

Mom hums as she takes the tea bags out of the cupboard. A dull, droning song rings in my ears and makes me dizzy.

The teapot screeches and Mom's arm darts out, grabs it, and I watch a stream of boiling water arc through the air. I close my eyes just as the scorching liquid splashes across my face. I can hear myself screaming, far away as if I weren't in my own body. High-pitched. Inhuman.

The blisters spring up instantly, bubbling in painful liquid pustules. I fall off my chair, shaking and scuttling on my side across the floor like an insect sprayed with poison. I cover my face with my hands, not quite touching the skin because that's too painful, but hovering shaky inches away as I rock back and forth in agony, curled into a fetal position, my sobbing so intense that I can't form any words beyond "Mommy!" Even in this moment, I can't help myself. I want to be comforted by my assailant.

My eyelids crack open just enough to see her face, a disgusting, proud smile gracing her lips. She takes the pan, holds it over me, her hand steady and the tiny sizzles of the oil whizzing above me. My eyes bulge and my mouth drops open, but I can't make a sound.

"Look what you made me do. You're one of them, and I know it. I'm not as stupid as you think I am. When did they get to you?"

Without a moment of hesitation, she tips the pan and I watch the stream of oil cascade down to my raw, burned skin. I hear it sizzle as I claw at my damaged face and arm, trying to wipe it away, but it's no use. The pain jumps through my brain like a white-hot flash. I try to squeeze my eyes shut, but as I thrash, the oil runs into one and I howl. My hand reflexively grabs at my face and the skin sloughs off from my cheek in a sticky sheet. The sensation of thick liquid oozing out of my injured eye, streaking warmly down the scalded flesh, causes terror to pulse through my being. I vomit down my shirt. Scrabbling to get up, run away, the slippery floor catches me, my feet slipping beneath me, my torso toppling hard against one of the kitchen chairs.

I no longer cry for Mom. She's a monster, and in that moment, I decide I never want her again.

"Daddy! Daddy!" I wail. I know the house is awake, but where are they? Is Brendan sleeping through my screams? Where's Dad to save me? On hands and knees, my far-off screams soften, fading into a pathetic puppy whimper. I have no energy to cry out for anyone anymore, only to ball up and attempt to disappear.

The world is a cotton ball muffled mess, but I make out the sounds of Mom boiling more water. I wince but cannot move away. The soft padding of a cabinet shutting. She's making tea, for real this time.

It's an eternity before Dad's heavy plodding footsteps finally enter the room. By then, I can't move. I can barely speak. Barely breathe.

"Winnie, oh god, what happened?"

They're fighting, back and forth, cursing and cussing, crying and screaming. It's all jumbled in my pain-numbed mind, but I know she's trying to convince him, like always. I see him take her in his arms from the corner of my eye, both shuddering with deep, guttural sobs.

He's bending over me, his hot breath against raw skin.

"Daddy, help." The words croak out through my hoarse, raw throat and my lips crack and burn with the movement. "I need to go to the hospital."

"Oh god. No, no, I can't. I'm so sorry." He's crying, his tears stinging my raw flesh as they fall, salt in my wounds. I don't understand, so I repeat my refrain for help again and again, even though the words hurt so much to form.

"Give me a minute to think," he says and stands up, paces. Mom is crying, huddled against the cabinets in the corner, as if she weren't to blame. I beg again for help. Why isn't he helping me?

"Daddy, why? Please help." Now my own tears sting and stain my face.

"Don't you understand? They'll take her away, Winnie! We have to fix this another way."

The breath leaves my lungs, my throat, my mouth, and I am empty. I want to die, and I think maybe I will. The betrayal turns my body to ice. I shiver uncontrollably.

Red lights flash through the kitchen window, lighting up the night. Dad is swearing and Mom is crying harder than ever.

"Fuck, the neighbors must've heard. Goddamn it, what are we going to do?"

He's not talking to me. I lay forgotten on the kitchen floor. No, worse than forgotten. I am trash. Lower than trash. The way they look at me and then each other, I wish I would die already.

Dad is bending down, hushing me and pretending to comfort me, but then he rattles off a list of demands. *Don't tell them what happened. You slipped and fell while cooking. It was all an accident.*

More cars arrive outside, their sirens screeching in the quiet night air. Banging on the door. Angry, worried, deep voices. I pass out, and when I come to, I'm in an ambulance. Alone. He didn't come with me. Nobody did.

"A PLEA TO THE PUBLIC: HELP ME FIND MY SISTER"

BRENDAN CAMPBELL
EXCERPT FROM *THE DAILY SUN*
DATED: JAN.30

You've heard of my sister, Winnie Campbell, even if her name is quickly fading from the spotlight. I can guarantee you've read at least one article about the "runaway teen murderess" with her occult interests, her bad reputation, and the gruesome details of the crimes. Crimes that the public has already decided she's committed without even giving her a chance to defend herself. It's no wonder she's still missing. I'd stay missing too if I read all those things about myself. But I'm begging you to pause and listen for a moment, so I can tell you who my sister really is. Then maybe someone out there might care enough to help me find her.

I won't lie. She can be annoying, arrogant, and a bratty younger sister, but she's not a monster. She's very caring and did lots of things to help our family. A bookworm, she's super smart and always got good grades. There are tons of reasons to admire her, and though I know some horrible things have come out about her, you need to understand what life was like for us growing up. Especially her. It wasn't easy.

I'm sure you've seen her scars in the pictures plastered across the news. Our own mom did that to her. For no reason. She was just a kid back then. We both were. Our house was a warzone and Winnie didn't take shelter from the storm in time. It was terrible. I stayed in my room when it happened, trying to pretend that none of it was real. That was what life was like for us back then. Survival was all I could manage, but I failed her. I'll always live with that.

Winnie, if you're reading this: I'm sorry. I promise I live with the shame and regret every day.

Maybe you're thinking, "Sure that's a sad story and all, but everyone's been through rough times. It doesn't excuse her crimes." I beg you to stop judging her when we don't have all the facts. I believe in my sister's innocence. The media wanted a juicy story, so they clawed into the idea of Winnie as a killer and haven't let up, but it isn't true. She certainly struggled with her mental health, but that doesn't make her a killer. She lived through so many horrific experiences at the hands of our parents, some so intense I can hardly believe they happened. I lived in denial for years, but I'm in therapy now, and finally waking up to reality. Yes, there's truth that she found solace in the dark and twisted, but I know she's *not* a murderer.

Winnie burdened it all alone, with nothing but a shell of a family who only offered the smallest shred of support. I know because I was part of it. All I can hope is that you might see she's a victim too. She needs our help and understanding, just like any other victim.

She's out there, scared and alone, hoping that someone can see past this vicious trial-by-media and give her a chance to tell her story. *You* can help. If you see her, you can reach out to her. She's not the monster you've been led to believe. Or you can reach out to me, even anonymously, using the website I've set up to give me any clue where she might be. Don't worry if you aren't sure. I'm checking out every lead. I won't give up.

This is my last chance to help her, after all the times I failed. Let me tell you just a little more about my sister, this supposed "monster" you all want burned at the stake. This girl we've all abandoned, ignored, then blamed without even considering other theories and possibilities.

Let me tell you a story of the Winnie I love, who's just a normal kid. The same as anyone's sister, daughter, niece. It's my favorite memory of Winnie, from a couple of years ago. We went to the big fair on the outskirts of town. Dad gave us pocket money and dropped us off. It almost felt like we were like a normal family.

Winnie was a surprisingly good shot at all those fake gun games and ended up winning this big pink rabbit for Lilly. And we ate so much cotton candy and funnel cake, I thought we were going to puke for sure, especially after riding the Scrambler so many times in a row.

I remember how happy both of my sisters looked, big grins spread across their faces and Lilly's long, black hair whipping around behind her. Winnie noticed this, and ever the nurturing, concerned sister, she kept trying to tie it back in a ponytail, saying she didn't want it to get stuck in the ride, but it wouldn't stay. Her hair was too silky. Silky and wildly free, the hair band gone almost instantly while the ride jostled us. Winnie was so worried, but Lilly just laughed and laughed. She laughed because it looked like the carts were going to hit each other, but they never did. Her cheeks were so red from giggling. I remember how young she looked with her one front tooth missing and the very edge of the new tooth just coming in.

And there next to her was Winnie, smiling despite the halfmoon of a healing black eye and the shiny scar tissue that trailed down her face. The worry was still there, wrinkled between her eyes, but she was smiling because she loved Lilly so much, and in that moment, we were all a family. A real family. A happy family.

She was always taking care of Lilly like a mother. Honestly, much more than our actual mother ever did. They looked beautiful together. I cherish this moment with my sisters. At that fair, we were there for each other. Loved each other. Protected each other. But as soon as we were home, things were back to normal, and I was the shitty brother I'd always been.

Please, I'm begging anyone reading this: Help me find her. Let's give her a real chance to tell her side of the story, and maybe you'll learn she's not a monster after all. Help me find her so I can have one more moment with my sister to tell her I love her.

To tell her I'm sorry.

WINNIE

AGE 16

Today begins the same as every day: I open my eyes, hold my breath, and wish as hard as I can that things will be different. They never are.

I get up, dress, make breakfast, iron Dad's work shirt, dress Lilly, go to school. It's so mechanical, so rote, I barely even notice time passing until I'm at school.

Sitting at the black lab table, tapping my pencil, I watch Gabe walk in. He struts more than walks, his green-tipped mohawk brushing the top of the doorframe and his handsome yet pockmarked face wearing a smirk. He's got that kind of effortless punk look that I could only dream of achieving. I notice he's wearing a bit more color than usual today, sporting some bright red Chucks. They must be new since we share so many clothes; I know his wardrobe inside out.

He sits down next to me, relieving the anxiety building inside me about finding a lab partner for the day. Often, he doesn't bother to show up to class at all, and sometimes he chooses someone else. That's always painful, but I don't know that he gets that. I think he does it just to mess with me. Says he likes to "branch out" occasionally, always with a playful wink, like I'm in on the joke. That's just his brand of fucked-up humor.

Mr. Jenkins is passing out the fetal pigs. This is it, the reason everyone looks forward to taking biology: the big dissection.

"Psst, look what I got last night," Gabe whispers and pulls down his collar, pointing to an obvious hickey halfway down his neck.

"A new guy or still seeing Jake?"

"New guy. I met him a few days ago. Wait, I didn't text you about him? You wouldn't believe the amazing weekend we had. Spent the whole time at his art studio downtown."

"Never mind that, how'd you get the new shoes?"

"The guy bought them for me," he says. I raise my eyebrow and smirk. He just laughs. "Fine. I borrowed some cash from the guy's wallet. Who cares?"

Mr. Jenkins gets to our table and places the tray down. The smell of formaldehyde causes us both to lean back, but we soon recover, gently exploring the tiny pig with gloved hands. Gabe examines our toolset, taking out a scalpel while clicking his tongue ring against his teeth.

"Nobody begin until I finish giving all the instructions," Mr. Jenkins says, looking at Gabe as he says it. Gabe puts the scalpel back on the table.

"So, what's the new guy's name?" I whisper.

"Dhruv or something," Gabe says, laughing. "I asked him to pronounce it a few times, but I'm still not sure. I probably won't see him again anyway, so it doesn't really matter."

"Because of those?" I ask, pointing at his shoes.

"Nah, not that. He was so wasted all weekend, I'm sure he thinks he spent it all himself. Plus, he's rich, so he won't care. Honestly, he was cool and all, but said he travels a lot several times, so I think he just wanted a fun weekend," he whispers in my ear as Mr. Jenkins walks by again. "But who knows? I'd see him again if he wants. It was a great time, if you know what I mean."

I nod and turn back to the piglet just as Mr. Jenkins finishes speaking.

Grayish pink and about the size of my hand, its tiny tongue sticks out. Its unborn eyes are closed in a peaceful way, never to open. It never really lived at all. I pick it up and turn it over once more, taking in all the angles, before I lay it on its back, little snout toward the sky.

Gabe takes the scalpel and carefully cuts at the legs and under the arms so we can pin them back and gain access to the tiny belly, full of the major bodily systems we've learned about. I take the scissors and cut a neat line from throat to tail, successful in not nicking any organs. We take turns, snipping and pulling, revealing the secret depths. One step at a time, we remove and examine the heart, lungs, liver, and intestines while making note of each in size, texture, color, and connection to surrounding organs. Our pig is soon an empty shell. His calm face pointed toward the sky while his ribcage is pulled taut like internal wings stirs something inside me. A dark excitement bubbles in my stomach and my head swims with grotesque delight. I try to explain this to Gabe, but he is too preoccupied with carefully opening the heart chambers to listen. I look up to the clock and see we've finished just in time.

"Please leave your pigs how they are, and I will dispose of them for you. I hope you all took detailed notes as next week we'll have the final test of the gross anatomy unit," Mr. Jenkins tells us, then graciously dismisses us five minutes early. I suppose some people might need that time to settle their stomachs.

"I'll see you at lunch in a bit. I have to go do something first," Gabe says, and I shrug as we file out the door.

The mixed smells of disinfectant cleaning products and mass-produced food assault my nose as I enter the cafeteria. Mindlessly, I get a tray, slide past the lasagna and cups of soup topped with greasy skins, and finally settle on a sad tuna sandwich with one limp leaf of lettuce hanging over the edges. Add an apple, a milk I most likely won't drink, and my lunch is complete. I so rarely eat this junk; I feel a twinge of guilt each time I checkout.

On the way to my usual table, Patrick bumps into me, probably hoping I drop everything. It wouldn't be the first time, but thankfully I don't. I just nod at his fake apology and keep going. I swear I hear him laughing as I sit down.

With a monotonous rhythm of bite, chew, swallow, pause, I keep my eyes on the latest thriller I picked up from the library. Then Gabe finally comes to lunch, tall and brooding, checking the spikes of his hair with his hand as he walks over.

"Okay, I'm back," he says, sitting down across from me. He grabs my apple, biting into it with a loud crunch. "I had to go get this out of the car because I knew you'd want to see it."

He puts a small black box on the table and pushes it toward me. It's the new tarot deck he'd told me about last week.

"Sweet." I open the box, gently removing the cards. The detail is stunning, and I pour over each one, noticing every tiny flower, intricate pattern, and character's facial expression. I love the crisp, new feel as I shuffle through them.

"Wanna do mine? You're so good now, it almost seems *real*. Plus, I still need tons of practice before I could ever trick some dumbass into giving me money for their fortune. Show me your ways, Mistress of Fate."

"Sure, but remember it's not real. Don't be so creepy about it like last time. It's just fun."

"Come on, just do a simple one." Gabe grabs the cards from my hands and shuffles, shutting his eyes halfway through. "Tell me my future, Mademoiselle Fortuna."

"Okay, fine. Just a simple one," I say, laying out four cards: the past, the present, the future, and lastly the signifier, which gives the overarching theme of the reading.

"I'm ready," Gabe says as he hovers over the cards. I turn over the first card, representing the past. It's the Lovers, naked and beautiful in a garden reminiscent of Eden. I bite my lip. Definitely true of Gabe's past.

"Your past is full of many lovers. Heh, we both know that," I say with a smirk. "In the past, your life has been full of relationships and sex as you tried to figure out the meaning of love."

I flip over the next card and reveal the Knight of Swords. I love this one, gallantly charging out to battle on his steed. I've always liked the knights best.

"Your present contains a Knight of Swords. He's independent, funny, smart, and unique. He fights for what he wants. He's the life of the party, but he's known to abandon people unexpectedly," I say, gently caressing the card.

"Hmm, so is this a guy I already know, or will I meet him soon?" he asks, but I just shrug.

"How should I know?"

I turn over the future card and we both freeze for a second, holding our breath. The Tower is struck by lightning, flames licking the night air and people flinging themselves to their deaths. I feel a little guilty and wonder if this one stupid card will ruin his good mood. Still, I continue, even though I'd rather we just forget the whole thing.

"The future holds a great loss. A devastating event beyond your control will occur," I say, but I don't look up, as

I can feel Gabe's eyes burning into me. He flips the final card, the signifier representing his life's overall theme, and it shows a figure on a throne holding a sword: Justice. I let out a sigh of relief and I feel Gabe's tension dissipate.

"Justice rules your life and will right the wrongs you encounter. I think that's a pretty good overarching card, don't you?"

"Yeah, plus this is all just stupid guesses anyway. But it's fun and all." He takes the cards and shuffles once before returning them to their box. "I want to do yours soon."

I laugh, but it gets stuck in my throat when I suddenly see Gabe glaring at something over my shoulder. I twist to see Patrick and some girl I don't know walking toward us. I turn away, but my face glows hot. Don't talk to me, please, don't say anything at all.

I hear them whispering and I can't make out the words, but the girl starts laughing. My stomach backflips inside me and I nervously pull my hair to the corner of my mouth. Then the bell rings and I hear them walk away, still laughing. Thank god he didn't pull anything like last week. Gabe is saying something to me, probably trying to tell me it wasn't about me at all this time, but I'm not listening. I'm too in my own head to listen to anyone.

The rest of the school day is a blur. I spend it locked in my mind, composing different possible versions of my future, making lists of things I need to do, and of course, fantasizing about how I could embarrass that asshole Patrick, make a fool of him like he's done to me so many times.

Before I know it, I'm home again. Evening chores, make dinner, get Lilly ready for bed, the usual monotony that I breeze through like it's a dream. Dad gets drunk and passes out in his chair. Thank god. That means no punishment tonight. In bed, I hide under the covers and close my eyes, pretend I'm dead. That's how I always fall asleep. It's more a wish than anything. To die and never wake up, or to wake up reborn. Someone new. I couldn't wish for anything better.

WINNIE

Days and days pass by me, so similar that they blend into each other. I hardly notice time anymore; I spend so much of it inside myself, dead to the world. Over the years, I have learned to "deaden" myself at will. It makes everything easier. Deaden is the only word I can think of to explain it. For example, yesterday, I stood in the kitchen and deadened myself when I heard Dad's heavy footsteps and the curt way he spoke to Brendan. It was not one of his good days.

Then he was next to me, screaming, veins bulging, red faced, but I wasn't really there. It was just him, yelling into the air as the pasta boiled over. When I deaden myself, each slap gets reduced to a heavy rag dragging my face to the side in slow motion. Each blow becomes just a dull ache, only as painful as an old broken bone before rain. It still hurts, but only when it's over and I'm in bed, tracing the red marks and gently testing the tenderness of the bruises. I've been doing it for a long time, but only recently have I really mastered deadening myself. I'm almost proud of it.

Today is Saturday and sunny, warmer than usual for this time of year. After my morning chores, I go outside and lay in the long grass of the backyard. I like it there; I can hide away and listen to bugs scuttle along the earth. But I don't get to enjoy it for long. Brendan is calling for me. I don't want to get up. I'm as tired as our grandmother used to describe; my old age already upon me at sixteen. I try to ignore him and stare at the sky. It's perfect like a child's drawing, sapphire blue with fluffed cotton ball clouds. Brendan is on the back porch now, still calling my name. Resigned, I sit up in the grass.

"What?"

"Hey, I've been looking for you all over. Come here. I need you for something," he says, and goes back inside. I give up my solitude and drag myself inside, closing the screen door harder than usual. I don't dare to slam it.

"Come over here." He gestures to the kitchen counter he's leaning on, and I obey. "I know it's the weekend, but I never got around to writing this makeup assignment for Mrs. Smith. It's some dumb paper about the Civil War. Here's the prompt," he says, and then he just leaves. He doesn't even wait for me to agree to write it.

As he stomps down the hall, he shouts something about going to a friend's house to Dad, but I don't really care enough to listen. I don't care about this paper either, but I know it needs to earn a passing grade. It's difficult to write Brendan's papers and not make them sound too good to be his own writing. I play with the prompt, twisting it, folding it, trying to force myself to put it aside, but finally, I give up and carry it to the computer. Get it over with. Booting up the computer, I read it over and pull some ideas together.

"What are you doing?" Lilly asks. Startled, I almost scream as I wheel around in the computer chair to face her.

"You scared me. I didn't hear you come in. I'm just writing something for Brendan."

"Will you come play ponies with me? I'll let you be Glitter Princess. She's the best one."

"Not right now. I have to work on this." I turn back to the computer and open the word processor.

"Come on, please Winnie. You know it's more fun to play with me. Please." She juts out her bottom lip in a pout.

"No, Lilly, I really can't right now. Maybe in a little bit."

She stands there, staring at me.

"I'll tell Dad you didn't play with me."

I laugh a little. "I think he'd understand this is more important."

She pauses. A smile flickers across her lips. "I'll tell Dad you pushed me."

I stare back at her.

"Why would you do that?"

"I'll tell Dad you pushed me down and made me cry."

She's staring at me with small, hard eyes, breathing louder than normal. I feel the corner of my mouth twitch.

"Sorry, yeah, yeah, you're right. I'll play with you. That sounds like fun. I'll just finish this another time," I say, trying to appear unfazed. Lilly still stares at me a little while longer before finally turning to lead me back to her room where her many ponies lie strewn across the floor.

We sit on the floor to play with the sparkly plastic ponies, my pretend falsetto voice squeaking out their imaginary words, and yet somehow it doesn't feel like it's enough this time. Lilly isn't bouncing around like usual, eagerly organizing the ponies into complicated stories of love and betrayal. She's more watchful. Her eyes dart to me every few seconds, like she thinks I'll disappear if she doesn't check. I try to tickle her, but she bats my hands away. I try to stack the ponies up like a cheerleader pyramid, but she pushes it down immediately. I even try to start a new storyline, but she grabs my arm holding the pink unicorn and pulls it to her.

"Winnie, you're not playing right. You are messing up the whole game. Glitter Princess is supposed to be at the party over here!" Then hits me hard on the arm with her doll.

"Ow, stop it." I grab the doll and hold it away from her.

"Give it back! Give it back!" Lilly shrieks, jumping on my shoulder and slamming her knee into my chest. I hurl her off me and onto the floor, then panic as I see it's knocked the breath out of her. She gasps and gasps before her lungs recover while I slowly back toward the door. Looking me straight in the eye, she cries in that piercing high-pitched way that makes every mother's heart jump at playgrounds.

Dad bursts into the room and pulls me by my hair. I claw at his hands, but he's dragging me out of Lilly's room. As I struggle, his grasp tightens, my scalp burning as hair roots rip free. Lilly hardly seems to notice and just continues to wail. Dad slams my head into the hallway wall before he forces me past all the other bedrooms to his own. He throws me on the bed and locks the door. I don't dare cry or plead. I hardly dare to breathe.

"That's it. You've been pushing all my buttons lately, but making your sister cry? Unforgivable!" He leans over me, bodies almost touching, his face inches from mine. There's an animal rage in his eyes yet I can't look away. He bends over, searching under the bed for the cookie tin. I clench my jaw, my teeth grinding painfully against each other.

"Take off your clothes." I follow his command and undress to my bra and panties.

"Lie down." Like a starfish, I spread my arms and legs. He finds the cords hidden under the mattress corners and binds my hands and feet. I close my eyes, my face scrunched up as tight as possible. He takes the first clothespin and pinches it open. Lightly tapping my right inner arm until

I can't help but flinch slightly, that's where he allows it to snap closed. Then the next and the next. All along my inner arms and thighs, in places always hidden beneath clothing, dozens of wooden pins dig into me. It stings now that the deep bruises are always there, but the real torture isn't until they're all on and he leaves. I never think to check the clock as he drags me into his room, so I'm never sure how long he leaves me, but it always seems like an eternity.

Minutes drag by like hours as the pins burn into the already bruised flesh. My limbs are bound so tightly that I can't move enough to dislodge even a single clothespin this time. I try to deaden and leave this pain, but I've let it get too intense for even that. I stifle my groans and busy myself clasping and unclasping my hands. Curling and uncurling my toes. Slowly shaking my head back and forth. Moving helps somehow, giving the tiniest relief imaginable.

Finally, Dad returns. His demeanor is calm now. His face drained back to the usual pallor. He removes each clothespin, pinching it open and placing it back in the cookie tin. They fall in with a soft clink, one by one. Then he goes to each corner and unties the knots, placing the cords back in their hiding spots under the mattress. Only once everything is returned to its rightful place am I allowed to stand up and dress myself.

"Oh Winnie, I wonder if you'll ever learn," he murmurs as I finish dressing and leave his room, shutting him behind the door. I notice the hall is dark. It's night now. I don't remember how long I played with Lilly or know how long I was punished, but I've somehow wasted the entire day. I walk to the kitchen, open the pantry, and search for dinner options.

"No use in cooking. Dad already ordered a pizza. There's some crusts and maybe a piece still in the box for you," Brendan tells me from the kitchen table.

"Thanks," I mumble, closing the pantry.

"Didn't write my paper, huh? I don't see it saved anywhere."

"Sorry, I ran out of time."

"Yeah, whatever. It's just a dumb history paper. That's why I didn't worry about it earlier." Brendan grunts, but then his face softens. "I really did save you a piece. Seriously." I walk over and open the pizza box. He's telling the truth. "Sorry you had a hard day. I still want you to write that paper tomorrow."

"I will."

"Well, I'm going to my room. Goodnight."

"Goodnight," I say, devouring the pizza as soon as he's gone. I didn't realize how hungry I am until now. I move on to the discarded crusts and eat them all. I check the trash can but there's no more. A soft thud catches my attention. I stop. Another thud and I peek into the hall.

It's Lilly, stumbling around with closed eyes. Sometimes I don't think she really sleepwalks. Sometimes I think that she's trying to spy on me and get me in trouble. I know she knows about the punishments and probably thinks they're entertaining or something. That really bothers me.

One time, Dad made me scrub every inch of the floor in the entire house because he found a tiny spill in the kitchen. Just a few drops of milk that someone neglected to wipe up, and I had to clean until my fingers were raw and blistered. I'm never allowed to wear gloves. That time, I saw Lilly peeking around the corner of the door each time I moved to a new room with a new floor to scrub. She was holding a glass of milk.

I could never hate my baby sister, but that day, I wished she had never been born. I know she's only a kid. She's just turned six. There's no way that she meant anything malicious by it. Still, it hurt, and I had a hard time even looking at her for weeks.

I hope she is just sleepwalking. She has no idea how bad the punishments can be. Lilly is a princess like in all her pretend games and I'm her lowly slave. If this family could allow themselves to forget the charade of normalcy and times gone by, we probably wouldn't even be allowed to fraternize. I pick her up and she goes limp in my arms as I take her back to bed, tucking her in under her chin. No kiss goodnight this time though, and as I close the door, I see her open her eyes just a sliver to watch me leave.

WINNIE

I spent the morning writing Brendan's essay, and it actually turned out really good. I was able to weave in some interesting quotes to give it that special flare that will earn him an A, or at least a B. He didn't even read it. Just snatched it out of my hand as soon as I brought it, printed neatly, with no errors, six whole pages of work. No thank you. Not a word. Just snatched it and cut my palm slightly as he did. A sharp sting and a flinch of pain. No blood got on the paper, or he surely would have spoken to me then. I don't know why I ever expect anything different. It's always the same.

Now I'm at the park by myself. Krystal didn't pick up. Gabe sent me to voicemail after one ring. Neither answered my texts. Even Lilly didn't want to go for a walk because of the rain last night. She didn't want to get mud on her shoes. I don't care about mud, and I love the way the earth smells after the rain, damp and alive.

As I walk down the dirt paths, the park feels desolate despite the people I pass. A man jogs by with a big white dog on a leash. A woman pushes a stroller, the baby inside fussing. Another woman I vaguely know from the neighborhood and her young daughter pass by, the girl's blonde pigtails bobbing happily as she skips next to her mother.

Something bubbles under my skin, and I scratch at my arms to make it stop. That girl has no idea how lucky she has it. A loving mother who dotes on her, takes her on walks. Even before things got so bad, I never saw Mom's eyes light up like that when she looked at me. Maybe when she looked at Brendan. Sometimes when she looked at Lilly. Never me. I was always in the way, too messy, making too many mistakes. I think about the picture Dad used to have of Mom holding me as a tiny baby, and my heart aches at the expression on her face. Yes, I think she might've truly loved me then. When I was so tiny. Before I could make trouble. The rolling boil below my skin calms to a mild itch and I realize I've been staring.

Just then, the girl turns back towards me and as we lock eyes, there's something familiar about her, like I know her from another lifetime. It's such an unsettling feeling, I almost want to approach her, but she turns away again before I do.

Who is she? The question rattles in my skull until finally, it dawns on me. She's a friend of a girl I've babysat. That brat Julia. I think her name was Leigh or something. I can't quite remember. What's wrong with my mind lately? I'm always groggy, out of it, like I can't wake up fully, can't think straight. The feeling passes and I return to a sort of loneliness, thick as fog. I sit on a bench, try to read a little on my phone, but I can't focus. Instead, I just walk. Walk and think.

After about an hour, I leave the winding path and go into the woods, stepping over the newly sprung mushrooms. Wandering farther into the woods, I never feel lost, even as I lose the view of the path. The sun directly overhead shines down, dappled shadows cast by the leaves dance along the forest floor. A tiny frog jumps from a wet pile of leaves, and I bend down, trying to catch him, but he's too fast. I go much farther into the wilderness than usual. I know I have all day to find my way home, and these woods aren't as large as they seem, so it doesn't matter if it takes some time to find my way back out.

Suddenly, I trip over a root buried in the thick leaves and slide down a steep ridge on my stomach and left arm. At the bottom, I sit up and brush the black leaves off the scratches, blood seeping down my arm. I slap away the bits of rot sticking to my jeans and the back of my shirt but, instead of falling off, they smudge and smear deeper into the fabric. *Dammit.* I'm sure the stains will set by the time I get back, and that means there will be a punishment if I can't figure out a way to hide them from Dad. Another reason for him to be ashamed of me.

Pulling my knees to my chin, my eyes well with tears but I try not to be a crybaby. Punishments are just part of life. I shouldn't feel so sorry for myself. A few drops roll down, but mostly I've managed to keep them in. I refuse to let it get to me.

With my hands now flat on the ground behind me, I let my head drop back with a sigh. Something hard cuts into my palm. Pulling away, I search the ground, brushing the rotten leaves out of the way before finally finding a small snail traveling in the black slime of the forest floor.

I pick it up, turn it over in my hand, and poke at the wet, undulating body. It writhes in a pathetic dance as it attempts to free itself. Teasing it, my finger hovers before I jab at the eyestalks, forcing them to retreat completely into the gelatinous head. I smile a little as it struggles, then poke it again.

"Stupid snail."

I put it back on the ground. Frantically, it tries to crawl away, but escape is impossible. As I stand up, the snail retreats into its shell. My shadow hovers over it. I place my sneaker on the shell, just barely resting on it. Slowly, as slow as possible, I shift my weight onto the foot and feel the shell crack, give way, and then completely surrender beneath me. I increase the pressure and feel the snail flatten against the earth, its body popping slightly as its slimy skin bursts to release the tension.

I wait until I'm sure there's not even the smallest bit of life left before I remove my foot and assess the damage. Some murky liquid flows from the broken shards. I smile wider. Almost laugh. A wild heat rises through my body.

I search through the leaves, find another snail, and crush it the same as the first, but even slower. I pretend the pain of the snail flows into my foot, into my leg, through my bloodstream. It courses through me, becoming part of me, strengthening me. *Oh, poor little snail, you can't get away. You can't do anything at all, can you?*

With a third snail, I crouch as I crush it, my head as close to my foot as I can get without tipping over. I'm hoping for something to satisfy this feeling, perhaps to hear the pop of skin or a tiny squeal of air or pain. I don't hear much though. I search for more snails, but don't find any. They must have sensed the fates of their brothers and found a way to hide. I figure that's enough for one day anyway.

I climb up the ridge easier and quicker than I could have before. It's the adrenaline, a chemical high. My cheeks are tight with restrained smiles. I feel like I could burst out laughing, but I keep myself under control.

Meandering through the woods, back in the direction of the path, I pick up a branch and hit the trees, haphazardly breaking off moss and bark. I try to smash a trio of white mushrooms, but their caps only sag slightly, so I stomp them to broken stalks before moving on. Striking the branch as hard as I can against a sapling, I watch a line of ants fall and scatter. Tiny piles of ruin mark my zigzagging way back to the trail.

Stepping back onto the fine brown gravel of the path, I take a deep breath. Then I feel overcome with the urge to stretch like I just woke up. Something about that private rampage felt great. I walk, almost skip, to the bus stop outside the park. I never knew destruction would be so enjoyable. Maybe if I'd known, I'd have started long ago. The bus comes and I have just enough change to get me there and then back home.

Through the window, the clouds grow darker as the bus arrives at Krystal's street. It's freshly paved, with identical cookie-cutter houses on either side. I try to remember which is hers, glancing from house to house, before a familiar ugly lawn gnome gives it away.

I knock on the door and at first no one answers. I wonder if she knows it's me and my heart sinks. I knock again, harder. There's rustling inside. Krystal cracks the door just barely, but then recognizes me and pushes it wide open, standing with her hands pressed against the doorframe. Her blonde spiral curls bounce around her head, framing her face with its perfect little turned-up nose, rosebud lips, and deeply sun-kissed complexion.

"Winnie! I didn't know you were coming over," she says, a bright smile flashing across her face.

"Yeah, I just thought, why not? I haven't seen you in a while," I say, smiling back.

"Come in. I'm going to my friend Miranda's birthday party in like an hour, but we can totally hang out until then," she says. I step forward, being sure to scour the bottom of my sneakers against the brown mat declaring "Welcome!" I look back for an instant and see the tiny bits of snail shell I left behind are barely noticeable.

"So, what's up? How are things at school?" Krystal asks as I follow her to the kitchen. Reaching up on tiptoes, she takes two glasses out of the cabinet. "Want some iced tea?"

"Yeah, sure. Thank you. Uh, things are good. Normal, I guess. You remember how it is there." I sit down and watch her pour the heavy pitcher, almost spilling it.

"Yeah, I gotta admit, I don't miss that place at all. But I do miss you!" she quickly adds with a surprised, apologetic look. I just nod and take the glass she offers. Only a small sip and already my teeth ache from the sugar. Definitely her mom's iced tea.

"I miss having you around, especially being right down the street. Three houses away seemed so far away back then," I say, forcing a laugh at the end.

"Yep, those were the days, but I'm really not that far," she says, leaning across the counter and resting her head in her hand. "I mean, it's only a ten, fifteen minute bus ride, and if your dad ever lets you get a car, it'll be even less."

"Yeah, well, taking the bus everywhere is a drag, but I doubt I'll get a car anytime soon. At least your parents let you drive the van sometimes. You could always come pick me up."

"Yeah, totally," Krystal says, almost whispering. Her smile drops and she looks away.

I nod and suck on an ice cube, spitting it back in my cup with a clink. A wall of silence forms between us. We both look down at our hands.

"How are things at home?" She tiptoes over the words, then looks wide-eyed up at me.

"Not too bad. Brendan's still an asshole." We both giggle.

"What about Lilly?"

"She's becoming kind of an asshole, too. It's pretty annoying," I say and take another sip of tea. It's Krystal's turn to nod and look away.

"What about…your dad?"

"He's the same as always. But enough about me. How are your folks?"

"The same as always here too, I guess. Oh, I told you about the drama with my mom and Aunt Ruth last time we talked."

"Yeah, but that was like a month ago."

"Oh yeah. I guess it was," Krystal says, pulling a coil of hair between her fingers. "It got better. They're talking again. Hmm, yeah, I guess nothing else has really happened. It's always boring around here." She shifts her weight to her other foot and leans back across the counter, again holding her chin in her hand.

"How's babysitting? You're still doing that, right?" She smiles and slips a fingernail into her mouth, nibbling at the edge. She still has that nervous habit, I think to myself.

"Yeah, it's going okay. The families in the neighborhood seem to really like me. I think I might not be charging enough, but I've managed to save up kind of a lot of money. I'm thinking about splurging on something cool, like a new outfit or tarot deck."

"Oh yeah, I remember back when we used to do that all the time," she says. "You were the best at making it feel so real and, I don't know, *sinister* or something. We should do that again sometime. I know! You should totally bring them next time I have a party and do it for everybody. That'd be so fun! Everyone would love that."

"Yeah, maybe. Gabe and I are thinking about starting, like, a business, trying to make some money from it. I taught him how and he's had tons of people asking him to read their fortunes. Maybe he could come and help," I say, smiling and taking another sip of tea.

Her own smile strains a little. "Yeah, sure. I didn't know you guys did that together."

"Yeah." I don't know what else to say. She clears her throat and tries to flip her hair off her shoulder and onto her back, but the honey curls bounce right back where they were.

"So, you and Gabe are super close now, huh? I always thought he was kind of mean, but I guess maybe I just don't know him well enough. Like, maybe it's just a kind of 'protective shield' thing. I mean, you always liked him, even back then."

"Yeah, he's not mean. He's just different. Doesn't fit in, you know, like us," I say, but I immediately regret saying it. Krystal is no longer the way she was, even just last year, and we both know it.

Thick silence catches in our throats, and we look at each other. I'm biting at my lips. She's chewing her nail. Nervously, I trace the scar tissue down the side of my face, then notice what I'm doing and pull my hair down, fluffing and pulling at it.

"I'm sorry. I know I've been too busy," she says and her voice quavers like she might cry. "You're still my best friend. I know I don't always text back. I don't mean to be like that. It's just hard to—"

"No, it's fine," I interrupt her. "Of course we're still best friends. That's why I came over." I smile. She blushes slightly. "I guess we need to read some new books or see some movies or something, anything, before next time we hang out, so we'll have something to actually talk about," I joke but she doesn't laugh, just paints on a feeble smile.

"Yeah."

"Well, call me when you're not too busy. I should go before it starts raining again," I say, turning to leave. She doesn't stop me, and I wonder why I thought she would.

I hear her call "Bye Frieda!" after me. I roll my eyes. Those stupid nicknames we came up with in seventh grade.

We thought we were so unique and quirky. We barely even use them anymore. Hearing it actually makes me feel worse.

On the way to the bus, the rain starts again. Just a light drizzle. A gray snail pokes his head out of the grass, sliding his body onto the slick sidewalk. I crush him in a hurried step, as if I didn't really mean to at all, and smile.

KRYSTAL SCHUMACHER

POLICE INTERVIEW TRANSCRIPT

DEC. **18**

Det. Garcia: What is your relationship like with Ms. Campbell?

Schumacher: We're friends. Like really close friends. Pretty much best friends since the second grade. I still can't believe any of this is real.

Det. Garcia: So, you're telling me this was completely unexpected? She never talked about being angry with anyone? Maybe there was someone she wasn't getting along with? Violent tendencies?

Schumacher: No, she never seemed angry at all. Even when people were jerks or whatever, she never lashed out. Okay, sure, it's true she'd say some sarcastic stuff after they'd leave, but never anything beyond that. She was one of the most loving people I've ever known. People thought she was so tough because of the way she dressed, but it just wasn't true.

Det. Garcia: Do you remember her acting differently lately? Did she seem more agitated than normal, or possibly spending more time by herself?

Schumacher: No, I swear, she was exactly like always. We talked on the phone just a week or so ago and she seemed like her normal self. Actually, maybe it was more like two weeks...

Det. Garcia: So, you haven't spoken to her for a couple weeks then?

Schumacher: Well, yeah, I guess. But only because of her dad. He'd been stricter with her lately. She told me he'd been, uh, well, just really strict.

Det. Garcia: What do you mean by strict?

Schumacher: He wasn't... well... he's not here, right? Like, he's not like in the next room over or something? I don't know if I should say anything...

Det. Garcia: If you're concerned for your safety, don't be. I can promise that you're safe here.

Schumacher: Okay, I guess. It's not just me I worry about, it's Winnie.

Well, he was just a horrible father. I don't know how else to describe it. But he'd been worse lately. I mean, she ran that house even if he was technically the one in charge. He was probably freaking out that she was basically grown, so he started putting all kinds of rules on her.

She cooked all the meals and did all the cleaning, but it was never good enough. I think he kind of blamed her for what happened with her mom or something. Or at least that's what I got from what she said. She really didn't like to talk about it very much.

Det. Garcia: Can you clarify? I'm not sure I know what you mean by a "horrible father".

Schumacher: Like, okay, let me give you an example. This one time I was over at her house, and she had just finished cleaning the kitchen right before I got there, and it looked great. Seriously spotless. But then her dad came in and he started yelling at her about the tiles being a little yellow. Can you believe that? Like he was really yelling, as if she had any control over that. They were just yellow because they were old.

And then, well, then he picked up the kitchen trash can and dumped it all over the floor. The floor she had just spent all that time scrubbing. And there were all kinds of gross things in that trash. I just couldn't believe he would do something like that.

She didn't even say anything, just started cleaning again. I had heard her talk about stuff like that before, little stories here and there, but that was the first time I really saw it. It was shocking. I guess I'd never really believed it before then. I didn't know what to do so I just left. Jesus, I should've helped her, but I just left. God, I feel sick about it now.

Det. Garcia: Do you know if he was ever abusive? Physically, or possibly sexually?

Schumacher: Oh my god, no! I don't think he ever would do something like that. Like... touch her... in that way.

But, yeah, I know physical abuse definitely happened. I think it happened a lot. Way more than she ever told me about. I hated him for it. What kind of a dad does that? As if her life wasn't hard enough. And she told me always only hit her around her chest and stomach, so nobody ever saw those bruises unless she showed you. She showed me sometimes, but I think it happened more than she let on. She didn't really like me talking about it.

She said one time he was hitting her; she fell down, and he just started kicking her. Like really hard. Just kicking over and over again, right in the stomach. She told me... well, she told me she shit blood the next day. I think she was actually scared, that's why she told me about that.

I saw the bruises that time. Almost black, and she couldn't touch them, not even lightly, without wincing. She said just her clothes rubbing against the skin was agony. That's how bad it was. Poor Winnie.

I told her she should call the cops or something, but she'd never do that. She wouldn't even go to the hospital because she was afraid they'd call you guys. I was going to tell my parents, or call the cops myself, but she begged me not to. She made me swear on my mom's life not to tell a soul, so I didn't. God, I should've done it anyway. She showed me and opened up about all that, and I didn't do anything...

Det. Garcia: Can you tell me a little more about that last phone call you had with her? I know it was a couple weeks ago, but it might help us find her.

Schumacher: Yeah, um, let me think. It's hard to think right now, knowing about everything that happened. I feel so shitty. I should've been there for her.

I guess it was a pretty normal phone call. I don't really know what you want me to say. She didn't tell me anything about running away or anything like that.

Det. Garcia: Just tell us what you two discussed. Do you remember anything at all?

Schumacher: Yeah, I think I remember most of it. She called in the evening. It was right after I had finished doing the dishes from dinner, and I was glad she called because I wanted to complain about my mom. I went on and on about something stupid. She just listened, completely quiet. She's such a good friend, letting me vent like that. When I was finally done, I asked her why she called.

She told me her dad had thrown out the dinner she made again. It was the second time that week. Then he took her brother and sister out for burgers or something, but left Winnie there. They were still gone when she called.

It was kind of weird. She didn't seem that upset. I guess I figured she was just starting to realize that's how he's always going to be or something. In my mind, I always thought that if she made it through high school, she could leave and never see those assholes again.

I remember she seemed kind of depressed. Like, she told me she didn't think she wanted to go to college anymore. I asked her what she was going to do instead, and she said she didn't think she'd ever be anything at all. I thought she was being melodramatic and didn't take her seriously. I tried to comfort her, remind her that with her grades, she was sure to get into a decent school. Then, she told me her grades had maybe been slipping a little, and I remember I didn't know what to say. I mean, what do you say to that anyway?

God, now that I say all of this out loud, I was being so selfish. I just wanted to complain about my own stupid problems, and I was honestly barely listening to her.

Det. Garcia: Well, you're helping her now by talking to us. Who knows, you might remember something that will help us find her. Now, is there anything else you discussed during that last phone call?

Schumacher: Um, I can't really remember. I'm sorry. Can I have a tissue? Thank you.

Well, she didn't seem really upset, even about her grades. She didn't say anything angry or violent, just a passive kind of acceptance. But that's depression, isn't it? I thought depression doesn't make you violent. It takes away your will to do anything at all.

I remember she said, "Talk to you tomorrow, Koo Koo." That's what she called me. And I said, "Night-night, Frieda."

We made up those nicknames from our favorite movie, *Freaks.* That's what we always felt like. Total freaks.

She was always there for me; I really should have been there for her. I just got so caught up in everything at my new school. God, I miss her so much already. Please, please, let me know when you find her. I need to talk to her.

Det. Garcia: Thank you for your cooperation, Ms. Schumacher. Call us if you remember anything else that might be helpful in our investigation.

WINNIE

It's an especially hard day at school. Mrs. McCord stops me
after class to lecture me about participating more.

"You're a bright girl, Winnie, and some days you're so
active in class, but others you just don't seem to care. I've
noticed you've had a lot more of the latter recently."

"Sorry, Mrs. McCord. I'll try to be better," I mutter,
staring at my shoes, noticing the mud still caked on the
side of the left one.

"You know, once you get to college, the professors
won't be as lenient as me. Participation is often part of your
grade, and the content is harder. You won't just be able to
slide by without studying, only doodling and daydreaming."

"Mmm," I nod, sucking my lips between my teeth.

"I hope you're taking me seriously, Winnie. I want you
to succeed. You are so smart, have so much potential." She
pauses a moment, her eyes gliding up and her lips pinched
like she tasted something sour. "What do you think about
a meeting with you, me, and your dad?"

I hold in the chuckle that bubbles up my throat. "I don't
think that's a good idea."

"Are you sure? Of course he wants you to succeed as much as I do, and I know you've had a tough time since things happened with your mom and all…" She lets the words trail off, and a hot blush burns my cheeks. I hate to think of them talking about me, about my family.

"Sure. I'll ask if you want."

"Thank you, Winnie." We stand, swaying in the awkward silence for a moment, but then the bell rings and I scurry away.

The idea of a parent-teacher meeting with Dad haunts me the rest of the day. It's so absurd, it simultaneously makes me giddy and sick to my stomach. Even if she does call, I know he'd never show. It'd just mean another punishment. That reality takes the humor out of it and leaves me achingly hollow.

Gabe offers to drive me to his house. We can finally watch that Ted Bundy documentary he's been hyping up forever.

"Mom'll still be at work, so we won't have to worry about her."

"Yeah, that sounds fine."

Under the tacky blacklight posters and through the haze of smoke, we watch the small tv in Gabe's room, first the Bundy one, which is pretty good, just like he promised, then some random true crime stuff. A blob of blood splatters across the screen with the title "Murder and Mayhem" written in drippy letters. I sigh, knowing this would certainly be a cheesy one full of bad reenactments.

"These guys are so fucking dumb. They make every mistake imaginable." Gabe snorts, sinking back into the beanbag chair.

"You think you could kill somebody and get away with it, huh?"

"Yeah, I do. Just look at all these serial killers who got away with it for years. You've just gotta pick someone random, or better yet, someone nobody cares about."

"Okay, sure, but most people don't want to just kill someone for no reason. They've got someone in particular they wanna take out. Do you think you could get away with that? Killing someone you actually know?"

He looks at me with a stupid smirk that makes my arm hairs bristle up and a shiver run down my back.

"Easily. Like I said, I'd just kill someone nobody cares about," he says, winking and then turning back to the tv like it was nothing.

In that moment, I hate him. Everything about him. His stupid, fake punk persona. His cruel little comments and jokes. His charisma. The way his mom just lets him run wild and do whatever he wants. I feel like running away, slamming his bedroom door so hard that the frame breaks, tearing down his posters and kicking in his stupid little tv. But I don't. I just sink into my own beanbag chair, its stink of old smoke and body odor closing in around me, and keep watching the show. One actor is pretending to stab another over and over, but it's glaringly fake, retractable knife and everything. I channel the anger at the idiots on the screen, jeering along with Gabe at the closeup of the victim, her face smeared with a ketchupy sauce that doesn't look even a bit like real blood.

"You'd think they'd try a little harder than that," I say and Gabe nods, shoots me a knowing look, and I'm not mad anymore. We both know what blood looks like. Real blood and real pain and the kind of real anger that boils in your head so hard you know that with just a fraction more pressure you could lose it and really kill someone. That's why I forgive him.

WINNIE

My eyes unfocus and the passing scenery becomes a blur of color as I daydream, staring out the bus window all the way downtown. I get off at a random stop and it's exhilarating. For a second, I wonder why I never did this before. Then I remember. There will be a message from the school about my absence. There will be a punishment. One worse than last night, and all I did was accidentally knock over Brendan's drink. I even cleaned it up right away. It was a bad one. An especially painful one. I spent the whole time imagining that Dad and Brendan had turned into snails, and I was slowly crushing them until their innards were forced through bursting skin and up through their mouths.

I shiver a little as I walk down the street. Should've brought a raincoat. Aimlessly, I walk around the alleyways and side streets of downtown, stomping in the puddles. The rain stops periodically, but never long enough for anything to dry. It's a light drizzle that makes everything smell like mold and earth. I watch as earthworms wriggle across the sidewalk. I consider stepping on them, but I don't really feel like it.

I walk down a narrow alley, made even more confined by dumpsters jutting out from either side. I run my fingers over the cold metal and draw shapes in the droplets running down. Suddenly, I feel like screaming, and I don't know why. Squatting down against the wall, I put my head in my hands.

My brain is throbbing, and each throb sends a jolt of electric pain through my teeth. I can't describe the emotion behind it, but something is squeezing my stomach, tossing it against my ribcage. I don't realize I'm pulling out my hair until I look down to see clumps all over the ground. I force my hands down and stand. Down the alley, there's a large gray cat. It stops grooming itself and stares back at me.

Leaning against the bricks, I bang my head backward once, twice. Roll it from side to side, then frown. It physically hurts to exist, yet paradoxically, actual pain makes it seem more bearable. I want to disappear.

The cat is closer, staring at me. Yellow, glassy eyes with elongated pupils. I push off from the wall and walk closer. Raising my lip, I hiss and spit at it. The cat takes a few steps back, arching its back. Still staring.

I take cautious steps forward, almost on tiptoe, but it stands its ground. Suddenly, I sprint toward it. It hisses, eyes wide and afraid. Before it can get away, I kick it hard in the belly. It tries to cling to my foot for a moment before taking flight, landing perfectly a couple feet away. A whimpering mew echoes in the alley as it scrambles from me. I pound after it, imagining us as the hunter and hunted.

The cat turns and hisses, lashing out its claws. I run closer, try to kick it again, but miss. Adrenaline pumps through my veins. I can't stop. We're both mere animals as we race down the alley. The cat runs out into the road just as a car speeds by.

Thud.

There's no other noise but the pattering rain and tires sloshing through puddles. Ashamed, I shuffle closer. The soft body is limp, strangely contorted, almost deflated-looking.

Mouth open, sharp teeth jutting out. Brain matter spills out in a pile where the top of its head was just seconds ago. I feel sick to my stomach, but I can't stop staring. The gray pile of mush and the half-open eyes beckon me to look.

Silence slowly surrounds me, drowning out the rain. Minutes pass. People walk by. No one cares about the cat or me.

Eventually, I go back the way I came, back to the bus stop. At home, I sit quietly by myself on the couch, staring at the black screen of the TV. I can't tell whether I feel guilty. Honestly, I just feel empty.

I used to have a pet cat when I was five. Izzy. I loved her. The way she pressed herself against me and purred was my favorite thing in the world. I remember I was devastated when she died. Trying to force tears from my dry eyes, I think of Izzy and focus on the guilt I should feel. I should feel horrible. Only a bad person would do what I did. Although, I didn't know a car was coming, I couldn't have, and I didn't want it to end like that. But what had I wanted?

Brendan comes home, slamming the door behind him, and stomps into the room.

"What are you doing? Why weren't you at school?"

"I couldn't go today. I needed to figure some things out," I say, but my voice sounds thick and rusty.

"What? What things? Don't you know how pissed Dad will be if he finds out?" I sense the combination of anger and pleasure in his tone. The sadistic bastard probably secretly loves it when I'm punished.

"I know."

"Winnie, you can be so stupid sometimes. I don't know why you want Dad to hate you so much. Maybe he'd lay off a little if you weren't so fucking weird." He sits, almost collapses, on the couch next to me, and I fall a little towards him. Digging his hands into the cushions, he finds the remote. With the press of a button, the TV comes to life, and he's cycling through the channels too fast to recognize any of the shows, searching for god knows what.

I think about how much I like the comforting blue glow of the room when the TV's on and the curtains are drawn. I turn slightly to Brendan and see the images from the screen flicker in his eyes. His mouth hangs open slightly. He'd be shocked if I told him about the cat. Little Winnie, lover of all animals, tortured and killed a cat. Inadvertently, but still.

He suddenly winks at me. "I know, I'm so good looking you'd rather watch me than TV." I crinkle my nose with disgust and turn away, basking for a few more minutes in the blue glow.

There's no more time for idleness. I get up, go to the kitchen, and start preparing dinner. As I take apart the chicken, I drift away, lost in its cold bumpy skin.

"Hey, are you okay?" Brendan asks. My head snaps up toward him, startled. I didn't notice him come in.

"Yes, I'm fine."

"What were you doing just then? You've been acting kind of weird lately."

"I was just spacing out, okay?"

"Okay, whatever. What's for dinner?" he asks, rummaging through the pantry behind me.

"Chicken and corn and mashed potatoes." My voice is cold and mechanical in my mouth.

"Mmm," he says. "Sounds great."

I hear him opening a bag of chips as he walks back to the living room, and I bristle with anger. He won't be hungry after eating all that, and then Dad will think he didn't like my cooking.

As I season the chicken, I imagine what it would be like to butcher the big gray cat. A smile blooms across my lips as

I picture serving it to my unsuspecting family. Roasted golden brown and as juicy as a Thanksgiving turkey, even served Mom's special occasion silver platter for the bastards. Their greedy teeth ripping through the skin and flesh. Crunching on the bones, getting every morsel. Licking their lips and fingers, making disgusting, satisfied moans. Then I'd show them the head. I grin, humming while I peel potatoes.

Dinner is uneventful, which is pretty much the best I can hope for. Everyone eats in almost complete silence, after Dad tells Lilly to shut up when she whines that she doesn't like corn anymore. Otherwise, an occasional "pass the salt" or "hand me the butter" are the only words spoken. Dad doesn't say a word about my skipping school.

I clean the dishes, the table, bathe Lilly as she yells at me that she's too old for that, and yet again, tries to drain the tub without having washed her hair. Then I ask Dad if I can run over to Gabe's really quick to borrow a book I need for homework. He waves me off, eyes glued to the television, back glued to the recliner. Slipping out the front door, I wonder if he would care if I never came back.

I text Gabe to meet me at the gas station a few blocks down and head out. While I wait, I buy some gum and a Coke with some of my babysitting money. I sit outside on the curb, drinking and smacking away.

I feel happier than I have in weeks. A ridiculous, manic type of happiness. I can't quite place why, but I feel like some invisible tension has been released. I turn and see Gabe walk down the sidewalk. I wave, but he goes inside first, emerging with his own Coke and a pack of Camel 100s.

"How do you always buy those? Did you actually end up buying that fake ID?" I ask. "It didn't even look like you."

"Come on, it doesn't look that bad. But, yes, as a matter of fact, I did. And guess what, it's worked at like four out of five bars I've tried it at. But dude, this place never cards anyway. At least not for cigs."

"You're just Mr. Too-Cool-For-School, aren't you," I say, laughing at my own dumb joke.

"Pfft, you were the one who didn't even show today," he says, lighting a cigarette. "And you seem weirdly happy. What's up with you?"

I play with my hair, pulling it over my mouth, and smile. My eyes dart to him and away.

"Did you get laid?" he asks, leaning in.

"No!" I shout and playfully hit him.

"Good, because I haven't gotten any for days and that wouldn't be fair." He play punches me back.

"I just feel better somehow. I feel like I am kind of coming into my own, you know? Becoming my real self. Maybe this is what growing up is supposed to feel like."

"So, you're finally realizing that you don't have to take all that shit, huh? Well, at the very least, take it for much longer." He takes a slow drag and blows it into the street. "Your family is full of jackasses, and you should just run away with me. Anything would be less boring than this shit-hole town." He looks at me, but I just smile and shake my head. "Well, I guess you have to wait it out for two more years until college. Although, if I were you, I'd have run away ages ago."

"Yeah, well, you're not me, and I love my family. Even if they are assholes. Plus, who would take care of Lilly if not me? Hey, can I have a cigarette?"

"Big time rebel now?" he winks and offers me one. "I've only ever seen you smoke in the throes of depression." He says this with a mocking flourish, but then looks at me very seriously. "You're not going to kill yourself or something stupid like that, right?"

"No, dummy! I am genuinely feeling, well, hopeful," I say and watch the plume of smoke rise from my lips.

"Mm-hmm. Well, I know what would really make a rebel like you happy: sneaking out to the club with me. That one I told you about, where they don't ID. Like, not at all. Dumbasses." He coughs a little but plays it off.

"I don't know. I mean, Dad's been easier on me the last couple of days. He didn't even say anything about my skipping today. I don't want to mess it up."

"Come on, what have you got to lose? You know he'll turn into a drunk monster again any day now." The words make me flinch, but when I turn to him, he doesn't seem to notice.

"Fine. I mean…maybe."

"If you go with me and just try it out, then next time you'll get to pick what we do. Even watching lame old movies." He sticks out his tongue at me.

"Okay, fine. You're right. It'll probably be fun. Maybe I'll even meet someone. I mean, I haven't been with a guy since Jeremy, and that was months ago." I sigh. "Sometimes I feel like you're the only person who gets me at all, Gabe." My half-smoked cigarette drops into a puddle near my feet and hisses as it dies. "Hey, don't forget to turn down your music when you come get me, by the way. Last time, Dad was suspicious after he heard the noise outside, that's why I couldn't get out."

He shrugs and pulls out another cigarette. I lean against his shoulder, and I'm so relaxed I almost fall asleep until Gabe nudges me and tells me to go home before it gets too late.

WINNIE

I stare in the mirror, trying to focus on the radio as it drowns out that inner voice of self-criticism. I lean forward, examining myself as close as possible. Concealer rubbed over my blemishes, rosy blush swiped across my cheekbones, thick black eyeliner, all topped off with that new mauve lipstick I'd swiped from the drugstore. I turn my head and look at my reflection in profile, then smirk. I can't believe it. For once, I don't hate the way I look. At least on my good side.

It's been forever since I've felt this way. My long blonde hair, strategically styled to cover the uneven texture of my scars as much as possible, cascades down my back and over my shoulder. Thank god my bangs have finally grown long enough to hide my bad side pretty well. I pout my lips and give my reflection the sultry stare I've practiced a thousand times. The tight, black dress, the pushup bra and fishnets I borrowed from Krystal, plus my favorite chunky heels, all combine to form a satisfactory illusion. I don't feel quite "beautiful", but definitely at least moderately desirable. I entertain the idea that maybe Gabe was right to push me into this.

Turning down the music and grabbing my purse, I sneak out the window. It isn't difficult, but I still don't dare to do it often. Around the corner, Gabe is waiting in his beat-up jeep. He wolf-whistles as I get into the car. I can't help but smile just a little as we cruise toward downtown.

"Are you ready to get shitfaced?" he asks, laughing. I guess I forget to laugh, and he lightly punches my arm. "Come on Winnie, cheer up. I promise this will be fun." He glances at me and adds, "What are you worried about? Is this about your Dad? He'll never find out."

"No, not that at all. Don't talk about him. I just…"

"What then?"

"Nothing. I don't know. What if they ID me? I don't have a fake."

"They never ID there. I told you. Trust me," he says, getting out of the car and heading straight to the door. Really more of a dressed-up shack than a bar, but it's his favorite for some reason. I now realize that's probably only because they never check ID. I walk behind him, almost tripping on the curb. Gabe turns around.

"You okay?"

"Yeah, yeah. Sorry." I look down at my feet.

"Good," he says, already facing away and going through the door. Inside it's dusty and loud, but I sort of like it. It reminds me of a movie or something I'd seen on TV but can't quite remember.

Right away, Gabe's ordering vodka shots and flirting with the bartender. We do shot after shot of the cheapest vodka. After three or four, we're on the dance floor making fools of ourselves to some horrible top 40 songs. I keep reminding myself to smile and stay present. I should be having a good time, and yet it feels so forced. At least I look alright.

We dance together for a while before Gabe's lured away by a tall man with a dazzling smile. I resent the man a little because now I have to pretend alone. I try to keep dancing, but I feel simultaneously on display and invisible. Moments later, the tempo quickens and someone starts grinding on me. That's it.

After pushing my way back to the bar, I down two more disgusting shots. The room threatens to start spinning, so I steady myself with a hand on a stool. The guy next to me says something, but his words are drowned out by the music and buzz of conversations all around.

"What?" I shout but can barely even hear myself.

"You're smoking hot!" he shouts, the words just audible over the music. My face is instantly forced into a flattered grin. I look around and notice a backdoor. I motion, and he follows me outside to the patio.

We step into the quiet night sounds of crickets and faraway traffic. There's only one other couple outside, and they're in the corner making sucking sounds and stifled moans. Away from the chaos, I take the time to truly look at this admirer of mine.

He's older, but not "old." I'd guess mid-20s. Chestnut hair hardened with too much gel, mild unibrow, goofy smile, and glassy eyes. He's obviously very drunk, and very not-my-type, but even I know I really came to this dive for validation, not love. I realize Gabe was right. This does make me feel a little better.

He grabs my hips, pulling me against him. I stumble the half step, but he doesn't seem to notice. He kisses me softly at first, but soon it turns sloppy and rough. His tongue slides down my throat. Too much spit. His hands are grabbing my ass, kneading it like dough. I feel ridiculous. I'm drunk, but not nearly drunk enough for this amateur fondling. He shifts his hips to press his erection against me while simultaneously biting my lip. I flinch. Such a Prince Charming.

"Oh babe, you're so hot. I want you so bad," he whispers into my face. His breath nauseates me, and I can tell right away he's not a talented conversationalist, but I love feeling wanted nonetheless.

"What do you like about me?" I ask in my B-movie actress seductive voice. I try to stroke his hair, but it just crunches.

"I don't know, babe, you're just hot. Oh man, so fucking hot. Do you want me as much as I want you?" He's breathing hard and practically moaning. He kisses me again, and I pull away a little.

"Heh, slow down a sec. What's your name?" I practice my flirty trill of a laugh.

"Brent. What's yours?"

"Winnie." I can barely answer before he's jamming his tongue into my throat again. I feel drool slip past his lips and onto my face. I pull away.

The night air is cool, and I breathe it in deeply. Two deep breaths, two staggering steps back, and I'm tripping on the bench behind me. Brent reaches out but misses and I fall back, hitting my elbow hard against the concrete floor.

"Whoa, that must've hurt," he chuckles. My face and ears burn as I stand up.

"Whatever," I murmur. He's still laughing a little. I scowl at him, but I think he's too drunk to even register it. He snorts another laugh then pulls me to him for a kiss, but I turn my head away.

"Do you wanna fuck or what?" I fire the words like bullets.

"Wait, what?" He lets go of me and searches my face. "What did you say?"

The words shoot out again, sharp and precise. "Do you want to fuck me in the bathroom or not?"

His drunken brain is obviously taking a second to understand the question since his whole face contorts into a squished look of confusion. I feel my attempt at a come-hith-er expression distort slightly as it tries to mask my rage. Real-ization finally washes across his features.

"Yeah. Yes. Yes! Whoa, that's just...crazy. Yes, let's go!"

He's still answering while I drag him inside to the sin-gle-occupant women's restroom. Once inside, I work quickly and without emotion. I decide I just can't stand to be pene-trated by this buffoon, no matter how beautiful he thinks I am in his drunken stupor.

I kneel. Unzip. Suck. Fake moan. His hands are rub-bing all over my head, tangling my hair into knots. Then he's pulling it. I stop; tell him to knock it off. He apologizes. I continue. He's thrusting like an asshole and I'm gagging. I'm going to vomit. He's jabbing the back of my throat and then, one or two thrusts away from a lap full of puke, he finally finishes. It slips down my throat in a few disgusting squirts, and finally, he lets go of my head.

I smile up at him, a smile of genuine accomplishment and pride. I expect him to shower me with praise, or at least gratitude, but he doesn't. He nods, timidly smiles back, and cleans himself up.

"Pretty good, right?" I ask with a wink. He nods again and turns away to zip up his fly. What a strange sense of modesty.

"Um, yeah. Thanks." I can tell he doesn't want to look me in the face anymore. I wonder if the hair-pulling ruined my attempt at disguising my scars. My self-esteem crumbles.

"Do you want my number? Maybe I'll do it again sometime," I say, giggling like an airhead, but inside, I hate him. I feel my face glowing hot again.

"Sure. Um, yeah. Sure, okay. Here, put it in," he says, taking out his phone and handing it over without looking at me. Pursing my lips, I put my information in.

"It's Winnie, don't forget! Text me so I'll have your number too, okay?"

"Yeah, sure. Fine." His text only says one word: *hi.*

I text back: *Best blowjob you'll ever get. Call anytime ;)*

He blows air out his nose in a polite substitution for a laugh. He looks up at me and then quickly away, but I saw it. It's not my face, but some kind of deep shame. Probably one of those guys who never thinks he'll cheat but really would if the occasion presented itself. I look down again and feel all the tension in my muscles relax. So it wasn't about my scars. Thank god.

"Wanna go have another drink with me?" I ask, just to be polite.

"Um, naw. I gotta go home. I work in the morning. You know how it is." He's laughing but also already backing away as he answers. I frantically nod. "And oh, um, can you maybe not text me unless I text you first? You see, I'm kind of seeing someone…and she's not nearly as chill as you. I mean, I definitely want to see you again, but just wait until I text you. Okay?"

I knew it. The guilt seems to have quite a sobering effect.

"Of course." I pout in an understanding way.

He sighs, almost inaudibly, but I sense the relief.

"Okay, sweet. Thanks. I'll see you around." Then he slips out the door like he's escaping imminent danger.

I spit in the sink and rinse out my mouth. I don't cry like I would have in the past. I've grown accustomed to the tinge of regret that accompanies most everything I do. Then I think of how I had actually hoped this time would be different. Not just the same old scum and fake compliments. I thought that was middle school bullshit. Stupid Gabe. I can't believe I fell for his slick, gilded sex stories. He's not just one to embellish; he's a total liar. It's the same as it ever was.

Then again, Gabe seemed to be having fun earlier. That guy he was with might have been a little old, but at least he was handsome. You could tell he really wanted Gabe, too. It's always better when they really want you. I wonder if they're even still here. Probably not. Suddenly, I'm nauseated. I stagger to the toilet and the entire content of my stomach hurls itself into the water in three heaves.

I stand and wipe my mouth. I turn to the mirror. The face I see looks completely different from the one I remembered from my room. No more illusion. My foundation caked on my cheeks and forehead, patchy with pimples sticking their white heads through the layers of carefully applied camouflage. Black globs of eyeliner cling to the corners of my eyes. Clumpy mascara. My lipstick, fully erased from the middle, now forms a dry, crinkled circle that smears outward past the border of my lips. Tired, haggard eyes with fine lines already appearing in the corners, creasing the thick foundation in obvious cracks. Flyaway hairs and tangled knots frame this prematurely weathered face. I try to push it away, but emptiness swallows me. I freeze for what must have been a long time and only snap out of it when some girl pounds on the door, loudly proclaiming that other people need to use the restroom too.

Suddenly, I'm going to be sick again. I feel it build up in my stomach and I vomit all over the sink, some even splashing onto the mirror, smearing across my reflection. The girl is still pounding on the door, ordering me to open up, but I can't do anything but purge the burning liquid from my stomach down the drain before me. Dizzy and shaking, I realize I'm crying, and I hopelessly try to smudge the makeup back into an acceptable face. Once more my stomach heaves and liquor mixed with acid gushes from me.

I'm sobbing, deep, disgusting, guttural sounds when Gabe gets them to unlock the bathroom to get me, dragging me to his car to take me home. He glares at me and turns the radio almost all the way up for most of the ride. Somehow, it helps a little.

Finally, I stop shaking and rub at my throat, as if that could soothe my sore esophagus. I feel myself glow red as I slide down into the seat, into the coat Gabe wrapped around me, pushing it into my mouth to stifle my cries as he rushed me from the bar. I'm sobering up and embarrassment creeps into my throat, closing it tight. I burrow down deeper into the coat and try to disappear, but it doesn't work.

WINNIE

As soon as I wake up, my head explodes in pain. I definitely overdid it with the vodka last night. I text Gabe, but he doesn't answer. Probably still sleeping, like a normal teenager on a Saturday morning. I, however, am required to make breakfast and tend the house as usual. There are no days off here.

As I set Dad's plate of fried eggs in front of him, I secretly commiserate with him as I can see he's even more hungover than I am. Lilly begs for pancakes and Brendan wants biscuits and gravy, so breakfast takes all morning. Thankfully, my queasiness and headache fade as I clean up the kitchen, and I feel back to normal by the time I'm scrubbing the bathroom. After all my morning duties, I try to sneak out to go somewhere, anywhere. Maybe walk around the park, downtown, really anywhere but home. Lilly stops me at the door. She stands in front of it, smug with arms crossed against her chest.

"No, Winnie, I don't want you to go. You're always gone now."

"What are you talking about? I'm always at home. Don't be silly. I'm just going out for a little while."

"You're always busy or gone. Please stay and play with me. Just for a little while."

I try to slide past her to the doorknob, but she grabs my arm and hugs it.

"Why don't you go over to one of those neighbor girls' houses, like Ally or…what's her name, uh, Danielle? I'm sure they're more fun than me," I say as I pull my arm free.

"Dad doesn't let me go over there anymore. He says I can only stay in the house or backyard," she says as she shuffles her feet. "Please, just for a little while? I'll let you pick what we play." I look down and desperation emanates from her tiny frame. She really is that lonely.

"Fine, we can play," I say, and she squeals with glee, pulling me by the arm into her room. As we walk through the door, an acrid stench hits me.

"Lilly, it smells weird in here. What is that?" I cover my nose with my sleeve as I speak. Lilly shrugs, but I search her room.

"Stop it! Stop and come play," she whines behind me, but I keep looking. Nothing under the bed, in the toy box, in the hamper. Then I see something shoved behind her nightstand.

"What's this?" I ask as I pull it out, but Lilly is on me instantly, trying to pry it from my hands.

"Don't tell Dad. He was so proud I'd stopped. Give it back," she whispers as she grabs at it, trying to pry the cloth with all her strength. I let go, and she falls to the floor. Her bug-eyed, surprised face delights me, and I yank the cloth from her before she can register what's happened. Unfurled, I see right away that it's one of her dresses. A wadded pair of panties drops to the floor, half-soaked in stale urine.

"Lilly, what is this? Why didn't you tell me so I could wash this for you?" I snap, but she just scrunches her nose and glares. She wore this dress two days ago. I remember thinking it was suspicious that she changed midday, but I figured she was too cold in that skimpy sundress she'd decided on. It's not even laundry day until tomorrow. She didn't stink when I gave her a bath that day. Must've washed up beforehand. These thoughts all race through my head like lightning.

"Don't tell Dad. I hadn't had an accident in so long," she half whispers, half whines. "He says I'm 'too old' to be 'pissing my pants all the time.'"

"Lilly! Don't say that word. It's not a nice word," I say, and her face softens into embarrassment. "Well, I'm glad I found this. Did you think you could just hide it forever?"

"No, I was going to wash it myself. I just couldn't figure out the machine."

"Well, if you want to know, I'll teach you how, but seriously, you have to tell me next time." I try to sound as if it's for her own good, but the lump in my throat comes from the knowledge that it wouldn't be Lilly who got in trouble for this cover-up. I open the window, hoping some fresh air might circulate in and diffuse the smell.

"Want to come learn how to use the washing machine?" I ask, but Lilly's already face down on her bed, sulking. If she had only told me, we could have avoided this mess.

I grab the towel hamper in the bathroom and place the soiled clothes in it, carefully covering them with the rags from this morning. I calm myself by repeating over and over in my head: *If Dad asks, I'll say these towels smelled too gross to wait another day*. He loves a clean house and a "useful" woman. I roll my eyes at the thought.

Dad is back in his room, door closed, probably sleeping off the rest of his hangover. As the washing machine lurches to life, I peek around the corner and watch his door. Nothing. I guess the noise isn't bothering him. I unfold the plastic chair in the tiny laundry room and sit down.

I can't go anywhere until Lilly's secret is successfully taken care of, for both of our sakes. I take out my phone, but Gabe still hasn't answered. I open the browser and search for random things but quickly run out of interesting topics. Who was that cool scientist Gabe told me about the other day? I rack my brain but can't remember.

Putting the phone away, I close my eyes and indulge myself in forbidden fantasies. I'm dissecting that gray cat, extracting all its organs, then cooking it and serving it to my unsuspecting family. I'm running away with Jeremy from last summer and we're at a sleazy hotel, fucking on the bathroom counter. I'm buying a gun, loading it, walking into my Dad's bedroom; he falls to the ground, crawling and shocked. Begging me to stop. He's kissing my feet. When he looks up, I shoot him right in the face. I'm tying Brendan to the bed, covering every inch of his skin in clothespins, then jumping on his chest and stomach until he throws up. He spits blood and wheezes for help, but I pretend I can't hear him. I'm burning all of Lilly's toys in the gas grill, one by one, while she screams, helplessly tied to a chair. The washer chimes and I'm back to reality. I put everything in the dryer, then lean back and start all over again.

By the time the towels and Lilly's clothes are finished, I have an idea of what I'll do today. Folding towels, I think over my plan and grin. Crushing snails is not quite satisfying enough, but something bigger might be. A dog would be easy to find and lead away. There are plenty of dogs in our neighborhood. Then Gabe could come, and we could dissect it, just like in class. It'd be so much bigger and interesting than that piglet. Maybe I could be a surgeon someday. This could be great practice and give me a better understanding of the bodily systems than most other students. A real leg up on the competition. Plus, didn't Leonardo da Vinci dissect animals he found and even rob graves for human cadavers? Nobody thinks poorly of him.

I put the towels away and toss the folded pile of Lilly's clothes on the bed next to her. She's still sulking, or perhaps hiding her embarrassment.

As I grab my bag, throwing a few things into it, a new fantasy forms in my mind. I'm a famous surgeon, the leading expert on organ transplants. I save hundreds of lives with my skill and live in a fabulous mansion. Dad comes to me and begs me to help him out. His work fired him and now he's penniless. I laugh in his face and toss him a penny. Problem solved. I almost laugh out loud as I head down the driveway.

As soon as I'm a few blocks away, I start scouting yards for a potential victim. There's an old dog sleeping on a porch of an ugly yellow house with too many windchimes. I whistle to him, and one ear perks up, but his droopy face stays placid and full of sleep. I'm about to open the fence, when a rubber ball comes out of nowhere and whacks me in the side of my head.

"Ow! What the hell?" I yell, just as a little girl comes running across the road, hands outstretched and eyes wide. It takes me a second but then I recognize her as Julia's best friend, Leigh. I had to babysit them both for a couple hours when she showed up for a playdate Julia's mom forgot to cancel and I wasn't even paid any extra. When I remember this, a slimy kind of anger burbles in my gut.

"Sorry!" She scrambles for the ball, clutching it against her chest, long blonde hair falling across her face. "It was an accident." I can tell she doesn't remember me from the way she backs away like I'm the kind of scary stranger her parents have warned her about. Or maybe she's just embarrassed about hitting me in the face. There is a light red glow across her nose and cheeks which could be a blush. As I look closer at her, a high, tinny sound rings in the back of my head, like a faraway siren. There's something about her. What is it? I shake the feeling away. I'm sure I'm just tripping from the adrenaline of the surprise attack mixed with my macabre quest being interrupted.

"It's fine, but you need to be more careful. You didn't look both ways before you ran across the street."

"Okay," she calls out, looking down the street this time before running back. I look back at the sleeping old dog and know I have to let him go. She'd remember me. I sigh as I rub at the place where the ball hit, even though it doesn't hurt anymore, and keep going.

After a snaking path down streets less and less familiar, I come to an old house with peeling paint and a dirty salt-and-pepper dog roaming around the yard. Approaching the waist-high fence, the dog happily ambles over, tongue hanging out of his mouth. I've never seen him before, but he seems like an easygoing old-timer. He's not wearing a collar. Maybe he's just a stray, I tell myself, and somehow got into this yard looking for food. He whines softly, slobbering on my hands as I lean over the fence to stroke him. His fur is wiry and unpleasant to touch, but I can't bring myself to stop petting him when he leans into my hand and joyfully thumps his foot.

He's such a friendly dog. For a moment, I consider trying to find a meaner stray, one that would be put down at the pound anyway. Then I realize the heightened difficulty in catching and leading a dog like that, so I decide to deaden myself. This is necessary. This is exactly what I need. No turning back now. I take out the old clothesline I found in the laundry room and tie a loop large enough to fit over the dog's head.

Glancing around, making sure no one is around, I open the gate to the fence and the dog happily bounds out, jumping at my legs and whining. I slip the rope around his neck, and to my surprise, he doesn't resist at all. I easily lead him away from the house and down the street, as if he was my own pet I was taking on a walk.

We get back to my house, and I quickly sneak him through the backyard and into the woods. The dog follows obediently, only stopping now and then to sniff, and immediately picking up his pace again when I yank on his makeshift leash. We go quite far, farther than Dad or anyone usually goes, to make sure it'll be a private place. I tie the dog to a tree and he sits, whining at me as I stand a few feet away from him, beyond the reach of his tether.

We look into each other's eyes and I'm not sure what to do next. I hadn't thought through the necessary steps between finding a dog and dissecting its carcass. Rubbing my hand across my lips, I think. What would be a fast, easy way to do it? I don't want to hurt him, although dying seems like a painful process no matter what. I definitely don't want him to screech or howl and cause any curious people to come out here. Especially Dad.

A gun would probably hurt the least, but that'd be loud, plus I don't have one anyway. I wouldn't even know where to get one. I look at the flimsy clothesline and decide it's much too weak and thin to strangle him with and would probably cut his neck and hurt him quite badly. He might even try to bite me. I think of other possible weapons at the house, but I don't want to stab or beat the dog. He's been so nice to me. Much nicer than most people I've known. Finally, I decide poison is the only acceptable answer and I walk back to the house. Nobody seems to notice as I slip in, digging through the cleaning chemicals under the sink, and then the food in the fridge.

Back with the dog, he whimpers as I pull the raw ground beef out of my bag and unwrap it, putting it in an old, cracked mixing bowl Dad wanted me to get rid of any-way. He whines louder and paws at the ground, licking his chops. I take out the package of rat poison, almost a full box of teal pellets, and mix them into the meat with a stick, then give the bowl to the dog. Snorting with pleasure, he devours the entire meal in seconds. I spend a few minutes petting him, trying to make these last memories tolerable, and then I go home. I'll try to forget about him until to-morrow. That should be more than enough time. I hear him whine a little behind me, but I don't stop walking, and soon I'm too far away to hear anything at all.

GABRIEL WALSH

POLICE INTERVIEW TRANSCRIPT
PART 1

DEC. **18**

Det. Garcia: Hello Mr. Walsh. I'm Detective Garcia and this is Detective Wilson. As you might've heard, we're investigating the disappearance of your friend Winnie Campbell. Thank you for agreeing to speak with us. I do need to let you know; we are recording this conversation, just in case there's anything important we need to review later.

Walsh: Of course. I assumed as much. Do you think she's okay?

Det. Garcia: At this time, we can't say. We know you're close with Winnie. What can you tell us about where she might've gone?

Walsh: Unfortunately, officers, I don't think I'll be much help to you.

Det. Garcia: Oh yeah? Why's that?

Walsh: I mean, I don't know anything. She probably just ran away or something, but she didn't tell me anything about it.

Det. Garcia: She didn't? Because, if she didn't say anything, why would you think she ran away?

Walsh: I don't know. She was just impulsive like that, I guess. But I really don't know. She could be anywhere, I suppose.

Det. Garcia: Hmmm. You suppose?

Walsh: I hope she isn't hurt or anything. I've heard rumors about what happened... Are those true?

Det. Garcia: Unfortunately, I can't tell you anything about that. We just want to ask you a few questions. Mr. Walsh, did she have any reasons to—

Walsh: Can you just call me Gabe?

Det. Garcia: Okay, Gabe, what do you think could have made her want to run away?

Walsh: Well, I mean, I guess she talked about running away in the past. A lot. You know, her dad is a real asshole. Beat her up and shit.

Det. Wilson: Oh yeah? How do you know that?

Walsh: Jesus, everybody who knew her at all knew *that*. She always had bruises and shit. Even broken bones a couple times.

Det. Wilson: Hmm, we don't have records of that. Garcia, go double-check if we have medical records or—

Walsh: No, okay, maybe not everyone knew about the shit with her dad. He never let her go to the doctor, and he was really good about mostly just hitting her where clothes would cover it. But she told me and even showed me a few times.

Det. Wilson: Hmmm.

Det. Garcia: So you're saying she ran away to get away from her father?

Walsh: How would I know? But, sure, yeah, I could see that being the case.

Det. Wilson: Do you think she has family or friends who are helping her? Maybe hiding her somewhere? Or maybe her dad gave her money to get out of town?

Walsh: No, no way! That jackass probably set this whole thing up to frame her and have her take a fall for something he did.

Det. Garcia: And what do you think he did?

Walsh: Well, duh! He set this whole thing up. I've heard the rumors, and the way you're acting, I know they're true. I know what happened. Fuck. He's a conniving bastard like that.

See, I've known Winnie a long time and she would never do something like that, but that asshole would. He's almost killed Winnie before, so he has it in him, and who better to take the fall than his punching bag of a daughter? That's probably why she ran away. She probably knew you guys were going to railroad her and her own dad was gonna testify that she did something that he damn well knows she didn't. You should be talking to him right now! That's what I think.

Det. Wilson: Now, hold on there, Gabe. What makes you say that? We haven't released any information about what happened. I know there's been talk but...

Det. Garcia: Has Winnie been in contact with you? Has she told you something?

Det. Wilson: It's okay. You can tell us. We don't want to hurt her. We just want to speak to her.

Walsh: No, I already told you I haven't seen or spoken with her at all. Come on, as if news like this doesn't get around?

Det. Wilson: True.

Walsh: All I know is what I've heard, and what I know about that fucked up family. Honestly, maybe I'm wrong about the whole thing and she's lying dead somewhere in a ditch, just waiting for somebody to find her, but I still think, even then, her dad did something. He's a mean old bastard.

Det. Garcia: Now, Gabe, just wondering here. What sparked this whole framing theory?

Walsh: Listen. I just know Winnie really well, and I've heard all about the way her dad treats her. He's either killed her or is trying to pin this on her.

Det. Garcia: I just think it's interesting that you're so sure it's someone in the Campbell family involved in this.

Walsh: Well, I watch enough true crime shows to know that's where to start. Random wackos aren't too common. I mean, you must be looking into this dad thing too, right?

Det. Wilson: Don't worry. We're following all possible leads. Now, can you tell us anything else about Winnie that might be helpful? Like where she might have gone if she ran away.

Walsh: I don't know. She doesn't have a car, so she'd probably take the bus. She used to take the bus downtown a lot.

Det. Wilson: We have police looking for her in the city, stopping traffic to search, and even combing the woods.

Walsh: Then I have no idea. Um, she had a lot of money saved up from babysitting. Maybe she took a greyhound somewhere? Have you looked into that? Maybe her dad put her on one.

Det. Garcia: We're checking the records of all planes and buses that left around the time she went missing. Does she have any friends or family that she might head to?

Walsh: I don't think so.

Det. Garcia: Hmm. Gabe, can you tell us a bit more about your Mr. Campbell theory? It sounds like you've thought about it a lot and your input in the case could be very helpful.

Det. Wilson: What are you—

Det. Garcia: Stop it, Greg. Maybe we should listen to him. Let Gabe here tell us his theory. He obviously has insight into the family we don't. You know we can use all the help we can get in this case.

Det. Wilson: Okay. I guess you're right.

Walsh: Of course, officers. I'll do anything to help.

WINNIE

I look at my phone and still nothing. It's been over a day since I've heard from Gabe. I really messed things up, I'm such an embarrassment. That was his favorite place. I know he was mortified. What I don't know is how to make it up to him. Maybe the dog thing will help. We've always both been fascinated by the intricacy of the venous system, the reliability of the heart, the efficiency of the liver. This will be more a gift to him than anything else. I need to do this to win him back. I justify it that way over and over in my mind, a thinly veiled denial, not even fooling myself.

It's past lunch and my stomach grumbles, but this morning Dad said I didn't need to eat today. He said I should be "plenty full" when he discovered the missing ground beef after requesting sloppy joes last night. I claimed I didn't know what happened to it, but I'm a horrible liar. My back burns from the belt lashing and my stomach churns, empty save for acid. I try to keep my mind off the pain by immersing myself in the true crime paperback Gabe lent me, the cover ripped off and the yellowed pages worn and buttery beneath my fingers, but the hungry pangs interrupt me again and again.

I hear him playing with Lilly in the living room, probably Monopoly since they're joking about going to "jail". I busy myself with little chores and errands: organizing the spice drawer, dusting the bookshelves, a quick bus trip to the grocery store to replace the ground beef and pick up a few more ingredients Dad requested via a list on the fridge. I don't dare eat anything, even though he probably wouldn't find out. I've thought that in the past and was gravely mistaken.

At about four, I decide to go back to the dog. It's bound to be over by now. The distant howling from last night echoes in my head. Could that have been him? I sneak out the back, unnoticed.

When I'm close to the spot I remember leaving him, I hear an unusual rustling of leaves. Not the typical crunching of feet, but a constant shuffling back and forth. My heart pounds and my jaw clenches tight. I tiptoe closer to the clearing and can hear a weak whimper under the rustling of the leaves.

My breath freezes in my lungs when I see him. His eyes are rolled far back in his head, which rests in a frothy puddle of vomit. The whole body is rigid and convulsing. As I get closer, I notice a fervid heat radiates from him. I start to hyperventilate. His tongue lolls out and a tiny whine chokes from deep in his throat. I pull at my hair. *Why didn't you die?* My eyes dart around for anything.

I see a rock the size of both my fists and sprint to it, then run even faster back to the dog. I slip on the vomit and fall by his side, one hand trying to hold the rock, the other landing on his seizing, fevered flesh. I grimace and yank my hand away. His wriggling body and white eyes mock me. Mock my vain attempt at a good death. I retreat deep into my mind. Go to that emptiness, that calm, blank, nowhere place. Taking the rock firmly in both hands, I raise it high above my head, my arms shaking under the weight. Then swing down with all my strength. Again and again, I bring the rock down on his head. His skull cracks and blood trickles from the wounds, but he stops moving. At last, he's dead.

Exhausted, I drop the rock and crumple by his side. I wheeze and can't get enough air, but after a while, my breathing slows. I pull the soiled clothesline over his head and put it back in my bag. I wipe the splatter and vomit off my hands into his fur. His body is already cooling.

My hands shake as I text Gabe again: *Come to my house. I found something cool.* I hesitate then send another message: *Really sorry about the other day. Let me make it up to you.* Then I sit on the forest floor and wait.

Twenty minutes later, he texts back that he'll head over soon. The same excitement and pride pulse through me as before.

Before I leave, I look at the dog again. Its eyes are still rolled back, just the white sclera showing except for one dilated pupil which has inched down enough that it feels the dead eye is watching me. Something seems to call to me through this unseeing void. Something cold and sinister, beckoning me. A chill, like icy fingers tracing down my spine, and I shudder, then bend over and close the eyelids before I trudge back to the front yard, just in time to see Gabe walking up.

"Hey, I'm still pretty pissed at you about Friday night." The scowl he wears reminds me of Dad.

"I really don't know what came over me," I say, pulling a twist of hair over my mouth as I speak. "I guess I just got too drunk."

"You've never acted like that when you got drunk before, and I've seen you much worse." He sneers as he adds, "I don't usually hang out with people set on embarrassing me."

"I didn't mean to." I look down and bite my lip.

Gabe kicks a pebble across the driveway. "Yeah, whatever."

We stand in the driveway, our eyes darting around, unsure where to land. The tension slowly dissipates.

"So, what's this cool thing you found?" Gabe finally breaks the silence, his voice much calmer, almost playful.

"It's out in the woods. Come on, I'll show you."

I lead him through the branches, making sure Dad isn't watching from the window. It's a long walk so I hurry, hoping we get there before Gabe loses interest and turns back.

"Why were you out so far? We must've walked like a mile by now," he whines a few paces behind me.

"I don't know, I was just trying to get far enough away from my house to have some peace, and I found this."

"What's up with all the suspense?" he asks, but I ignore him and in a couple minutes we're there. The dog is exactly as I'd left him.

"Whoa! What the hell?" Gabe takes a step back, then curiosity replaces shock, and he walks over, prodding the dog with his index finger. "Jesus Christ, it's still kinda warm, Winnie." He looks at me with a stern yet inquisitive look. I shrug and so does he, an unspoken contract of silence.

"I was thinking, maybe if we could find the right tools, we could dissect him. Just like the fetal pig in Mr. Jenkins's class." I tap the dog's leg with my sneaker as I speak.

Gabe's eyes light up. "You know, that's actually a pretty cool idea. I think we could do it with some scissors, a knife, and some kind of stick for a probe. I could probably score us some gloves. Yeah, this could be great! It'll be like performing a real surgery."

"That's exactly what I was thinking!" I shout as validation washes over me.

"Sweet. I'll go grab some stuff at my house. Help me walk back to yours so I don't get lost on the way."

Within a couple hours, we have successfully opened and dissected the dog. Delicately handling each organ, examining the circulatory system, parting muscles to see how they connect. The tendrils of intestine are my favorite, slippery and warm. Gabe seems most fascinated by the heart, turning it over and over in his hands. We decide not to take out the brain since Gabe says he'd rather not explore the head at all. I don't argue with him, although I had hoped at least to glimpse the coils of the frontal cortex, but it's not worth it if it bothers him.

The empty carcass now lies on its back, its tongue hanging out and resting in the dirt. The organs and some muscles lie around it in a semi-circle, and I can't help but find a morbid beauty in the display. Gabe pours a water bottle over my bloody arms after I've removed the gloves, and I scrub them clean before returning the favor. As he packs up, I pick at the dried blood stuck under a fingernail where the glove split.

"That was intense," Gabe says, and pulls out a cigarette. He offers one to me, but I don't need it. "But, for real though, did you really just find this dog dead out here?"

I look at Gabe squarely in the eye, and that's all I need to do. He snorts a laugh and shrugs again. He pulls out his small flask as he puffs on the cigarette and takes a swig.

"Hey, so the other night, I might have noticed you accompanying a young man to the restroom, before your total and complete freakout, of course," Gabe says with a little wink.

"Yeah, he was a real loser though," I grunt as I sit on the wet forest floor, still picking at my nail.

"Did you get his number? We could prank him, like the good old days."

I smirk as I bring out my phone. "Oh yeah, I think I did. Actually, he said I shouldn't text him and should only wait for him to text me. Something about a girlfriend."

"Do it," he says immediately. I think for a minute about what I should say. Then I find Brent's texts. Almost six o'clock, he's certainly home with this girlfriend, probably exchanging pet names as he wraps his arms around her, kissing her neck as she stirs some chicken soup she's making for dinner.

I scoff and text: *Was so nice sucking your cock the other night. I def want to see you again ;) <3*

That should do it.

"Let me see what you said." Gabe grabs my phone and bursts out laughing before handing it back. "Good one."

"Whatever," I say, but I can't help but smile. He passes me his small silver flask and I take a long swallow. Tastes like gasoline.

"Gross! What is this shit?"

"I don't know," he says, snatching it back. "I take what I can find. Tequila is tequila."

"Ugh, well, I guess it does the job." He passes it back, and I take another swig.

My phone buzzes and I roll over laughing as I read the text: *Who is this? Why are you texting Brent?*

"Oh my God, classic!" Gabe cries out, almost doubling over in his laughter.

"Yeah, that jackass deserved it. I can't believe that worked! She must've been right there, watching his phone."

Gabe nudges me and says, "We're such bastards. Fuck 'em and leave 'em. To hell with everybody's stupid ideals of love. Like we need it." He laughs, but I force a smile.

We pass the flask back and forth a few more times. I breathe in the crisp air and I feel alive. The world is mine for the taking.

"Hey, don't tell anyone about this whole dog thing," I say.

"Duh." He rolls his eyes. "But I guess we should bury it or something. What if the owner goes looking for it?"

"We're way out in the middle of nowhere," I argue, but I know he's right. "Fine."

It takes a long time to dig in the mess of roots, but the earth is soft enough that we can do it with just a small trowel and garden spade I fetch from Dad's shed. We push the empty carcass in first, then scoop up the organs and throw them on top, careful not to get blood on our clothes. In the end, the dirt mound is barely visible, even if it's not very deep.

We walk back together as the sun sets. I imagine we're outlaws. Partners in crime. I feel my face glowing, prouder than I've felt in years.

WINNIE

I walk to school today. Brendan's car is in the shop and Dad says he needs to leave for work too early to take us. Of course, Brendan immediately decides to abandon me, catching a ride with some girl, leaving me to deal with Lilly. I text Gabe, but he's probably still sleeping since he doesn't answer. It's early, so I don't blame him. Unfortunately, elementary school starts earlier than most of my peers have even rolled out of bed. Since we never ride in the morning, the school bus doesn't even come near our street, and I don't see any feasible routes on the city bus to get Lilly to school on time. That leaves us no option but to walk.

First comes the two-mile trek to Lilly's school. I have to carry her on my back the last bit because she says her feet hurt too much to keep going. After seeing her in, I trudge to my own school.

As I push open the door, sweat trickles down my face and neck and I wonder if my makeup is still intact. My feet are sweating in these thick socks and leather boots, and I curse myself for dressing for the autumn weather instead of the inevitable exercise I knew was coming when I heard about Brendan's car trouble.

Inside my locker, I look in the tiny magnetic mirror and dab powder on the remaining foundation that hasn't sweated off, focusing the most attention to those thinly veiled scars down my cheek and neck. Eyes burn into my back, and I know someone's watching me. I shift the mirror slightly to see that asshole Patrick standing behind me. His locker isn't anywhere near mine, so I brace for some sort of comment, but he doesn't say a word. He just winks and then bursts into a laugh.

I attempt to ignore him as I take the cap off my lipstick and reapply a thick layer of the black cherry color. I hear him walking away, but he's still laughing. Rage bubbles up and I imagine slitting his throat, the blood spurting down his shirt while he claws at it with desperate hands. Then he'd stop laughing. Slamming the locker shut, I scurry to my class as his laughter echoes after me down the hall.

The day passes slowly, filled with half-ignored lessons and scribbled notes. Each teacher doles out disappointed looks to the students who neglected their weekend homework, myself included. As I step through Mr. Jenkins' classroom door and fail to place my copy of the Friday assignment in the homework folder, he stops me.

"Why haven't you been doing the homework, Winnie?" His brows knit, and his voice is warm with concern.

"I don't know. I guess I just keep forgetting," I say as I squeeze past him.

"You've excelled in this class all year, don't let it slip now," Mr. Jenkins says, his voice trailing me as I move for the empty spot Gabe's saving for me.

He's bent over a book, deeply enthralled. I try to read over his shoulder. He laughs at my awkward attempt and shows me the front. *120 Days of Sodom* is sprawled across the glossy cover.

"Oh, I've heard of that. It's supposed to be super kinky, right?" I ask, setting my notebooks down and taking my seat.

"Eh, it was pretty good for a while, but now it's just all about shitting on each other," Gabe says, dog-earring the page corner and shutting the book. I laugh and he shrugs. "So, want to hang after school today? We could catch a movie or something."

"I can't," I say, "Mrs. Carpenter called yesterday after you left to ask if I could babysit."

"Cool, whatever."

Mr. Jenkins' dry-erase marker scratches across the board and I open my notebook, ready to take notes. Gabe leans over and whispers, "Dude, your mutt totally topped anything this old geezer could ever show us." A blush spreads across my face and I smile. I copy down the loopy words cluttering the board.

After class, Gabe and I walk to the lunchroom together. He's beside me as I slide my tray down the line, snickering at some of the more unappetizing items, but doesn't take anything himself.

"Your mom forgot to put money in your account again?" I ask, but he just shrugs. At the end of the line, I take two cornbread muffins, my tray heaped with more than I can eat by myself. We sit at our usual spot and immediately Gabe grabs one muffin and unwraps it.

"Hey, did you bring your cards today? We haven't done that in a while and I've been practicing at home. Let me try to do yours."

Cornbread crumbs spray across the table as he speaks. I search through my bag while Gabe finishes the first muffin and starts working on the second. The cards are at the very bottom, held together with a rubber band, their worn edges rounded and soft from use.

"You should've brought yours," I say, removing the rubber band and shuffling. "The artwork is prettier. Plus, these are pretty much trashed at this point. I've been meaning to get some new ones."

"Yours work better because they're old, duh," he says as I continue to shuffle, weaving cards in and out, sliding their worn edges into each other. He smiles at the careful shuffling and adds, "I think they used to belong to a powerful psychic."

"Why would she give them to a thrift shop then?"

He shrugs and I can tell by his excited eyes, he's getting impatient. I close my eyes to concentrate, focus my energy on the cards, think about my future. I don't wonder about the usual things, like what my future husband will be like or which college I'll end up at, but instead focus on what will become of me. Will I ever get away from here?

After a minute, I feel they're ready, and I hand the stack into Gabe's eager hands. In either parody or showmanship, Gabe waves his hands over the cards and whispers some nonsense. I sigh and look around, making sure no one is watching. He sets out four cards for the most basic reading I've taught him. Flipping the first card reveals the past: the Eight of Cups. The golden cups shine in the moonlight while an old man in a red robe walks away, cane in hand, into the dark.

Gabe looks down on it and then at me, taking his time before saying, "The Eight of Cups shows dissatisfaction and a need for change. A past full of boredom and things holding you back. Like the man on the card, you have left this time behind you and are moving on with your life." I smile yet feel some unease about this card. Gabe looks to me with raised eyebrows.

"What?" I ask and cross my legs under the table.

"Am I doing okay so far?" His eyebrows rise farther, creasing his brow, a childish grin hinted on his lips.

"Yeah, yeah. Keep going," I laugh. He flips over the next card, representing my present situation. It's the Two of Swords with its blindfolded woman seated before the sea, wielding the pair of swords, her arms crossed against her chest.

Gabe looks at it for a minute, and I can tell he's struggling to remember its exact meaning. Suddenly, he jerks his head slightly.

"A time of rest and careful reflection before a conflict. Your sword against theirs, your will against theirs, and you must hold your ground and come out the champion. A preparation for combat."

I nod, and he seems pleased with himself.

The next card, my future, is flipped and he uncovers a man pinned face down to the ground with many swords, piercing into his flesh and standing tall against the darkening sky. It's the Ten of Swords, and I swallow hard when I see it. Not a favorite card to have in a reading.

I look to Gabe and he too seems disturbed to see it. I take a breath, prepared to laugh it off, when he stops me with his eyes.

"The Ten of Swords is nobody's friend," he begins, looking slightly away in an uncharacteristically sheepish manner. "It shows us complete destruction and a final fall. Your future holds the ending of something. Pain, failure, and stress will overwhelm you when this future unfolds, but at least there's hope. That's all one can cling to when the Ten of Swords rears its head." Gabe laughs a nervous giggle after saying this, trying to relieve the tension, but a sort of solemn importance has settled itself into this reading. He taps his fingers on the table and adds, "It's just a stupid card game. It's not real or anything."

My hand lunges out and I flip the last card. The Star, a symbol of hope and change. I breathe a sigh of relief. I touch his hand and force a smile.

"You did a great job reading them. I totally think you could have a booth at the carnival or maybe a webcam business or something. You have the spookiness necessary to make it feel real. And don't worry about that card, it's not a stupid game, but it doesn't mean anything that I didn't already know. Nothing to worry about. Plus, the Star as signifier helps. At least there's hope." I watch his smile ease from fraudulent grin to relief.

"Hey." He kicks my leg playfully under the table. "I *am* kind of spooky when I do it, right? Maybe I really could start charging people for readings. It's fun and who isn't eager to see their future? Maybe we could add some hoodoo magic if you find another animal like your dog."

"Shhh, don't talk about that at school."

"It's not like you killed it, right? We just did what any scientist would do," he says, winking and pushing back his bangs. "I was just thinking that some more intense props, like a real heart, would probably make some big money."

"Hmm, I don't know." I sigh and finally start eating my lunch, cold and gelatinous on my tray. I gag down a couple spoonfuls.

"Well, maybe we can talk about it after school. Wanna hang out at the park?" he asks, but I shake my head as I force myself to swallow.

"I have to babysit tonight, remember?" I rub my stomach a little, trying to force it to accept the slime. A grimace crosses my face before my stomach settles.

"That sucks. Maybe tomorrow," Gabe says, but he's already taken out his phone and is texting. I can't see the screen, but it's probably some hookup he's arranging now that he knows he's without evening plans.

After school, it's the usual routine of chores, cooking, and general slavehood until I remind Dad I need to leave right after dinner to watch the Carpenter girls.

"I was wondering why you made dinner so early. Well, you'll need to take Lilly with you this time. I'm going over to Jeb's later, and Brendan doesn't need to be doing all that after a hard day of school and work."

I don't even try to argue with him. It won't change anything, not in any way positive at least. I throw a few coloring books into my backpack, tug a sweater over my sister and, taking her hand, pull her down the street to the Carpenter's house. She doesn't protest but drags her feet the whole walk. We wait at the front door, my hand clasping hers beside me since she's already rang the doorbell twice.

"They're taking forever," she whines. "Are you sure they're even home?"

I ignore her, step back, and admire the brick archway. I love this house. It's one of the prettiest in our neighborhood with its red bricks and wooden garage. A beautiful house full of beautiful people.

The door swings open to reveal Mrs. Carpenter bouncing the baby, Allie, on her hip. It's a surprising image, a woman dressed in a royal blue sequined dress, hair carefully piled atop her head in an intricate updo, pearls around her neck, all topped off with a towel draped over her shoulder to catch the spit up of an almost nude infant clawing at her shoulder.

"Sorry, sorry," she mutters and pushes the baby into my arms in a way somehow both meek and domineering. We step inside, but she's already disappeared to another room. Up the stairs, the older girl, Julia, sings along to a karaoke game and I know from experience she's already decked out in her pink feather boa with plastic rings on every finger. A four-year-old rock star. Lilly looks to me and I see her yearning to join the girl but also her constraint to remain the cool older kid she wants to be.

"Why don't you go up and watch Julia for me while I take care of the baby?" I ask, granting her the perfect excuse. She runs up the stairs the second as I finish my sentence. Mrs. Carpenter reappears with a glittering clutch in her hand and no longer adorned with the vomit rag. Mr. Carpenter follows her in a formal suit, gold-plated cufflinks sparkling as he slides his hand across his hair.

"We'll be back by eleven at the latest," he says, and they're gone, barely waiting for me to move out of the doorway before they make their escape. I hear Lilly upstairs, joined in a falsetto, slightly sour harmony with Julia, and I bounce Allie on my hip the way her mother had done. White spit up gurgles over her lips and drips down onto my shirt, and I go looking for that rag.

WINNIE

"Hey, I'm really sorry about the other day," Krystal's voice rings into my ear as soon as I answer the phone. "I don't know why I was being so weird. I'm really sorry."

"It's fine. I'm sorry too. I was having kind of an off day, and it was rude of me to just show up unannounced like that."

"No! That was totally fine! That was great. I mean, it was great to see you! I was just distracted or something, thinking about the party later, and it'd been so long since you'd come over." She sighs. "I was being a total bitch. I'm sorry. You know I'm kind of jealous of Gabe, even though that's stupid and you guys still go to the same school, and here am I, all fake and stupid at this new school. You mean so much to me, Winnie. Really, you do. I know you think I'm different now, but I'm not. I'm still the same Krystal. I promise."

"The same great Krystal taste, but now in popular flavor," I say, trying to lighten the mood with a dumb joke, but I can feel her cringe through the phone and regret it.

"Winnie, just know that I'm sorry. I know you think I'm some kind of traitor or something, but I'm not. It's assimilate or die here. I didn't really have a choice. And honestly, it's also kind of nice to get a second chance and completely start over. It doesn't mean I'm not still that weirdo you've known since second grade."

"I know, I know. I'm happy for you. You're amazing and you deserve people to acknowledge that. You never had a chance here."

"Maybe you should think about changing schools. I know it's pretty far away, but if you could transfer here next year, I'd introduce you to everybody and you could be whoever you wanted here. Plus, you'd get away from that asshole Patrick. Don't even try to lie to me. I know he's still harassing you," she says. "I think he secretly likes you, but he'd never admit it. Not even to himself."

"It's too far, and it wouldn't be the same for me. You know it." I run my fingertips over the scars from my eyes, down my face and neck. I wait for Krystal to convince me otherwise, but she doesn't say anything.

"Do you want to hang out soon? You could come over and we could make popcorn and watch movies like the old days. We're way overdue for a movie night."

"I don't know. I'm always busy with all the babysitting and housework, it's hard to find time to do anything fun except for an hour or two after school." My mouth feels dry and sticky even though it's an honest excuse.

"I get it, but still, look into it. It's been too long. I hope your dad's not still treating you like shit. You said it was getting better, but that was a while ago that we talked about it."

"Yeah, it's not so bad. He's still strict, but that's just the way it is."

"Do you want to talk about it? You know I'm here for you."

"No, it's nothing. I should probably go."

"Winnie, he's not still…hurting you, right? You said he wasn't doing it anymore, but…" her voice trails off because she knows I'm not going to tell her. She's right.

"No, it's fine. I'll text you if I can get away for a movie night," I say. My heart swells with memories of Krystal, and suddenly I wish I was with her, and we could just run away together, something she'd never do. I know she cares, but she could never really understand. "Love you Koo Koo. Talk later."

"Okay, bye—" I hang up and cut her off. A sob builds in my throat, but I push it down and put back on the apathetic mask I wear at home.

Dad's yelling in Brendan's room, but I can't make out the words. My head spins and I swallow hard as I hear a door open then slam. Like a bull, he storms down the hall. I see his shadow at my door and quickly hide my phone under the mattress.

The door bursts open. Veins throb across his forehead and tendons strain in his neck. The empty, raging look in his eyes could almost be comforting, it's so familiar. I scramble to my feet, standing at attention. The thin gray hair, wiry, tall frame, taut face, fisted hands: this is the father I know. I can hardly remember when he wasn't like this, even though it was only a few years ago. He looms in the doorway, watching me.

"What are you doing sitting in the dark all alone?" he asks in a calm voice, clashing drastically with his appearance. I look at him, then down at the carpet. There's no right answer.

"Is there somebody in here with you? A boy maybe?" Without looking up, I shake my head furiously. He grunts and searches my closet, under my bed, peers outside the window. "There should be bars on this window. I know that's how you sneak them in and out of my house. As if I was too stupid to know what you've been up to."

He darts across the room. Footfalls rumble like a train. A calloused hand around my neck, menacing but not cutting off oxygen. Yet.

"You whore, I know you've been fucking around," he says, his face almost touching mine. "And smoking too. I can smell the stink on your breath." I force my eyes to stay open, fixed on the carpet. Our feet. Mine are dainty, nicely trimmed toenails painted a glittering azure. His feet are rough and hairy. They probably stink too. I'm better than him. In this way, I win. I am better.

The grip tightens around my neck, and I fight the urge to grab his hands. It only ever spurs him on. His grasp holds my head still as the blows cross my face. Deep within, I try to center myself. Withdrawing more and more. Relaxing the facial features. Looking down, but not disinterested or rebellious. Apathy is the only defense. A blow to my stomach doubles my body over in pain. Agony radiates through every nerve. The old bruises aren't anywhere close to healed.

"Why do you make me do this, Winnie? All I ever wanted was to be a good father, a good husband. You couldn't let me have it, could you?" he says and another blow lands lower, crashing into my hip. An airy gasp escapes my lips. "You won't follow the rules." Thud. "Won't behave." Thud. "You've even been corrupting your brother."

On my knees, I accidentally look up into his face. Something smashes against my skull and shatters. I can't see. I close my eyes. With my eyes closed, the total darkness isn't so scary.

I'm lying on my side, trying to disappear into the shag carpet. I drift away then back. I can sense time has passed. He's picking me up. Placing me on my bed. The sheet and comforter are gently brought over me, then tucked neatly under my body. Blood is trickling down my face. I turn my head the other way against the pillow, so it won't stain. Blood is so hard to get out. I open my eyes, but the dark remains, so I shut them tight again.

Footsteps leaving the room. A tap running far away. The sounds bounce through my head like a muffled echo, distorted as if underwater. Footsteps back and then a warm, wet rag is mopping away the trickle. He's humming. I can't focus well enough to remember what song it is, but it's familiar.

"Dad?" I ask, very softly, but he doesn't answer. He's still humming. "Brendan? Is it you? I can't see..." I say, but my voice is faint. I don't hear him speak as I fall asleep.

I wake up and my vision is back. The washcloth with my blood is on the pillow next to me. It's grown cold. Alone and tired, I glance around the room before I let myself sleep again. A perfume bottle is shattered where I had been lying. It's the one Mom gave me for that last birthday. I want to cry but I can't. It was almost empty anyway.

BRENDAN CAMPBELL

POLICE INTERVIEW TRANSCRIPT

DEC. **17**

Det. Garcia: Hello Brendan. Now, I know it's a very difficult time for you, but unfortunately, this is a time sensitive matter, so we need to talk.

B. Campbell: Oh god. No. I don't want to talk about anything. Just leave me alone.

Det. Garcia: I know you don't. I know. But we have to. We need to know everything to figure out what happened. We need to find Winnie.

B. Campbell: Do you—you think she could still be alive?

Det. Garcia: She could, so we need to find her fast. She might even be injured or in danger. I know you're hurting after what you saw, but we need to talk so we can figure this out, okay? Can you try to help us?

B. Campbell: Fuck. I can try, but I don't know anything about any of this.

Det. Garcia: We need to figure out if there are any clues about what might've happened. This could help us find her.

B. Campbell: It might help you find Winnie?

Det. Garcia: Yes. Listen to me, Brendan. You're dealing with a lot, but we need to know every detail we can to try to find your sister.

B. Campbell: I don't know. I just don't know!

Det. Garcia: Brendan, think hard. Do you have any idea where she could be?

B. Campbell: No. No. I don't know.

Det. Garcia: Can you tell us some places you'd expect her to go if she was scared and maybe needed help?

B. Campbell: Uh, I don't know... maybe Gabe or Krystal's house. She also liked to go to the park by our house a lot. I don't know. Oh my god, I'm so worried about her.

Det. Garcia: We already have police out searching, and unfortunately, we haven't located her with any of those friends. I'm not sure if they've checked the park, but I'll make sure they do immediately. Please, help your sister out and try to remember if she possibly ever mentioned any other people she might be staying with?

B. Campbell: No. But you need to find her. You need to find her soon! What if she's hurt or–or–

Det. Garcia: We're trying our best.

B. Campbell: I hope so. God, I'm so confused. Was she kidnapped? Is she even alive right now? I feel like I'm going to be sick.

Det. Garcia: That's why we need your help. We have to figure this thing out. Can I ask you a few questions about what life was like at home for your family?

B. Campbell: Yeah, I guess. Sure. Oh god. Oh shit. I'll tell you anything if it might help.

Det. Garcia: Brendan, what was the relationship between your sister and father like?

B. Campbell: Wait, you don't think Dad did this, do you? Oh my god! What if he did? No, no way! He was completely passed out before I even went out last night. There's no way he could've done this. He was snoring and spilling beer everywhere. I saw him. I saw him like that. I even took that can out of his hand and put it on the goddamn table so he wouldn't blame one of us for his mess the next day. There's no way it was him! Is that why you've got him in the other room? Is he under arrest over there? Oh god...

Det. Garcia: Calm down, Brendan, calm down. We understand that your father was very intoxicated, and no, he is not under arrest. We are just trying to figure out what exactly happened last night.

B. Campbell: Okay, I'm sorry. It's just—it's just so hard. I couldn't handle losing Dad. Not now.

Det. Garcia: Don't worry, Brendan. We are trying to make things right. We're trying to help you. When you're ready, just tell me what happened that night.

B. Campbell: Okay. Okay. Shit. Uh, it was a pretty normal night. Like I said, Dad drank a little too much after he got home.

Det. Garcia: About what time was that?

B. Campbell: I don't know. Like seven or something. I'm not sure.

Det. Garcia: Okay. What about your sisters?

B. Campbell: Lilly was normal. Bouncing all over the place. Winnie did seem in an especially bad mood, but I just figured something had happened at school.

Det. Garcia: Don't you two attend the same school? Uh, [redacted] High School?

B. Campbell: Yes.

Det. Garcia: Then wouldn't you have heard if something had happened?

B. Campbell: Oh no, probably not. I don't really hang with her. We uh—we hang with different groups. And people make fun of her sometimes.

Det. Garcia: Oh?

B. Campbell: You know, about the scars on her face and arm. Also, about how she's kind of fat. Her wannabe punk style. She's just not cool. God, I should've said something. I'm such a horrible brother.

Det. Garcia: You've heard students say these things to her?

B. Campbell: Well yeah. I mean, a few times.

Det. Garcia: Hm. Okay. So, she was bullied at school some-times. Tell me more about that night. What did Winnie say or do to make you think she was in a bad mood?

B. Campbell: Well, she was just being... I don't know... weird, I guess. She took forever to make dinner, and she made Lilly help set up everything, which was weird. But Dad didn't say anything, so I just ignored it.

Det. Garcia: It wasn't usual for Lilly to help with dinner?

B. Campbell: No, that's Winnie's job. Winnie always does the cooking and cleaning.

Det. Garcia: Why is that? Does she enjoy taking care of every-one?

B. Campbell: Yeah, I guess so. Or... actually, maybe not. I'm not sure. We never really talked about it. I guess Dad just kind of always made her do it since Mom left.

Det. Garcia: Uh, according to our records, your mom was hospitalized following an assault on Winnie, is that correct?

B. Campbell: Yeah.

Det. Garcia: So, your father made Winnie do all the house-hold chores since your mom's hospitalization?

B. Campbell: Yeah. It's pretty much been like that ever since. But, you know, I help the family out too. I work at the gas station. I give most of my paycheck to Dad to help with the bills and everything.

Det. Garcia: Yes, that's very good of you. So, Winnie made Lilly help with dinner for the first time ever last night?

B. Campbell: Yeah. I guess that's true.

Det. Garcia: Anything else unusual about last night?

B. Campbell: No. Well, wait...yeah, there was something else. It was after Winnie made Lilly help.

Det. Garcia: What was?

B. Campbell: Um, well, Dad punished her. It was really hard to watch. It was worse than usual.

Det. Garcia: What did he do?

B. Campbell: It was just really embarrassing. Even to me, and I was just watching. He, well, he pulled down her jeans and panties in front of us. Then he did like he used to when we were really little. He bent her over his lap and spanked her really bad. Like almost more beating her than spanking her. It looked painful, but mostly it was just super humiliating to watch. I mean, she's sixteen! That's way too old.

And we were just sitting there, Lilly and I, watching her get beat. I remember she scrunched up her face really tight, like she was trying not to cry, but she just turned bright red and couldn't help it. She was still crying for a long time afterward.

Then Dad went to the living room and got wasted, like I told you. Lilly went to her room, and I left at about ten to go to Brian's house. I couldn't be there after that. It was too awkward.

Det. Garcia: That must've been hard to watch. Do you think your father went a little too far with that punishment?

B. Campbell: Honestly, yeah. I mean, she's way too old for that. He did it to embarrass her more than anything.

Det. Garcia: So, this type of punishment was unusual, correct?

B. Campbell: Oh yeah. It's true, Winnie does get punished a lot, but never like that. It was usually just extra chores and stuff like that. Never that bad.

Det. Garcia: Your father isn't usually violent?

B. Campbell: Oh no! Not Dad. Sometimes me or Winnie get a slap or something for being a dumbass, but that's it. He just totally lost it last night. Winnie was pushing his buttons though, I guess.

Det. Garcia: Is there anything else you remember about that night?

B. Campbell: No. I don't know. Other than that dinner thing, it was just a normal night. Like I said, Dad passed out before I left, and Winnie was crying and cleaning up. I think she'd already put Lilly to bed. I don't remember anything else.

Det. Garcia: Okay, thank you for your help. I'll be back in a minute. I'm going to go check in on your father. Can I get you anything on the way back? A soda or a cup of coffee?

B. Campbell: No, no thanks. Not right now. I just want to go home. Or no, maybe not home...

Det. Garcia: Okay, I'll be back in a few minutes. You'll get to go soon enough.

WINNIE

"Hey Winnie, what's up with the shiner?" Gabe says, chuckling. I ignore him and set my tray on the table between us. He immediately grabs the biscuits on top and starts devouring them. His mouth still full of food, he tries to say something, but it comes out a mush of gibberish. I push my water bottle toward him, and he takes a big swig. "For real though, what happened?" he finally manages to get out between bites.

"Usual shit," I say and snatch one half of a pathetic turkey sandwich off the tray so I can eat something for lunch. Gabe grabs the other half immediately after finishing the biscuits, but I know he's just hungry, not trying to be rude. I notice the unused butter and jelly packets I got specifically for the biscuits and sigh.

Gabe swallows the glob of food in his mouth and looks at me very seriously. I fidget a little under the scrutiny. "I thought he only hit you below the neck," he says. I glare at him and start to stand up, but Gabe grabs my arm and pulls me back to my seat.

"Jesus, Winnie, I'm sorry. I was just messing around," he stammers out. "I figured you got in a fight or something. Well, I guess you kind of did."

He chuckles again. I tell myself he only does it to lighten the mood. I rest my head in my hands on the table and listen to Gabe as he munches on the apple from my lunch tray. He finishes eating then touches the back of my head, kind of stroking my hair. I guess it's a caring gesture.

"I just thought I did a better job covering it than that, okay?" I say, sitting up straight to pull my head away from his caress.

"Sorry," he says, in an actually genuine way. He pushes my hair behind my ear as he examines it closer. Rubs at the makeup a little, blending it outwards. "On your good side, too. What a bastard." I brush away his hand and shrug my shoulders.

"If anyone asks you about it, tell them you heard I got in a fight with some bitch at a party or something." I try to swallow the lump in my throat. "But don't worry, they won't ask. Never have before. They don't care enough to notice shit like that."

He just nods. "Want me to try to cover it better? I've done it for my mom before and I think I did a pretty good job."

I shake my head. There's no doubt we'd only make it worse with more concealer.

"It's really not that bad. I'll be able to hide it better in a day or two. Let's talk about something else. Is your Halloween costume done yet?"

"It's so freaking sweet, you have no idea." Gabe beams as he describes it. "The straight jacket is super realistic looking, but I'm able to put it on myself and get out of it pretty easy. Good call on that, by the way. The makeup is super freaky. Definitely professional-level zombie makeup, but not all old school cheesy like all that shit you usually see. You are going to be super impressed."

"Dude, I already told you, I'm not going to that party."

"Come on, it'll be great. The guy who's throwing it said there's going to be a huge crowd and lots of cute guys. Plus, I could still pull together an awesome costume for you." Gabe raises his eyebrow in his usual flirty way.

"No, I hate Halloween. Anyway, I already told Dad I'd pass out the candy, so you know, I'm kind of stuck at home anyway now."

"What kind of a goth hates Halloween?" he teases, but adds, "Okay, well, whatever. Let me know if you change your mind. I'm going no matter what. Hey, do you think you can grab a soda for us to share? I'm parched and this water's not cutting it." I shrug but get up and stand in the lunch line again. At least it's not very long now that lunch is half over.

As soon as I'm there, that asshole Patrick comes up behind me. Finally, I get to the salad bar and grab a few packets of crackers followed by a soda at the cash register. Patrick says something but thankfully I don't hear it. Probably something about salads and my weight. He's said shit like that before. Back at the table, I dump the crackers on the almost empty tray.

"Thanks," Gabe barely gets out before he digs into the crackers. "Dude, that really sucks about your dad."

"Just shut up about it. As if today doesn't already suck bad enough," I say as I open a packet of crackers. He smiles and starts to tell me about some love potion he found online and how he wants to try making it, but I space out a few sentences in and stay locked in my mind for the rest of lunch.

After school, the day drones on as usual until I get to leave right after serving dinner. Babysitting again, but this time with my new favorite. Nikolai is such a sweet baby and easy to look after. Babies are the best because you can get your homework done since, once you get them asleep, they don't get up every fifteen minutes asking for another story or a glass of water. Plus, they're cute.

I walk up the driveway where Mr. Johnson is already warming up the car. He doesn't notice me at first, but then I wave and he smiles. As I get to the front door, I notice it's already cracked open. Through the slit of light, I see Mrs. Johnson walking back and forth between rooms, frantically getting everything ready. Opening the door a bit more, I poke my head in.

"Hi Winnie," Mrs. Johnson says as if she wasn't running around like mad trying to leave on time. "I think everything's ready for you. Nikolai has been fed and has a fresh diaper, so it should be an easy couple hours. We'll be back by ten. Oh, and here's for today and last time. Sorry again about that." She places sixty dollars in my hand, which is ten dollars more than we agreed to. Mrs. Johnson is always generous like that. I almost dispute it, but I know it was intentional, so I put the money away and move toward Nikolai, cooing in his playpen. Mrs. Johnson says some sort of goodbye behind me, but as I turn, the door clicks shut. They're always in a hurry, but the Johnsons are good people. You can tell that they love their baby Nikolai the way parents should. They absolutely spoil him, even if it means they have to cut back on their own indulgences. He'll always have everything he could ever want.

I look at the dark-haired drooling baby then pick him up, cuddling him in my arms. He continues to coo happily. After some bouncing and peek-a-boo, I put him in the playpen next to the coffee table so I can start on my homework. He gurgles and sucks his toes as I wade through pages of geometry followed by three chapters of *Of Mice and Men*. By the time I'm finished reading, he's half asleep, barely able to keep his eyes open.

Standing over the playpen, I smile down at the beautiful baby. His tiny, upturned nose and long-lashed eyelids are nothing short of perfect. Not only are the Johnsons exceptionally nice and caring, but they're also beautiful. Beautiful people with a beautiful child. They have no idea what it is to struggle, to be despised, to hurt. Their perfection stirs an anxiety, almost a hatred, inside me, but I push it down.

Cradling the sleeping baby, I hold him to my cheek, the soft, unscarred one that can still feel. A sense of calm washes over me as I breathe in his infant smell. Why do babies always smell so good?

I walk him up the stairs into the nursery, gently rocking him in my arms to keep him asleep. The room is dark and cool; a soft night light hums with soothing white noise in the corner. Anyone would want to sleep in this room of soft blues and powder-fresh smells. Nikolai makes a noise in his sleep, kind of like a grunt, and I giggle. I pinch his little nose closed and he opens his mouth to breathe yet doesn't wake up. A shadowy feeling passes through me.

I take the burp cloth carefully laid across the rocker's arm. I look at the little embroidered elephants dancing along its edge.

Then I cover both his nose and mouth with it.

Pressing firmly, I feel his mouth gasping, trying to pull in air through the thick weave of cotton. I pull the cloth away and he pants in small wheezing breaths. His dark eyes open wide and stare up at me before he begins to cry. I rock us back and forth, hushing him and pulling his trembling body close to my chest, letting him hear the comfort of my heartbeat.

After a few minutes, he's calm again and drifting back to sleep. I continue the peaceful rocking until I'm sure he's out, and then I gently place him in his crib. Looking down at him, I'm struck by the helpless and fragile nature of his existence. He needs me. In his designer crib, away from his parents, in this one moment, he's mine. I watch his slightly parted lips, his chest breathing a little heavier than before in his deep slumber, and my hand hovers over his face. I could take away his breath if I wanted.

"Did you know you're mine, Nikolai?" I whisper. "You just keep sleeping, oblivious and calm. You don't even know that you could be in danger." My body trembles. I place my cupped hand gently over his face and feel his small breaths in my palm. "This is what God must feel like." He pulls the air from around my skin then pushes it back in warm tiny gusts.

Taking away my hand, I step back from the crib. My head suddenly aches. I feel foolish. Turning on the baby monitor, I walk downstairs where the screen displaying his slumber rests on the kitchen table. I listen to his steady breathing until the Johnsons come home.

"I hope he was good for you, and not too much of a crier tonight," Mr. Johnson says when he walks into the kitchen. Mrs. Johnson is behind him, smiling and slightly red-faced. They've obviously been drinking.

"He's been super easy. Just sleeping away up there as I finished some homework," I say, forcing a smile in return.

"You made sure to check on him often though, right? Just to make sure he's not too cold or anything," Mrs. Johnson asks. She has a nervous habit of twirling her necklace in her fingers and tilting her head to the side.

"Of course. We played for a while, but he's been sleeping like an angel almost all night."

"Thank you, Winnie. We're so lucky to have a babysitter like you in our neighborhood. We'll let you know when we need you again."

I nod and leave, walking out into the cool night without buttoning my coat. A crisp wind blows, and I shiver, then take a very deep breath and smile.

WINNIE

I used to love Halloween when I was a child. The costumes, candy corn, and spooky atmosphere, along with the cooler fall weather, made it the perfect holiday. I remember dressing up as Cinderella when I was five, complete with itchy blue petticoats and roll-on silver glitter. At six, I was Sleeping Beauty in a pink satin gown, my gold hair cascading down my back. Seven-year-old me chose Arabian princess, complete with face veil and a midriff-baring belly dancer outfit. Mom put my hair up in an elaborately teased topknot. At eight, I transformed into Snow White and Mom even let me wear a short black wig, powdered my face, and painted my lips with her brightest crimson lipstick. Nine was Snow White again because Mom didn't have time to shop, but at ten-years-old, Rapunzel seemed only natural. My long blonde hair reached almost to my lower back, and I melted under the soft fingers of my mother as she braided into a rope of gold. The velour dress we found at the thrift store, with a lace-up bodice threaded with black ribbon and flowing bell sleeves, partnered with my hair to form the most dazzling of all the frilly costumes from my entire decade of Halloweens. Even Mom, who sparingly gave compliments, said I looked like a true fairy-tale princess.

Then eleven came, and two months before I could become a princess for a night again, my face was irreparably damaged. Dad got me a mask, one of those long-faced ghouls from horror movies, and a black cape, but I just went through the motions of trick-or-treating and gave all my candy to my brother. At twelve, I told Dad I was too old for trick-or-treating, even though Brendan was still going well into his midteens. He just nodded. By then, I was merely a nuisance and maid-in-training. By thirteen, I seemed like someone who would cherish Halloween as the most sacred of holidays, donning my goth fashion and wallowing in macabre interests, but I let it pass almost unnoticed. Now, three years later, Brendan goes out to parties, Dad takes Lilly around the neighborhood in her own fantasy ensembles, while I sit here in a chair near the door with a bucket of candy, just waiting for the doorbell.

The half-broken doorbell buzzes faintly and I answer it. Finally, some kids. Feels like I've been waiting here forever. Behind the door is a ballerina, some kind of monster from a television show, and a toddler Mario with his mom.

"Trick or treat," they buzz through their teeth, almost as annoying as the doorbell.

"How adorable," I say, dumping a few pieces of candy into each of their buckets. I don't recognize these kids from the neighborhood at all. I wonder if they came here from a different neighborhood to get better candy. They thank me and walk away.

I go back to slumping in my chair and trying not to eat the candy. The doorbell buzzes again within a few minutes. Glancing at the clock, I notice it's almost eight. The Halloween rush hour. Dark enough to make glow sticks and jack-o'-lanterns appropriate, but not so late that kids are up too much past their bedtime.

This time I recognize the girls behind the door. Julia and her friend Leigh. Two adorable little four-year-olds who can be either sweethearts or fucking demons, depending on their mood. Their faces beam with wide grins.

"Trick-or-treat, smell my feet, give me something good to eat," they sing and burst into giggles. Julia's mom, Mrs. Carpenter, is behind them, blushing fiercely and mumbling something about 'being polite' while she bounces the baby girl, Allie, dressed like a chubby pumpkin, on her hip.

"Hi Winnie! I'm Cleopatra," Julia says with a twirl. "Don't I look just beau-u-u-u-tiful?" She stretches the word out in an annoying way.

Leigh smiles brightly and proclaims, "Well, I'm Cinderella. You can tell because of my shoes." She pushes out a socked foot squished into a translucent, sparkly jelly sandal from under her petticoats. She laughs, eyelids scrunched closed and sparkling with roll on glitter.

When she opens them again, I fall into the depths of their cobalt blue. My breath is sucked away as I tumble in, mouth gaping like a suffocating fish, as I hurtle through the darkness of her dilated pupils. I want to look away, but I can't, locked in this terrible eye contact like a prisoner. A creeping dread claws across my scalp and down my arms. I shudder. *What is it about her?* Whatever it is, it's terrible and fascinating. I'm instantly, hopelessly, embarrassingly addicted. Thankfully, she looks away, breaks the spell, and I exhale as my blood begins to pump again.

"Wow, I can definitely tell," I say as I drop the candy into their plastic pumpkin buckets, eyes on the driveway, trying not to look at either of them again. "You know, I was Cinderella for Halloween when I was about your age too." The girls both burst into giggles and adjust their royal headwear as they skip down the driveway back to the sheepish mother. I see her wave goodbye while averting her eyes.

As they walk down the street, I can't stop watching Leigh as she walks up to the next house, still giggling, her blonde hair floating dreamily around her shoulders. The realization hits like electricity through me. I see myself in her. It isn't just the costume or the hair or any little part of her that reminds me of my past. I *was* her all those years ago, looked just like her, before all the bad things happened. Before my life became this. Thinking about it makes me want to vomit. The terrible dread passes over me again like a shadow, my hair standing on end. I can't tell if I hate her or love her. I shake the feeling away. My mind's just playing cruel tricks on me.

I sigh, shut the door, and wait. Not as big of a rush as I expected. I guess a lot of the kids around here are getting a little old for trick-or-treating. Then there's a knock at the door.

"Twick-o-tweat!" an excited boy shouts, jumping up and down, his pinned-on tiger tail flopping behind him.

"Whoa! A real tiger! I better be careful," I say, my hand quaking in faux fear as I deposit the candy in his bag. He laughs and then growls at me, making his hand into a claw as he scratches the air. I jump back and he laughs again, the whiskers bending around his apple cheeks. His mother shouts a 'thank you!' at me from the sidewalk while he shrieks with delight and runs down the driveway.

I sit back in the chair and play a mobile game while I wait. Nobody comes for twenty minutes or so, but then I'm forced to forfeit my high score when the doorbell forces out a pathetic buzz, so soft I barely hear it in time.

"Trick-or-treat!" a group of five neighborhood kids shout. I recognize most of them, but a couple have masks. They're covered in fake blood and wield fake weapons. A murderous clown, hockey-masked killer, zombie soldier, vengeful mummy, and what could only be some kind of werewolf all stand before me, begging for candy. I'm impressed by their dedication to their characters. The zombie is groaning, and the clown lets out a creepy chuckle.

"Nice costumes," I say and dole out candy. They thank me before heading toward the next house.

Another hour passes and only three more trick-or-treaters show up. At ten, I figure I can stop, setting the candy bucket on the kitchen table for Brendan to inevitably eat when he comes home hungover tomorrow. Lilly and Dad walk in right as I'm putting the chair back.

"Get a lot of candy?" I ask. Lilly nods, but her drowsy eyes don't even attempt to open completely. It's way past her bedtime. Dad takes a couple of Snickers from her candy pail and eats them. He almost seems like the loving dad I remember from my childhood when he's with Lilly. She's his favorite and he basically worships her. He pretends that he doesn't, but Brendan and I know it's because she looks so much like Mom.

I give Lilly her pajamas from the top dresser drawer she can barely reach, and she changes and crawls into bed. I tuck her in and refuse to read any bedtime stories. It's already too late.

"I wish you would have come with us, Winnie," she sighs and cuddles into her pillow, hugging a plastic pony to her chest.

"I'm too old for trick-or-treating, silly head," I tell her as I flip on the nightlight.

"Do you remember when you were Rapunzel, and I was a black cat?" she asks. I nod. "That must've been fun. I was so little back then. I don't really remember; I've just seen the pictures."

"Goodnight Lilly. Sleep tight. Don't let the bedbugs bite," I say as I shut her door and see her fall asleep before it's completely closed. I hear Dad in the kitchen, bottles clanging. He can't even go one night without.

In my room, I listen to the soft rock station, turned down low enough that Dad can't use it as an excuse to punish me. I turn my head and stare out the window, squinting my eyes, trying to see the stars past the bright aura of streetlamps. It's no use. I can only make out one or two and they're probably satellites.

Dad's footsteps thump down the hallway. He stumbles past Lilly's room. Past Brendan's room. I hold my breath. He's slowing down. My throat tightens and lungs burn. I start to feel dizzy as I continue to hold my breath, as if releasing it will break the spell and allow him to enter. He stops. My eyes water. He continues to his room, closing the door with a sharp snap. I release the painful breath, emptying my lungs then gasping, though I try to keep it quiet. He's not asleep yet. A few minutes later, snores rattle our shared wall, and I can finally relax.

I text Gabe: *Hey dude. Happy Halloween!* He responds: *You too! Let's hang tomorrow. Or you could sneak out and come to the party. Night's still young ;)* I grin and reply: *No way. See you tomorrow.*

After I plug in my phone, I melt into my quilt, listening to the wind whistle through the forest behind the house. I love that it's finally cold enough to warrant turning the heater on. That warm dry air always comforts me for some reason. My phone vibrates. I pull it to my ear, careful not to unplug it. It's Krystal.

"Hey, what's up?" I whisper.

"Oh, is it too late? I don't want to get you in trouble," she whispers, as if her volume is as important as my own.

"No, it's fine. I just should mainly listen." I wheeze out an airy laugh.

"Well, I was just wondering how you're doing. We haven't talked much. I miss you."

"Yeah, I've been alright. I miss you, too. Why'd your family have to move so far away?"

"It's not *that* far away," Krystal says, still whispering.

"It's far enough." I roll onto my back, still attached to the wall. "Hey, remember that Halloween we went trick-or-treating together?"

"Yeah! I was a weird fairy-witch hybrid, and you were a belly dancer."

"I was an Arabian princess, like Scheherazade."

"Oh yeah. Wait, she's not a princess, right?"

"Yes, she is." I hear myself say it and it suddenly feels wrong.

"Oh well, whatever." Krystal does her bubbly, anxious laugh. "I remember your mom took us. That was such a good Halloween."

"It really was." I close my eyes and picture seven-year-old Krystal with her pointy black hat and butterfly wings strapped to her back.

"You should've come over. It was a pretty fun party. I'm sure your dad would've let you. It didn't even go that late and you could have still passed out some candy to the late-night stragglers."

"No, I don't think he would've."

"Well…" Her voice strains. "You should have at least asked."

"Next year, Koo Koo," I murmur. She doesn't say anything. "I should probably go. Dad stopped snoring. Maybe I'm being too loud."

"Okay. I wouldn't want you to get into trouble. Call me soon," Krystal says, back to a whisper.

"Sure. Goodnight."

"Goodnight." I hang up the phone and put it back on the nightstand. My head sinks back and silent tears run from my eyes into my hair, soaking my pillow.

WINNIE

I take the bus home from school today. I don't want to see Gabe or Brendan, not even for the duration of a ride home. I want to be alone. I get off the bus and walk home, kicking rocks along the way. My phone buzzes in my pocket. It's Mrs. Johnson. She wants me to babysit. I agree even though I don't feel like babysitting. I don't feel like doing anything. But the money is good, and I need it if I'm ever going to get out of this fucked up place.

As I hang up, I frown and kick a rock as hard as I can. It goes flying across the street, skipping onto the sidewalk. I wish I could dissolve into a million pieces and be blown away by the wind. My feet drag as I walk up the driveway.

Brendan's not home. Neither is Lilly. I can finally be alone for a few hours. Back in my room, I fall face-first onto the bed then breathe deeply into the quilt, enjoying the sense of near suffocation. I pull my arms up and cradle my head in them before drifting to sleep. I just want to sleep forever.

I wake up to the sounds of Brendan and Lilly walking around, slamming doors, and complaining about being hungry. With a groan, I force myself up and go to the kitchen. As I cut up the carrots, I pretend they're Brendan's fingers and smile to myself. When everything is cooking, I sit down at the kitchen table and almost fall asleep again, leaning into my hand.

"What's wrong with you, sleepyhead?" Brendan laughs and smacks my arm off the table. I awaken with a jolt, barely keeping myself from falling to the floor.

"I don't know. I've been extra tired lately," I say, putting my elbow back on the table. "I have to babysit for the Johnsons tonight. Can you put Lilly to bed?"

"Aw man, again? Can't you just take her with you?" he whines and pulls a soda out of the fridge.

"I guess if you really can't watch her. I don't think the families like it though."

"Fine. I guess I can, but only if you give me ten dollars of your babysitting money."

"What? That's so much!"

"Five."

"Sure, whatever." I roll my eyes. "Gotta be the easiest five bucks anyone ever made."

"Hah! You got it," Brendan says and leaves the kitchen.

Dinner is ready just in time for me to get it on the table before Dad comes home. I grab my backpack and get to the Johnsons' house right on time, but they act like I'm late, practically pushing past me, coats in hand, as soon as they open the door.

"Nikolai just ate so he should be fairly easy tonight," Mrs. Johnson says, pressing the baby into my arms. "Bye-bye, cutie pie! Mommy and Daddy will be back in a couple hours."

I take the baby to the living room, bouncing him a little and humming an impromptu lullaby. He gurgles and smiles. Drool oozes down his chin as he happily flaps his arms up and down. I smile back and wipe the spittle with the hem of my shirt.

We lie down on the blanket under his baby gym, and he reaches for the toys while I make up a story about the little happy animals hanging above us. He laughs and laughs. After a while, I pick him up, turn on the radio, and dance with him across the living room. He squeals with joy. A diaper change comes next and then we read a story. He chews on the board book corner, happily cooing.

We play peek-a-boo, but I can tell he's getting grumpy. Time for bed. I take Nikolai in my arms and carry him to the nursery. Pastel blue curtains, white carpeting, dozens of baby toys littering across the floor, and the smell of wipes and baby powder embrace us in this most comforting of spaces. I lay him down in the crib and smile at him.

He yawns, and I smooth his fuzzy hair. My hand caresses his fat, pink cheek. I place the tip of my finger in his tiny mouth, and he pushes his tongue at it. He gurgles happily. Then I place my palm firmly against his face, covering his nose and mouth. He thrashes his arms and legs. He tries to move his head away, but I apply pressure. My breath quickens. Then I take the hand away.

Eyes closed, mouth open and panting, his little chest heaves up and down as his limbs relax. He drops his head to the side, but once again I caress his chubby face, tracing my finger across his eyebrows, around his tiny eye. Then I take his face firmly in my palm, cutting off all air once again. My head swims, watching his flailing arms and legs. The rush of adrenaline overwhelms me. Just a little longer. With a tiny sigh, I press down even more, and his body goes rigid. His stiff legs kick in tiny arcs, but then he completely relaxes. I take my palm away. He's not breathing.

Suddenly, I realize what I've done. Panic shoots through every nerve in my body like a thousand needles. I grab the limp body from the crib and set him on the floor.

I try to remember the CPR lesson from health class, but my mind's blank. I pinch his tiny nose and blow into his mouth. That's the only step I can visualize from the video we watched.

His chest inflates, overly full, round, tight, and then as I stop, he completely deflates to a flatness I've never seen before. I try again. It doesn't seem to be doing anything at all. Tears rim my eyes as I look down at his slightly blue lips and the tiny dribble of blood coming from his nose. Wiping the blood away with the edge of my shirt, I put Nikolai back in his crib. I lay him on his belly, turning his head a little to the side, and he looks peaceful. I caress his tiny cheek again but quickly pull away, shocked by how rapidly his body is cooling.

I pace the nursery a few times. Back and forth. Back and forth. Biting my nails frantically, my mind races. Why did I have to play that game? I knew it was dangerous. I never meant to actually kill him. Oh god, the police will not think that's a good excuse. Mr. Johnson has a gun, I think. What if he shoots me when he gets home and sees what I've done? A hundred questions race through my brain, every synapse firing.

I run back to the crib. He looks like he's just sleeping. Maybe they won't notice right away. I realize I've bitten my index fingernail to the quick and it's bleeding. I suck on it and decide to pretend I didn't know. Don't babies just mysteriously die sometimes? I've heard of that happening. I turn on the baby monitor camera and place it on the dresser right next to the crib. Then I take the screen and bring it with me to the kitchen.

My backpack is slumped in a chair at the breakfast table, and I decide that's how I can bide the unbearable next hour and a half before the Johnsons come home. In English, we're reading Kafka's *Metamorphosis* and I throw myself into the story, burying my reality beneath its surreal horror. I begin to calm down as I read on. The language hypnotizes me, lulling me into apathy and surrender. I almost forget about Nikolai and instead focus on Gregor. I see myself in him, that pathetic, tragic toy of fate. I know I've been changing against my will as well. I can't control myself anymore either. We're not evil, just misunderstood. The time flies by as I read, stopping to jot down notes for the essay I'll write tomorrow. They're late. It's almost 11.

Finally, I hear a car pull into the driveway. Headlights momentarily shine through the window, blinding me, then darken as quickly as they appeared. Doors close. Laughter. Stumbling steps. They've been drinking again. Maybe they won't notice. They're still laughing as they open the front door, pawing at each other. I glance up at them and flash my innocent smile.

"Have a good time?" I ask. I'm surprised my voice doesn't quaver or crack.

"Yes, wonderful. Thank you again for babysitting," Mr. Johnson says, taking out his wallet. "Now let me see... here's for a job well done." He hands me the cash and I pocket it.

"Anytime. Nikolai is such a good little boy. I put him to bed about two hours ago. I checked in a couple times, and he was just sleeping so sweetly every time. You two are blessed to have such an easy baby. Well, it's a school night, so I should head home," I say, a little too quickly. They don't seem to notice, eyes half-closed from too many glasses of wine. I pack up my homework and walk out to the street.

A cold, sharp wind tousles my hair as I walk home. I look back to the house twice, expecting the bereaved parents to bolt out the door and chase after me. "Murderer!" they'll yell and tackle me to the ground. Beat me into oblivion. Both times my hair tries to veil my view, but there's nothing to see. The house gets smaller behind me and soon I'm too far to keep checking. They haven't noticed. They don't know. The knot in my stomach loosens slightly.

I creep into my house, careful not to step on the creaky floorboards. The stillness of sleep and night fills the house. I lay on my stomach across my bed. I think of Nikolai, the same but lifeless, in his crib. I didn't mean to hurt him. Did I? I guess I did mean to hurt him. I loved him though. The easiest baby I've ever looked after. Cheerful disposition and adorable face. I smile when I think of his gurgling laughter then immediately feel sick. I can't figure it out. I can't explain it even to myself. Was it the thrill? The control? The power of his life in my hands? I loved that baby, and yet, somehow that moment of omnipotence outweighed anything else. I guess I'm really a bad person. The kind of person that should be locked away and forgotten. Just like my mother. My phone buzzes in my pocket. It's one in the morning.

"Hello?" I whisper.

"Oh Nikolai, my angel! My baby! He's dead! He's dead!" the voice barrels out. It's Mrs. Johnson.

"What? Are you sure? Call an ambulance!" I feign surprise and anguish, all while keeping my voice loud enough to hopefully sound genuine yet soft enough to avoid disturbing my family. Real sobs swell inside me, and I decide to let them out as quietly as possible. Let her hear me crying.

"Larry did. He already did. Oh Nikolai! No, this can't be real. Tell me, did anything happen while we were gone? Was he breathing differently? Was he acting sick?" she wails through her questions like an injured animal, a sound I've never heard from a person before.

"He was—he was totally fine when I put him to bed! I checked on him, and he was just sleeping. How did he die? How could he be dead? What happened?" I answer in breathless suspense.

"I don't know! We don't know! He's dead. Oh Winnie, he's so cold! My baby, my baby boy." Her voice transforms wholly into beastly howls, and I can't understand her anymore.

"I'm so sorry, Mrs. Johnson. I don't know what to say," I mumble. She continues her strange cries, and I can't help but listen, mesmerized. A feeling of electricity jolts through my body as I hear her sorrow manifest in choking sobs and grunts. I let her melancholy engulf me and remember Nikolai helplessly fighting for air. My conscience tells me that I loved him, and I care for these parents. This ideal family should never experience this. My stomach twists itself and I think I could vomit. Yet, deep down, in some hidden dark place, I feel satisfied and incomparably savage.

"Call me if I can do anything at all," I say, but I don't think she hears me above her own voice. I hang up and return to my prone position on the bed. As I drift to sleep, my mind sifts through the guilt, fear, and ferocity to conjure up unspeakable dreams.

COLE CAMPBELL

POLICE INTERVIEW TRANSCRIPT

DEC. 17

Det. Wilson: Thank you for coming in to talk to us today, Mr. Campbell. I'm Detective Wilson and, just so you know, this conversation is being recorded in case we need to clarify any details at a later date.

This morning you witnessed a very upsetting scene for your family and, as you know, we are currently still searching for your daughter Edwina Campbell. Do you have any idea of her current whereabouts?

Campbell: No.

Det. Wilson: The crime scene doesn't seem to indicate foul play in her disappearance at this point, such as kidnapping. We think she may have fled the scene. Right now, it's unclear whether she was possibly involved or was just trying to get away to protect herself. Is there anyone she might have gone to if she's alone and afraid? A relative perhaps, like a cousin, aunt, uncle, or grandparent.

Campbell: No. We haven't seen any of our extended family for years. I don't think she even knows where they live.

Det. Wilson: Okay. We'll still need you to give us any addresses and phone numbers so we can check.

Campbell: Of course. [personal information redacted]

Det. Wilson: Thank you. I know it's been a very upsetting morning, Mr. Campbell, and I know this must be exceedingly difficult, but could you please walk us through yesterday? Anything you remember could prove helpful in finding your daughter.

Campbell: I guess I can. I feel like a zombie or something though. Nothing feels real.

Det. Wilson: That kind of feeling is completely normal after such a traumatic event. Please, just try your best.

Campbell: Well, let me think. Yesterday morning was just the same as any day. I woke up and got ready for work like usual. Winnie made breakfast and got Lilly ready. Brendan drove them all to school, the same as always. Uh, then I guess they were at school all day while I was at work.

Det. Wilson: Okay, hold on and let me get this all written down. And where do you work Mr. Campbell?

Campbell: I'm a bioengineer at [redacted].

Det. Wilson: Okay. Did anything unusual occur that morning?

Campbell: No, it was just like always. Just a normal morning.

Det. Wilson: Okay, so it was a normal day for everyone, as far as we can tell, at both work and school. Then what happened that evening?

Campbell: Well, it was a typical evening too, I suppose. The kids all got home before me, which is normal since I usually work late. Winnie had dinner going by the time I got home.

Det. Wilson: What time was that?

Campbell: Oh, about seven, uh, seven thirty.

Det. Wilson: Do you know what time the other children returned home?

Campbell: Well, let's see. Winnie usually comes straight home, but Brendan had told me she'd been going out with that friend of hers, Gabe, more and more after school, so yeah, I guess I don't really know what time she came home.

Det. Wilson: What about the other children?

Campbell: Brendan works at that gas station after school until six or seven, I think. He only works a couple hours a day and he's usually home before me. Lilly stays at that after school program until four and then takes the late bus home or goes over to a neighborhood girl's house if Winnie's not home yet. Um, what was that lady's name... Yvette Sanders, I think? I really don't know if she went over there or not.

Det. Wilson: Okay, so all the children are pretty much home by around six every day, including yesterday. Is that correct?

Campbell: I think that's right.

Det. Wilson: Then you came home around seven, or sometime before eight. Tell me a little about last night, after you got home.

Campbell: Like I said, Winnie made dinner. I remember she was in a weird mood. Kind of irritable, I suppose.

Det. Wilson: This behavior was unusual?

Campbell: Yeah, that's not like Winnie. She usually knows how to keep things to herself and be a good girl, especially in front of her little sister.

Det. Wilson: What do you mean by irritable? Was she acting aggressive?

Campbell: Well, not aggressive exactly, but more just plain rude. She forced Lilly to help set the table, plates and silverware and all, even though that's her chore.

Det. Wilson: So she had her little sister help set the table, and you thought it unusual she had Lilly help with dinner this way?

Campbell: Yeah, it was wrong because that was Winnie's job.

Det. Wilson: Was Winnie in charge of the other household chores besides dinner, or did the other children help around the house too?

Campbell: Well, Brendan has real work at the gas station so, of course, I don't make him do anything else. He's almost a grown man, and those things around the house are really more women's work anyway. And Lilly, well, she's too little and delicate to help out with that stuff. Her whole life she's been a sensitive girl, you know what I mean, very sensitive. I've always had to protect her a little from the world.

It just broke my heart to see her carrying those plates because Winnie was too lazy to do it herself. Making her little sister work like her own personal slave or something, even when she knows Lilly is so sensitive. That's why I punished her after dinner.

Det. Wilson: You punished Winnie after dinner last night?

Campbell: Well, yes.

Det. Wilson: Do you mind describing what kind of punishment this was?

Campbell: Well, the kids' punishments have always varied, especially for Winnie since she has a penchant for getting into trouble, but the usual sorts of things. Sometimes grounding her, sometimes taking away something like her phone, sometimes other things. This time it was, well, a spanking.

Det. Wilson: A spanking?

Campbell: Yeah. I had to do *something* to really teach her a lesson. So, I bent that girl over my knee and spanked her with my own belt. Not very hard or anything. Just like anyone would spank a child who's been misbehaving.

Det. Wilson: Mr. Campbell, isn't Winnie sixteen years old?

Campbell: Detective, I don't think it matters how old she is. She's still my daughter, even at sixteen, and I still have the right to spank her. I know my rights and that's a parent's right.

Det. Wilson: Did the other children witness this punishment?

Campbell: Of course! The embarrassment was the most important part of the whole thing. It hurts a child's pride more than their ass. That's what makes it so effective and makes sure they learn their lesson.

Det. Wilson: How did Winnie act after the punishment?

Campbell: She was kind of sullen, like usual after a punishment like that. She just sulked around the house until she had to finish her chores before bed.

Det. Wilson: When did Winnie go to her bedroom?

Campbell: Well, uh, I don't know for sure. She puts Lilly to bed at nine, I think, and... I don't remem— it's hard to remember, okay? Honestly, I'm getting up there in age and yesterday was an especially draining day at work.

Det. Wilson: Mr. Campbell, I need to know, had you been drinking last night?

Campbell: Who told you that?

Det. Wilson: Nobody told me. I need you to be honest about this. Were you drinking last night?

Campbell: It was a Friday night and I'd worked hard all week. I'm entitled to a few beers. Not like I got drunk though. I don't suppose it's a crime for a hardworking man to have a few beers on a Friday night, is it?

Det. Wilson: No one is accusing you of a crime, Mr. Campbell. I just want to make sure I completely understand all the details. How many beers did you have last night?

Campbell: Well, I guess probably... a six-pack. Oh, plus a couple of bourbons on the rocks. I honestly don't really remember too much else. I must've dozed off before everything happened.

Det. Wilson: Who was watching your youngest daughter Lilly while you were intoxicated?

Campbell: I guess Winnie was—

Det. Wilson: What time would you say you "dozed off" last night?

Campbell: I really don't know. It wasn't very late. Ten or so.

Det. Wilson: So, you don't remember anything else from that evening?

Campbell: No, I guess not... I didn't mean to fall asleep. Maybe if I hadn't everything would still be the same. Not ruined like this...

Det. Wilson: I know you must feel that way, but right now we need to not focus on what anyone could have done and instead work on finding Winnie.

Campbell: I always knew she was trouble. When you find Winnie, you'll see, it's going to be all her fault. No way she's just a witness who ran away scared. Or a fucking victim like she always acts like. She did this. I know deep in my heart that she did. Ever since she drove my poor Theresa past her breaking point, she hasn't been the same.

Det. Wilson: Theresa. That was your wife, right?

Campbell: Yes, it was.

Det. Wilson: I think I have some notes on her. Oh, here. Yes, I see she passed away in a hospital four years ago. Looks like a psychiatric hospital according to these records. Hmm. Do you mind telling me a little about her mental illness? It could possibly be relevant.

Campbell: Well, Theresa was my wife. The best wife a man could ever want. I loved her more than I ever loved anyone. But your records are right, Theresa wasn't well.

She had always been very imaginative. That was something I really loved about her. She was a painter. I only worked so hard to climb the career ladder so fast because I wanted to take care of her and our children. Allow her the time and freedom to paint and stay home with the kids. All I ever did after I met her was try to make her happy. She was my inspiration to always try harder.

It wasn't long after Lilly was born though, that she started having a hard time telling fantasy from reality. She would think up these scenarios in her mind and then she'd get confused and start to believe it. I was trying to get her help when Winnie pushed her too far. I had just spoken with her earlier that day and convinced her to finally see a doctor. I just knew this time we'd finally find a medication to help her, and things would go back to the way they were before. But no, Winnie wouldn't have it. She confronted her about her... confusion and Theresa broke down.

I know she didn't mean to hurt Winnie. She was just unwell, but that's what happened. Next thing you know, she was locked away in that hospital forever. I only let the kids visit her a few times. It was horrible to see. She became unresponsive, uh, "catatonic" they called it, after a few weeks. She was never the same again. Then, when she got sick, she didn't even try to fight it. I couldn't bear anyone to see her like that. It was hard to visit even for me.

Det. Wilson: Thank you for sharing that, Mr. Campbell. I'm so sorry for your loss. Is there anything else you can tell us about your daughter? Do you know what Winnie's life was like outside of home? Was she involved in anything at school? On any teams or clubs?

Campbell: Winnie, she's a smart one, I'll give her that. She always did very well in school. When she was little, I used to think she might become an engineer like me someday. But no, she wasn't involved in anything else. She spent all her time either at school or taking care of the house. I don't think she really had any friends even. Brendan told me she got made fun of sometimes, because of the scars, but I don't think it bothered her that much. She always seemed stoic and cold to me. She's been like that pretty much all her life.

Det. Wilson: She didn't have any friends? I have here notes about a Krystal Schumacher and Gabriel Walsh as friends.

Campbell: Yeah, I remember that girl Krystal, but she moved away last year. I don't think they really talked anymore. And Gabe, he was a load of trouble. As soon as I saw him, I knew he was just like Winnie. But you're right, they were pretty good friends.

Det. Wilson: Mr. Campbell, can you tell me a little about Winnie babysitting for the Johnson, Carpenter, and Castillo families?

Campbell: What do you want to know? She loved taking care of kids. That was the only time she didn't seem so fucking cold.

A while back, she babysat for just about every family in the neighborhood. She used to babysit for the Castillos more, but I think they got a new babysitter, and then the Johnsons lost their little baby not too long ago. SIDS, I heard. So, I guess she only really babysits for the Carpenters now. She told me they have two little girls. She used to take Lilly over there sometimes when it was going to be a late night if Brendan or I weren't going to be home to put her to bed.

Det. Wilson: Did she ever talk about babysitting?

Campbell: No, not much. Like I said, Winnie was good at keeping to herself. I know she liked doing it though. She was really proud to be a babysitter for so many families. Jesus, can we take a fucking break? I could use a cup of coffee. My head is killing me. It all seems so unreal...

Det. Wilson: Of course. Let me go get you one. I think we're pretty much done here for now anyway.

WINNIE

I told Dad I have the stomach flu. He actually believed me this time and let me stay home. Maybe he didn't really believe me, but thought I was sick with grief. In a way, I am. I've been lying in bed all day, my stomach twisting, contorting, tying itself in knots more painful than any real stomach flu I've had. I'm lightheaded and feverish, but I know it's not an illness. It's Nikolai.

Nikolai. His tiny corpse haunts my every thought. I see his eyes snap open, bloodshot and vacant. His little hands clenched in stiff fists, a network of blue threads showing through his thin translucent skin. I imagine slowly reaching out, touching his chest and feeling the strange cold stiffness. No rising and falling in that familiar steady rhythm. Not one thud against his breastbone of that most constant of organs. Cool and still as if he was never a living thing at all but a stone, unchanging for all time. But I know better.

Inside him, even when he's resting deep within the earth in his protective box, he'll be changing. Embalmed and encased in a sturdy coffin. It might take years or even decades, but slowly his body will putrefy and disintegrate. His bones will become dust.

My guts squirm like the worms that will wriggle their way into his resting place when I think of it. Then I try to imagine his funeral. I've never been to a funeral, not even Mom's, so I can only imagine it from movies I've seen. I see his parents grieving in my mind's eye, and I feel even worse. Instead, I think of his last night alive.

There in his room, just Nikolai and me. Over and over, I relive those last moments, my palm pressed gently over his mouth and nose as he struggled. I had his life in my hand, and I took it. I held all the power, not him. An invigorating sensation simmers through my abdomen; however, soon the guilt and terror grip my intestines and pull me inside myself, back into the tension and pain. I groan, fling my head back against the pillow, stretch my neck long, claw at my gut. Death, I beckon, come take me. This torture is more than I wanted and too much to bear.

All day, I drift in and out of sleep. Sleep is the only respite from the suffering, but I cannot will myself to stay in that safe emptiness. Every hour or two, my body jolts awake, and I stumble to the bathroom, vomiting strings of bile or gushing burning diarrhea until I feel hollow again. I force myself to drink some water after each trip, knowingly fighting my own death wish.

The front door screeches open and slams itself. I look at the clock. Must be Lilly. Why didn't she go to her friend's house after school? I heard Dad tell her before they left. He didn't want her around me in case I'm contagious.

Soft feet pad around the kitchen, followed by clinking plates and the hum of the microwave. She turns on the television and the muddled voices and unintelligible words lull me to sleep again.

I wake to see Lilly sitting at the foot of my bed. A glance at the clock tells me I only slept fifteen minutes. I look back to Lilly, but I can't read her expression at all. My vision blurs in and out, making me dizzy. Dehydration is the likely culprit.

"What's wrong with you?" Lilly asks, raising her lip a little and poking my foot through the covers.

I try to speak but my voice fails me, and I cough violently to bring it back, pushing through the damage from digestive acids. Lilly waits impatiently, picking at her nails while she looks at me the way she would a bug she's waiting for Dad to smash.

"Stomach flu," I finally manage to wheeze out. She nods but stays on the bed, sneering. I try to ignore her, close my eyes and try to sleep, but her weight on the bed keeps me awake. I open my eyes again. "You'd better stay away. Dad said he didn't want you near me, so you don't get sick too." Her face crumbles into a dejected frown.

"Winnie, are you going to get better?" she asks and pokes my foot again. "I don't like Dad's cooking and I don't want to eat junk forever." I roll my eyes and turn over on my side, away from her. I hear her whimpering voice again. "Please get better. Very soon, okay? We need you."

"You need me to cook and clean, huh?" I say, and I hear her sniveling, wiping her nose with her hand and then spreading it across my quilt.

"Yeah, we need you," she sobs. "I like it better when you take care of me."

I sit up and glare at her and she startles, slips off the bed to her feet. She rubs at her eyes, but more tears fall despite her efforts, dripping onto the floor. I notice she's wearing mismatched socks and no tights under a too-short green jumper, all topped with an oversized fuchsia sweater. I wonder whether Dad dressed her in this clown costume or if she managed to pull the abomination together herself. Snot runs from her nostrils in a thick ooze onto her upper lip.

"Here," I say, handing her a tissue. "Blow your nose." She obliges, and I carefully get out of bed, my legs weak and trembling with exhaustion. My arms wrap around her, pulling her close. She hugs me back as tightly as she can and nuzzles into my stomach.

"I'll make dinner. I think I'm feeling better."

We walk to the kitchen, and I look at her porcelain face framed by dark hair, poking her tongue through the hole in her smile where one of her baby teeth is missing. A tiny bit of happiness runs through my veins. Everything aches as I pull a pan out from under the sink and ask her about her day.

"Well, Mrs. Schneider was mean, as always. She wouldn't let me sit next to Chloe again because she says we talk too much, even though we don't, but I did really well on my spelling test." She skids back and forth across the linoleum in her socks as she speaks.

"I'm glad all that hard work we did paid off then," I say, unable to conceal a proud grin as I unwrap the beef.

"I would've aced it anyway. I'm not a dummy. Anybody could spell those words."

"Oh yeah? Well then maybe I won't help you study anymore." I shoot her a look and start slicing tomatoes.

"That's fine with me. You're not very smart anyway. I should study with somebody who's actually smart, like Dad," she says, stealing a tomato piece from the chopping board. I briefly consider grabbing her hand and holding it down as I chop off a joint from her index finger, but I don't. Instead, I just huff a loud sigh.

"What are you making?" she asks impatiently bouncing near me. "I'm so hungry."

"Just a stir-fry."

"Aww, but I don't want that! Can't you make spaghetti? Please, please, please," she whines and steals another tomato piece. I slide the cutting board away.

"We don't have the stuff for that," I say, then add, "I'll go shopping tomorrow."

"But I want spaghetti! Please, Winnie, please, pretty please." Her whining rings in my ears like tinnitus. I try to ignore her, but she pulls at my arm. I push down the urge to slap her as her begging rises into long drawn-out vowels. "Pleeeeeeeeease. Wiiiiiinieeee. Pleeeeeease."

"Stop it! I said I can't make it today, I'll make it tomorrow," I snap and jerk my arm away. I grab an onion and mince it as she flops on the floor in a tantrum more appropriate for a three-year-old than a girl of seven. Brendan comes into the kitchen, red-faced and smelling like he's more likely been drinking with friends than at work.

"What the hell is going on in here?" he asks. I shrug and Lilly continues her fit, slightly more exaggerated now that her brother's there to witness. I see his eyes dart around the room, his confused little brain trying to decipher the situation.

"Oh Brendan, Winnie is so mean! Where's Dad?" she screams and pulls herself off the floor, running to his arms. He holds her and glares at me.

"What'd she do to you?" he asks Lilly. She pulls at his shirt, and he bends down to her. Cupping her hands around his ear, she whispers something much too long to be the truth.

"Go play in your room." He brushes her off toward the door, then looks back to me. I turn away. Keep chopping. Don't look at him.

He stomps across the room, and I can feel him directly behind me. Suddenly, he shouts, "How the hell could you hit your little sister!" and I feel him picking me up, carrying me over his shoulder like a firefighter. I'm kicking and scratching at him, but I can't wriggle free. We're in the hall. Then my room. He tosses me hard on the bed. I squeeze my eyes shut, bracing my entire body, but he just hovers over me. I open my eyes and see confusion in his eyes.

"Did you really hit her?"

"No! I just—I jerked my arm away when she pulled it." I shoot the words out at him. "She was freaking out because she wants spaghetti for dinner, but we don't have the right stuff! I can't help that." My hair falls across my sweaty face and I feel it sticking and try to wipe it away. Brendan looks at me, starts to speak but stops. He's staring at me, sheepishly. My clothes stick to my slippery, feverish body and I'm not wearing a bra under my pajamas. A burning blush spreads across my skin and I hate him.

"Well, I don't know what happened, but since you're not feeling well today, I'm not going to tell Dad. This time." His version of an apology. "I'll finish dinner. Lilly will just have to deal and you... should put some clothes on."

He finally leaves, and I wring the bed sheets between my hands before shoving a pillow over my face to muffle my scream. I vent all sorts of things that no one can hear. I scream "I wish you were never born!" to Lilly and "You're a dumbass fucker!" to Brendan. I scream until I have to pull away and gasp for breath. The pillow takes it all until it's damp and beaten.

Eventually, I get up and pace slowly, a prisoner in my own house. I could try to sneak out, but Dad might actually check on me tonight since he let me stay home sick. I text Gabe, but he quickly responds he's busy, and I know better than to bother him after such a quick reply. I text Krystal, but she doesn't respond for hours, and by then, I don't want to talk to her anymore. I try to read but my eyes are tired and dry and the words all blur into nonsense.

As I wait, I hear Dad come home and the family assemble for dinner. There are a few jokes about Brendan's cooking, but overall, they're happy and normal. I think about how ordinary they are without me. Just a family like any other. Listening to their small talk, I know they're happier without me. I don't hear anyone do the dishes though as they finish up. Shriveled vegetables stuck on plates and crusty forks will await me in the morning. That's how I fit into their lives. At least I'm good for something.

I lie back and put in my earbuds, but I can't find anything worth listening to on my phone. Eventually, I settle on spending hours reading random Wikipedia articles and listening to the night noises of my family settling in for sleep.

Dad is snoring through the thin wall that separates us, so I decide to sleep again. Just as I'm drifting off, my door creaks slightly. I open my eyes a sliver and see Lilly walking toward me.

"What? Go to bed. Didn't you already do enough?" I whisper, but she crawls up into bed next to me.

"I'm sorry Winnie. I didn't mean to," she says and snuggles against me. "Do you ever think about Mom?"

I don't say anything. I just fall asleep, purposely not holding her even as her small arms try to wriggle through my own.

MARINA JOHNSON

POLICE INTERVIEW

DEC. **22**

Det. Wilson: Hello Mrs. Johnson. I'm Detective Wilson. You spoke on the phone with my colleague, Detective Garcia, yesterday. I appreciate you allowing me into your home to talk.

Johnson: Yes, of course.

Det. Wilson: Now I know this is painful, but just for my records, your son, Nikolai, passed away on November 2nd. Is that correct?

Johnson: Yes.

Det. Wilson: And he was six months old?

Johnson: Yes. Just one week past six months.

Det. Wilson: I'm so sorry. I can't imagine how difficult it must be for you.

Johnson: Why exactly are you here, Detective Wilson? My son passed away from Sudden Infant Death Syndrome. It says so on his death certificate. Why are you asking about him? What is this about?

Det. Wilson: No, I'm sorry if I gave you that impression. I'm not here to talk about your son, not directly. You see, I'm searching for a missing girl, Winnie Campbell. I understand she used to babysit Nikolai for you. Is that true?

Johnson: Yes. Why? What's going on?

Det. Wilson: I'm just trying to find out more about her and her life is all. I'd appreciate anything you could tell me about her.

Johnson: That's terrible that she's missing, but I don't know much about her. She always seemed like a nice girl. Nikolai really seemed to love her.

Det. Wilson: Did Winnie ever bring her little sister Lilly along when she would watch Nikolai?

Johnson: Yeah, sometimes she brought her. I didn't mind. She also seemed very nice and polite. Winnie always made sure to bring snacks for her too, so she wouldn't have to eat any of our food. I appreciated that.

Det. Wilson: So, overall, you thought Winnie was a competent babysitter?

Johnson: I would say so. She really had a way with babies.

Det. Wilson: How did you go about hiring Winnie?

Johnson: The Carpenter family recommended her to me. They said she was great with Allie and Julia, and she wasn't as expensive as some of the other babysitters in town. I mean, she wasn't with an official agency or anything, just a neighborhood girl, so it was really convenient. She'd been watching Allie and Julia for over a year, so I figured she must be good.

Det. Wilson: How often did Winnie watch Nikolai for you?

Johnson: Uh, probably once every other week or so. Larry and I were trying to keep up with date nights whenever possible.

Det. Wilson: And how long ago did she first start watching him?

Johnson: He was almost three months old when she first watched him, so she was our babysitter for about three months or so.

Det. Wilson: I know this is hard, but can you walk me through the night Nikolai passed away?

Johnson: Why? What does that have to do with anything? She was there with him that night...

Det. Wilson: Please calm down, Mrs. Johnson. I'm just trying to find out all I can about Winnie so we can find her. I know it's difficult, but you never know what might be important to our investigation. Can you please try to tell us everything you remember.

Johnson: I don't know how anything about that night would be relevant. Larry and I went out and we stayed out a little later than we had anticipated. When we got home, Winnie was working on some homework at our kitchen table. She told us that she had put Nikolai to bed a couple hours earlier and she had the baby monitor next to her. He was always a good sleeper, since the beginning. We paid Winnie, and she went home. Then, after I had washed up for bed, I checked on Nikolai since I hadn't heard anything from the monitor since we got home. And— and— [crying].

Det. Wilson: I'm so sorry, Mrs. Johnson.

Johnson: I remember every detail. Tiptoeing into the room because I didn't want to wake him up. Peering over the crib and there he was, laying on his belly with his little face to the side. He looked like a sleeping angel. I reached over and touched his cheek and—it was cold. So cold... Larry called an ambulance. They couldn't save him. They told us it was SIDS and there was nothing we could have done to prevent it. I still feel so guilty though. I should have checked on him sooner. I just thought he was sleeping.

Det. Wilson: I am so sorry for your loss, Mrs. Johnson, and that you had to recall those traumatic details. That's all I need. I really appreciate you taking the time to speak with me.

Johnson: Wait, don't go. Do you think Winnie is alright? Why were you asking about this? I remember I called her right away and she seemed just as shocked and devastated as we were. She's such a sweet girl. I could tell she really cared about Nikolai.

She came to his funeral. I saw her run away during the burial. It was too much for her. She loved my little boy. I hope you find her soon. Her family must be devastated.

Det. Wilson: Thank you so much for your time, Mrs. Johnson. Again, I am so sorry for your loss.

WINNIE

It's a gorgeous Saturday with clear skies, slightly warmer than it's been. It's also Nikolai's funeral. The morning goes by the same as any other. Dad does ask a little about the time and location of everything, grunts something about how it's so very sad, but everything else is exactly the same. Bacon, eggs, black coffee, orange juice. Washing dishes, mopping floors, scrubbing toilets. Suddenly it's noon and I need to hurry to get ready or I'll be late. It might be suspicious if I'm late. What if they're already suspicious?

I swallow hard and hold my stomach, trying to calm the butterflies, while I look through my closet for my most conservative black dress. It hangs shapeless and baggy on my body. Looking attractive shouldn't concern someone attending a funeral though. The black stockings slide over my legs and my feet slip into my old black flats, their leather cracked and discolored. Then I dig through the green floral jewelry box, looking for my small cross. It's tangled with another necklace, and I waste minutes separating them. As I clasp it behind my neck, watching it hang against my breastbone, my heart flutters. It was a Christmas present from Mom. Maybe that makes it a perfect funeral accessory.

I stand back and look at myself in the full-length mirror. I push my hair forward, almost covering my right eye, trying to block the scars, and apply minimal makeup, just enough mascara to keep my eyes from disappearing into the white roundness of my face. I rub my eyes, lightly smudging the makeup and irritating my eyes enough to redden them. I should have made myself cry last night so I could showcase the swollen eyelids of a truly bereaved person, but I've been too numb to force out the necessary tears. Oh well, good enough, I think, and go bother Brendan until he finally pauses his video game.

"Can't somebody else take you? I'm busy," he says, jutting out his lower jaw.

"You know it's too far to walk," I say, drawing circles in the carpet with my big toe. "Come on. I've got to go pay my respects. You know I watched that baby all the time."

"Fine," he snaps.

"Can you help watch Lilly while I'm gone? I think Dad's maybe, um…" I lower my voice. "A little hungover."

"Well, duh he is, but no, I can't. I'm seeing Danica in a bit." He smirks.

"What? I thought you guys broke up." My face flushes. He knew about this funeral for at least the last couple days. He just continues to smirk. I hate him. "Okay, well, I guess I'll go get her ready and she'll just come with me."

"Cool." His eyes glaze as he returns to his game. "Come get me when you're ready."

Shit. Now I'm going to definitely be late. I trudge through the house looking for that snotty little sister of mine. Finally, I find her in the backyard, digging a hole in the soft mud near the forest edge.

"What are you doing?" I ask, taking in the bizarre scene. The shallow hole is filled with Barbie dolls, all in varying stages of undress, and her fanciful ponies circle round, peering down at the nude women. Lilly looks up at me and smiles, her silky dark bangs falling over her eyes. I should give her a haircut soon, but there's no time today.

"I'm having a funeral. Just like the one you're going to." She points to the hole. "I'm the priest and here is the sad family."

"That's…interesting," I say, but I can't help but add the question that bubbles up inside, "How did they die? There's so many of them in that grave."

"Oh, a car accident." She spreads her fingers over them nonchalantly. "And the flu."

"Hmmm, that's sad. Sorry dead Barbies, but your priest will have to finish your funeral later. She has to come to a real funeral with her big sister right now." I shrug toward the miniature mass grave, pulling Lilly up by her arm. "Come on, you've got to change. You're all covered in mud."

As we walk into the house, Lilly stops and pulls her arm back. "Why am I going with you?"

"Brendan and Dad can't watch you, so you have to go." She bites her lip and nods. Pushing past the too-small frilly dresses from past school picture days, I find a deep green dress and push it over her head, pulling hard to stretch it over her body, her peach fuzz arms straining against the cap sleeves. My old Christmas dress, now Lilly's only formal dress that isn't pastel and festive. Her knees peek out when they shouldn't and the seams threaten to bust, but there's nothing else.

"I don't like this dress, Winnie," she whines and pulls at the sleeve. "It's so itchy! And tight."

"Don't do that." I pry her fingers off the sleeve. "We have to go." I attempt to shove her arms into a white knit sweater, but she fights me off.

"I can do it myself," she huffs. I throw her cream tights to her and tap my fingers in a steady rhythm as she slowly pulls them up. Her only dress shoes, scuffed and dirty, are almost too small. I force them on, hoping the thick stockings will save her feet from blisters.

She resists slightly as I push her along in front of me into Brendan's room. He looks us over, leans his head back over his chair and stretches his arms wide. Without a word, he stands up and shuffles out to the car. I buckle Lilly in back while she scratches at her stomach, her hand reaching far up under her dress, her face lined with frustration. This is going to be horrible, I think as I get in the front, barely buckling my belt before Brendan speeds us off to the church.

"Whoa, I've never been here," Lilly gasps behind me. "It's beautiful!"

The white steeple pierces the sky, its vast shadow engulfing us as we pull up to the front door. Carved stone creatures peer down as we walk to the oversized ornate doors. Lilly stares wide-eyed at the tall, thin windows. Stained glass figures of green, blue, and gold hold poses, held in place by black rods and frames. Through the doors, we can hear the faint sound of the organ and choir.

"Listen." My voice hisses in coarse, squeaky whispers as I bend toward Lilly. "The mass has already started. We need to be as quiet as possible when we go in. This is a funeral. Remember that. You need to just be quiet and stay with me." She nods vigorously, but I pull her closer. "You remember Nikolai and the Johnsons? This is very important to them. Let's be respectful. Got it?" She nods again, slower.

"I liked baby Nikolai. He was so cute," she says and then looks at her shoes. I nod and run my fingers across her scalp, pulling them gently the length of her hair. We wait a couple minutes until there is a break in the music, some sort of transition, and then quickly slip through the door and sit immediately in the back pews.

The priest is talking, but I'm not listening, instead scanning the faces and taking in the room. Candles flicker around the tiny blue casket. Beautiful pillars and arches surround the altar and soft colored light falls on us through the stained glass. Mrs. Johnson is sitting in the front, her head wobbling slightly from stifled sobs. She turns to whisper something to her husband, and I notice faint black lines running down her face and wonder if she had not considered how waterproof mascara would be a necessity. Her lip quivers as she turns back, and my legs tremble in reply. Lilly squirms a little next to me, then pulls her foot under her dress and sits on it.

"I have to go pee," she says, squirming a little more.

"Can't you wait?" I whisper into her ear, pushing the hair back. She furrows her brow but nods, defeated.

The priest drones in Latin before sprinkling holy water across the casket with liver-spotted hands. As he finishes, Mr. Johnson and a man I've never seen lift the tiny coffin and begin the procession out to the cemetery outside. I can tell from the way they hold it that it's no heavy burden.

Nikolai lies inside and I imagine his tiny corpse, bluish pale to match his casket, with closed eyes, his long eyelashes fanning across the tops of his chubby cheeks. The choir bursts into a celestial song, their voices rising and falling, stirring my heart. The voices seem to flow not just around me, but through me.

Tears run down my face. Lilly looks at me curiously and then casts a worried glance toward the casket as it leaves the altar with the men. Not a word but a gentle tug at my dress and I look at her, and seeing the fear in her eyes, I pull her to me in an embrace.

I'm still sniffling as we follow the line of people outside where the freshly dug grave waits under a green tarp. The small blue box has been placed on straps that suspend it as we all gather around. I pull Lilly toward the front of the crowd, and we stand next to the broken husband and wife. I touch Mrs. Johnson's shoulder and she turns, then bursts into tears when she recognizes me. She hugs me, tugging me to her bosom and cradling my head there in a gentle sway. She wails in my ear as they start to lower the coffin, suddenly thrusting me away and turning to her husband, seizing his shoulders, and almost pulling him down on top of her. Mr. Johnson drops a bouquet of daisies onto the casket as it lowers from view and his wife's hysterical howls intensify into almost animal screeches.

Lilly runs from my side. Lunging after her, we run across the small graveyard, dodging headstones. Suddenly, she stops and crouches behind an ancient one covered in moss, and ducks out of view. I look back and see Mrs. Johnson has collapsed to the ground; her howls still tearing from her throat in an injured voice. Everyone has gathered around her, and no one seems to have noticed Lilly's desperate retreat. I walk around the grave and see Lilly crouching, holding her knees against her face, tights partially pulled down, and a small dark patch of earth forming under her. The smell wafts toward me. I step closer and as my shadow falls over her, she pulls her legs even tighter and I notice the meek whimper, muted by the dress pushed against her mouth.

I pick her up in my arms, almost falling, but then finding my balance. The wet warmth of her dress already cooling in my hands. She shivers as the autumn wind rustles through our hair and dresses. I carry her back through the church. Small drips mark our trail.

Out front, I set her on her feet, and she clings to me, hands clasped round my waist, as I text Brendan to come get us. We wait in silence, Lilly still wrapped around me and shivering the entire twenty minutes it takes for our brother to come.

WINNIE

"Wait, Gabe, wait!" I call as I step out of the restroom and see him closing his locker and walking away. He stops and turns slowly, cocking his head, hand on his hip.

"So now you suddenly want to talk?" His forehead creases as he raises his eyebrows. "You've basically ignored me for days, and today you haven't said a single word to me! Literally, not a word. What the hell?"

Towering over me, at least a foot taller, Gabe stares down at me. Disdain seethes in his gray eyes. His ash blond mohawk with green tips, lip ring, tongue ring, eyebrow stud, a fake rebel with all his store-bought punk accessories. I hate how much I wish I were more like him. He thinks of me as lesser, pathetic, a charity case. Would he even listen to me if I told him everything? Would he believe me?

I look deep into his eyes, trying to get him to read my mind. I pull my eyelids back even farther, trying with all my will to send him a telepathic message about everything. He looks down at me confused, still angry, and not understanding. I don't want to have to tell him. Why can't he just know without words being spoken?

"Something happened." My voice creaks in my throat.

"Well, obviously," Gabe scoffs but then something changes. His gaze softens. "How about my house, after school? Just come over whenever. You can tell me all about it." Then he quickly adds, "We can figure it out together."

As the day drags on with boring lectures and forgotten assignments, I wrestle with myself, trying to decide how much to let him know. There's no one else. I swallow the pain that wells in my throat as I measure out my solitude so finitely. But how much do I tell Gabe? Can I trust him? A part of him must care about me, would understand. All the possible outcomes play out in my head. I analyze each scenario, compare and contrast, rewind to watch them over again. I don't know. I just don't know.

The anxiety buzzes through my wrists, fingers, ankles, toes, tightening in painful twists. I run my fingers through my hair and pull out strands, one at a time. Jolting at the sound of the bell, I pack up my bag and a shower of plucked hair falls from my shoulders. My scalp aches and I curse myself under my breath. Like things aren't already bad enough, I think, rubbing my head lightly as I stop at my locker.

I look outside to the parking lot. Gabe's car is gone. No way he left that fast after the bell. I have no idea how he'll graduate if he doesn't stop skipping. I take the school bus home. Gabe doesn't live far from me, but it's strange walking to his house. He almost never wants to hang out there.

I walk across the overgrown grass, up the cracking driveway, and knock tentatively on the door. Inside, the sound of bottles clanging, a television blaring, an off-balance washing machine clunking in an erratic rhythm jumble together. I knock again, a little louder, and hold my breath. Gabe opens the door just enough to pull me inside.

We creep up the stairs and below us I glance his mom curled on the couch in a fetal position, as if she were protecting herself from the infomercial yelling full volume at her from across the room. In the pulsing blue light, empty bottles glisten and crusted Chinese takeout containers are strewn across the coffee table and floor. It smells like a dirty litter box, but I've never seen a cat here. Gabe pulls me along, not letting me linger and gawk.

A black door with glow-in-the-dark stars glued all over it looms ahead. As we tiptoe into his bedroom, he flips on the black light, and the walls, plastered with posters, glow magically down on us. Gabe pulls a green-swirled glass bong from behind some books on a small bookshelf in the corner. As he packs the bowl, I lie down on his bed and look up at more glow-in-the-dark stars fixed to the ceiling. I hear him take a hit, filling his lungs and slowly letting the smoke billow out from his lips. He offers it to me, but I shake my head. I already feel like I'm spinning in this neon room.

"Okay, so go ahead, tell me what happened?" he says, pulling a green beanbag toward the bed and flopping onto it. I close my eyes and inhale, taking in the musty, thick air, feeling the dust settle into my lungs. My mind reels and I'm spinning into oblivion. I'm so dizzy I could vomit. I sit up and look at Gabe. He's hunched forward, face resting on the top of his intertwined fingers. Part of me feels like we know each other better than anyone in the world, and part of me feels like we're complete strangers.

"Well, I did something," I say. He nods, gestures for me to go on. "It was something really bad. Horrendous. There's not a word for how bad it is. I—well, I don't know why I did it. I'm not a bad person you know... right?" I stop and reexamine his face. He's listening intently, but I can't read his expression at all, more a blank mask than a face. I want to stop, yet I feel compelled to go on. The confession boils in my stomach and forces itself up my throat and into my mouth, against my will.

"I killed that baby, Nikolai. I killed him." I say it, but I'm shocked at my own words, and break into tears. I'm gagging as I sputter out the words, "I'm so sorry." Snot and saliva flow down my face, mixing at my chin, dripping onto my shirt. I gasp in shuddering sobs. Gabe's holding me. His arms tight around me, I let it out completely. We sit like this for a long time as I quietly purge all the guilt and anxiety I've built up for days. When I'm empty, I begin to compose myself.

"Wow, Winnie," Gabe says as he holds my face to his neck, not minding the thick fluids streaming down us both. "What happened? How?" My arms hold tight for a moment, but then I pull away. I need to look at him while I speak.

"It was when I was babysitting. I'd done it before, this game. This stupid game. I don't know why. He was just a little baby. I just felt so much better when we played. I don't know why." He leans forward, tightens his lips. I force myself to continue. "It was just a game. I would, well… I would put my hand over his mouth. I did it before and nothing happened. I mean, I'm not stupid." My eyes dart up in a glare. "I knew it was dangerous. I didn't mean for it to go this far. It was just a stupid game."

He closes his eyes and massages his temples. When he finally looks back at me, he lets out a long, steady breath.

"So, you played a game where you suffocated him?" he asks, completely calm.

"Yes, I guess you could say that. But this last time, I must've been too caught up in it. I didn't know it was too long. He… well… he stopped breathing. And I couldn't bring him back." I force the terrible words into reality.

"Did you try to revive him? Like CPR?" he asks, tapping his chin absentmindedly.

"Yes! Of course! Of course, I did," I almost shout, but his eyes force it into a whisper. "He didn't come back."

"What did his parents say? You didn't tell them, right?"

"No! I don't want to go to jail! I didn't mean to do it. It was an accident, well, kind of..." My voice trails off, ashamed.

"Since you're not in jail, they didn't figure it out, huh?" he leans back, lacing his hands behind his head. I hate him for his apathy and yet somehow appreciate it.

"They think it was SIDS."

"So, you liked playing that game? Was it for the power? The power over another life in your hands?"

"What? Well, yeah, I guess so," I say, pushing my hair behind my ears, shielding my scars with a casual cupped hand, a trained reflex learned over the years.

"Well, I have to say..." He leans back a little, pushing his hair back over his head. "That is both amazingly fucked up and kind of understandable at the same time."

I sit stunned by his response. His eyes are burning in a way I've never seen. His smile more genuine than any that came before. He takes my hand, the scarred one, and massages it in his own, tenderly running his thumb over the ridges and craters.

"I mean, who doesn't dream about exerting that kind of power over another human being?" he asks.

"What?" I ask. "What are you talking about?"

"I wouldn't personally want to hurt a child, but I get why you were intrigued to try it. Most people won't admit it, but everyone thinks about it. Killing someone, I mean. I've thought about it before. Lots of times."

"I didn't mean to do it. It was an accident."

"Of course it was an accident, but it also wasn't completely accidental, right?" he asks, and I hate him for his attitude toward the whole thing.

"But that poor baby. He was so little, Gabe. You don't know what it was like." A tremor builds up inside me, but I press it down.

"This confirms it. We're all the same inside. We all think about doing horrible things, but we stop ourselves. You decided not to let that little voice stop you and did a horrible thing, but I don't judge you. Actually, I feel closer to you than ever. I've thought about just letting go and doing something many times…" He trails off into a mumble.

I'm visibly shaking now. "I'm scared," I say, and he snaps back to reality.

"You know, I wish I could do it. Just to know what it feels like. Plus, there are some people that the world would actually benefit from losing." He glares at the door. "What did it feel like?"

"Don't ask me that." I hold myself, rocking slightly, trying to stop my shivering.

"I don't know if I *really* want to or not." He looks at me again. "But I'm a little envious of you. Well, as long as you don't get caught."

"I'm so scared. I can't think about anything else." Hot tears run down my face into my lips as I speak. "I think—do you think I should turn myself in?"

"No, don't be stupid. You need to stop beating yourself up about this whole thing. It's all over now. Turning yourself in won't change what you've done. It won't magically cure the parents from their grief. Won't bring back the dead. It'll just ruin your life. Locking you away doesn't help anyone."

"Okay, okay." I exhale. "Yeah, I guess you're right." We sit in silence for a moment.

"Do you think you'll do it again?" he asks, his lips curling up into an unsettling smile. "Do you think you can just go back to being a normal person again?"

"No, never," I whisper. "No, it was an accident. Of course I couldn't do it again." My mouth is salty with tears and I can barely speak, I'm so hoarse from crying.

"Okay, I was just asking," he says as he lights the bong again. This time I don't turn it away, sucking its contents deep inside of myself. We sit quietly, listening to the television booming downstairs, muffled through the floor.

"We don't have to talk about it anymore. I didn't mean to piss you off," Gabe finally says. I shrug my shoulders. "But don't keep any more secrets from me. I really am your friend, Winnie. After all this stuff lately, the dog and now this, I think I'm the only one who gets it. Understands you. You should trust me. I just want to help."

As he finishes, I reach out and touch his arm. He holds my hand on it and then we lay back on the bed together. I close my eyes. Gabe clicks the lighter again and I finally let myself relax.

TRANSCRIPT FROM THERESA CAMPBELL ASSAULT ARREST

POLICE BODY CAMERA
FIVE YEARS PRIOR

C. Campbell: Stop! Don't take her! Don't take her!

Officer: Sir, you need to step back now.

T. Campbell: I need to go back in! They've brainwashed my daughter! I need to help her!

C. Campbell: No! Stop! She's sick. She didn't mean to.

T. Campbell: No, make them stop. It hurts. Stop touching me!

Officer: Ma'am, calm down. Sir, I need you to step back. Your wife is under arrest.

C. Campbell: She didn't do anything. It was an accident. Let her go!

Officer: Please sir, step back and calm down. I'm not going to tell you again. She is under arrest. Don't you think you should go back inside and be with your other children? They need you right now.

C. Campbell: No, let her go! She didn't mean it! It's not her fault!

Officer: If you'd like, I can help arrange a ride for you and your other children so you can be with your injured daughter.

C. Campbell: I don't want her! This is her fault! Let my wife go! Let her go!

Officer: I need you to go back inside right now, sir, or else I will be forced to arrest you too.

C. Campbell: Don't worry honey. I'll get you out. I love you.

JEREMY

INTERVIEW TRANSCRIPT FOR
THE DAILY SUN
WITH JOURNALIST NATHAN STEIN

DATED DEC. 22

Nathan: Thank you for agreeing to speak with us here at the Daily Sun. Just to be clear, your last name won't appear to help protect your identity, especially since you're a minor. So, how does it feel to know your ex-girlfriend, Winnie Campbell, is missing, presumed on the run from the police, and is a suspect in one or, recent updates indicate, possibly multiple murders?

Jeremy: Uh, I don't know about any of that. And she wasn't really my girlfriend or anything.

Nathan: Really? Our sources indicated you two were a couple.

Jeremy: Uh, no. We just, uh, messed around a few times. We weren't dating or anything. She was just a friend.

Nathan: Did she ever act violently towards you?

Jeremy: No. She was sweet. Honestly, I'm really confused about this whole thing. I was told she was kidnapped. Shouldn't you be out trying to find her? Or who took her?

Nathan: Did she ever reveal any violent fantasies to you, or did you witness any violent acts?

Jeremy: What? No, nothing like that. I just told you, she was a nice person. At least she was always nice to me. Seriously, isn't she a missing person? I don't understand this interview.

Nathan: She has a reputation as being a bit of a "rebel" or a "punk." Do you agree with this representation?

Jeremy: What even? I don't understand why you're asking me these things.

Nathan: Our sources also tell us she dabbled in drinking and drug use. Do you know anything about this? Could the murders have been a drug-induced rage?

Jeremy: What? I don't think so. Wait...what?

Nathan: Was Winnie sexually active? Were you two sexually intimate?

Jeremy: Seriously? Do I really have to answer that? I don't feel comfortable—

Nathan: No, of course not. You don't have to answer anything. I'm just throwing some stuff out there based on what other people have told us. We're just trying to find out more about her. She's a bit of an enigma. Not many people seem to have known her, even at her own school or in her neighborhood.

Jeremy: Yeah, she didn't have many friends.

Nathan: And why is that?

Jeremy: I don't know. She was just kind of an outcast.

Nathan: How did you two meet?

Jeremy: I don't really remember. I think it was at a park.

Nathan: Do you think Winnie could have committed these horrible crimes?

Jeremy: I don't think so, but I don't know. I told you, I always thought she was nice, and I'm pretty sure I heard the police think she was kidnapped, which is terrifying.

Nathan: We're getting such conflicted descriptions of her. She seems to have been this druggie rebel as well as a quiet student and responsible babysitter. Some people are saying she was a kind, caring person while others paint her as a crazy delinquent. Tell us anything you can about the *real* Winnie.

Jeremy: Um, well, she was nice, like I said. She loved science. She told me she wanted to be a doctor when she grew up. A pediatrician. Or a surgeon.

Nathan: What would you say to her if you could talk to her right now?

Jeremy: Um, you mean if she's not kidnapped? I guess that she should come home if she didn't do anything. And I don't think she did.

WINNIE

I keep walking this same route every day for almost a week. Down our street, take a right, follow the road until the sidewalk ends, and then another right, and I see her house: Leigh Bennings. I opened their mailbox once to see the last name. I can't get over how much she looks like me when I was her age, although a bit prettier, and her hair is more dishwater blonde than golden. Still, the resemblance is striking. A doppelganger. A bad omen, but an irresistible one.

It's been like this since I saw her at the grocery store Tuesday. Of course, I'd seen her around many times before, but I'd never really *seen* her like this. She was just walking with her father, picking up a few groceries after school, her little light-up pink sneakers flashing across the linoleum. Her hair was up in a perky ponytail, and it bobbed as she jumped around, trying to pull her father toward the candy aisle instead of the much less exciting canned goods. He was obviously trying to ignore her and her high-pitched whiny voice, but she was making such a fuss, I couldn't help but watch her. She was mesmerizing.

The demeanor, the visage, even the same aura I had at her age. It was more pronounced than ever. She *was* me, just younger. Happier. It doesn't make sense because it's unexplainable. A random encounter with my double, more than a decade apart. I remember my heart pounding and getting lightheaded as I frantically tried to decide if the resemblance was really as exact as it seemed and determine whether this was some kind of sign from the universe. I still don't know why I'm so helplessly drawn to her.

I stand now, facing their little house with its blue front door, pretending to stop to answer a text, but really, I'm watching. Around the corner of the house, I catch a glimpse of her running with a doll in her hand. My own hands are shaking. I take deep breaths to calm myself. I dab cold sweat from my brow and upper lip. Why am I so obsessed? Just because she looks like me? It's silly, and yet here I am, every day. Any possible meaning of this exact look-alike still eludes me, no matter how many hours I stay up at night analyzing it.

It must mean something.

I decide to approach her. She'll remember me as Julia's babysitter most likely, or at least as a neighborhood girl. Not a threat like a strange man, but a girl like her, only a bit older. She'll trust me, I know it, as long as I don't reveal this strange fascination bubbling beneath my skin.

Part of me wishes I had a childhood photo to show her, some sort of proof to explain my unusual connection with her, but Dad burned them all not long after Mom was taken away. Now there are only pictures of Lilly and she's not the same at all, dark and delicate instead of fair and feral like me. Like Leigh.

I look around. No one is looking out the windows of the house or any of the neighbors' houses, at least that I can see. I sneak around the corner of the house where a hose and other gardening equipment lies in an unorganized heap, through the grass that's slightly longer and less tended than the yard. I try to walk in a way that is stealthy yet not too suspicious.

The backyard is big and alternates between a lush carpet of green and grassless patches of dirt. It backs up to the same woods as our house, a wild untended place that no one seems to own. Leigh is playing near a sand pile, her doll prancing up and down, disturbing a line of ants.

I walk a little closer, feeling vulnerable in the open yard. Leigh freezes and glares up at me, body tense and doll suspended mid-leap. I smile and raise my hand in a timid wave.

"Hello! Whatcha playin?" I venture a few steps closer, but she raises her lip, looking like a cornered dog, her eyes darting from me to her backdoor in quick twitches.

"Who are you? Why are you here?"

"Don't you remember me? I babysit Julia. You're her best friend, right? I think I watched you both for couple hours one time. It was a playdate, at her house. Leigh, isn't it?" I ask, and she nods her head, uneasy yet lowering her guard. "Julia has told me all about you and how much fun you two have together. I remember you came to my house on Halloween. You looked so beautiful as Cinderella."

She smiles, a tinge of recognition in her eyes, and I can feel her relax even from across the yard. I walk over to her, then kneel down next to her, careful to avoid the ant pile.

"Yeah, I remember that. You gave us lots of candy! More than the other houses." She giggles. "But why are you in my yard? Are you looking for Julia?"

"No, I was just walking by and saw you back here playing. I thought it would be fun to stop by to say hello." I watch her face, searching it for signs of trust or anxiety. She opens her mouth but closes it again, thinking over my

response before answering. Finally, I see her accept my behavior as normal, as nothing to worry about, no stranger to
run screaming from, and she twists to reach a doll behind
her in the grass.

Pushing the cloth doll into my hands, she says, "You
can play with me if you want. Here, you can be Jasmine.
Just be careful not to rip her arm. See," she gently tugs at
the arm to reveal a busted seam with white stuffing pushing
out. "I don't want her arm to come off."

I accept the toy and carefully join her in bouncing our
dolls in the grass around us, talking in slightly altered voices
to give them life. I watch Leigh and breathe in every detail
of her. Her blonde hair is tied in a high ponytail with a large
polka dot bow. My mom tied my hair in twin bows atop my
head when I was her age. I even dressed like her back then, a
pink long-sleeved shirt, stained with various small splashes,
and jeans. I don't remember what it feels like to be so light
and small, but I guess I must've known at one point.

She sits with her legs splayed in a w-shape, the way
I was warned again and again not to by my kindergarten
teacher. At four years old, she must only be in pre-K, like
her friend Julia. Maybe no teacher has warned her about
sitting that way yet.

She's easier to play with than Lilly who's in her awkward phase when toys are still fun but also losing their ap-
peal. Lilly was more fun when she was younger. I probably was too. Leigh looks at me, her cheeks rosy and full of
health. I shake my head at how absolutely uncanny it is.

"Here, you can be both of these girls and I'll be Karina," she says and, before I can say anything, she runs across
the yard and through the sliding glass door into the house.
My stomach lurches, but I've done nothing wrong. Sure,
it's strange for a sixteen-year-old to be playing with a little

girl, one she doesn't know in any concrete way, but nothing that would warrant more than a sideways glance, maybe an awkward conversation.

I hear her mom yelling inside. She's saying something about "tracking in dirt" but she sounds like she's at the other side of the house. A couple minutes pass by and I consider leaving, but then Leigh comes running back with a stuffed turtle in hand.

"Hi Jasmine and Sasha! Let's go into town and get everything we need for the big birthday party." Leigh tilts the turtle towards the dolls in my hands, bobbing its head as it "speaks" before running off across the yard. I chase after her, holding the dolls in clenched fists ahead of me. Soon we're running circles around her backyard at full speed, laughing with the dolls held in front of us.

After a couple of laps, she stops near the woods and calls to the dolls again. We collect acorns, small white flowers, and dandelions as pretend groceries for the toy party. When everything is gathered, she fetches a small plastic tea set and we set up all the imagined treats to surprise a stuffed kitten she has waiting inside. She runs to grab the kitten, covering its eyes with her hands as she returns to our tea party, then reveals the feast to the birthday cat with a squeal of "Surprise!" We play like this for ten or fifteen minutes before I start to feel uneasy. Maybe this is too weird. I shouldn't stay too long. I shouldn't be here at all.

"This has been so fun! Can I come over and play with you again sometime?" I say, handing the dolls back to her. She nods and waves goodbye before returning her full attention to the pretend birthday celebration. I sneak out the way I entered, and even though the neighbor across the street is mowing his lawn, no one seems to notice or care. I walk all the way home, focused on my steps, trying to keep my pace steady even though I feel like running.

Exhilarated yet frustrated, my heart beats against my breastbone painfully. What is it about her? What do I even want from her? I feel a compulsion to slam my head against a wall, to hurt myself and stop thinking about this totally normal little girl, a stranger to me, but I resist. It won't help anything. I've tried it before. But why does it hurt so much to see her, to know her?

I reach my house and peek through the front window before I enter. Dad and Lilly are in the kitchen, and although the obstructed view prevents me from seeing what they're doing, from the excited voices I hear inside, I assume it's something like baking cookies. Dad always does things like that with her when Brendan and I are away.

I sneak away from the house and sit on the curb by the end of the driveway. I take out my phone and start to text Gabe, but I remember he's out of town with some guy. So unfair. I text Krystal: *Hey! :) Movie night tonight?* and then scroll for fifteen minutes before she finally responds. *Yeah! Come by @ 7 for dinner too.* I cringe a little. She should know better. I guess I could make something in the crock pot so it can finish cooking while I'm away. Maybe Dad won't mind.

Hours later, I'm finally walking up to Krystal's house, only a little late. Half an hour. I knock and wait for what feels like an eternity for someone to answer. The door makes a noise like lips smacking as it opens. That paint isn't even a year old.

"Hello Winnie! You're just in time. Dinner took a little longer than Cheryl had thought," the handsome middle-aged man says, the light from the hallway lamp forming a halo around his head. Always a perfect dad: Mr. Schumacher. As we walk into the dining room, Krystal's mom pops her head out of the kitchen with a smile plastered across her face.

"Oh, Winnie! We haven't seen you in so long. It's absolutely wonderful to have you here for dinner again like the good ol' days," she says as she wipes her hands on her apron. "It's gumbo on the menu tonight. I remember you used to like that. I hope you still do."

Her voice has that kind of sing-songy lilt that is almost grating but not quite to the level of annoying. Her big fake breasts jut out like torpedoes from beneath the low-cut black tee. She's so fake it's disgusting, but she's always been nice to me. Krystal always bitched about her a lot and apparently, she can be kind of controlling, but she seems like a good mom. I just wish she wouldn't dress like she's still a teenager or something. It's somehow more embarrassing that she's oblivious to how absurd she looks.

Mr. Schumacher yells up the stairs, "Krystal! Krystal, come down! Winnie is here!" which is quickly followed by a rapid stomping of feet down the stairs.

"Dad, when did she get here? You should've told me right away," Krystal says, rolling her eyes at her dad before running to me. "Oh Winnie, I'm so glad you came! And Mom's even making your favorite." I smile. It almost feels like the 'good old' days' never ended.

After dinner, I clear the table and am subsequently showered with the usual compliments from Krystal's parents, "Such a helpful young lady!" and "Krystal could learn a thing or two about manners from you, Winnie." Krystal washes her face and changes into pajamas while I search the enormous DVD collection. She shouts something about streaming movies, but I know all the best classics are already in her living room. I find the one and set it up.

Krystal slides over the back of the couch and bounces on the cushions as I snuggle into a blanket on the floor.

"Oh yes! *Freaks* is the best. I haven't seen it in ages. Man, you really made this just like the movie night from middle school," Krystal says. "Wait, pause it a minute. I'll go make popcorn."

As she runs into the kitchen, her parents call goodnight to us. They head upstairs to leave us alone and probably to have some much-needed quality time themselves. They seem like the kind of parents who still have sex occasionally. I hear the beeps of the microwave and almost let myself believe that things can go back to how they were, but then I hear Krystal on the phone. She's explaining how she can't go out tonight, but maybe tomorrow. *Old friend came over. Yeah, just movies or something like that. Too bad I'll miss out on the party.* I burrow deeper into my blanket and try to let it go. Just enjoy the moment. But I can't, so I pretend.

WINNIE

"That was total bullshit today. Really, why can't those bitches just leave you alone? What did you ever do to them?" Gabe says as he grabs the almost empty wine bottle and drinks the last bit. After he finishes, he tosses it to the ground, and it crashes to pieces. He's getting pretty drunk, but I'm only tipsy since I went easy on the first bottle. "Why would they write shit like that about you? God, it just really pisses me off."

"Tell me about it," I say. "I'm the one they said it about." The wind rustles the leaves above us and I shiver, prompting me to zip up my jacket and pull my sweater sleeves over my hands.

"Don't act like they aren't assholes to me too. Some-times it feels like everyone hates us." Gabe stumbles through the sentence, glaring at me. I bite my lip and nod in agreement, which seems to appease him, and he calms down a little. "I just—why? Why?"

"I don't know," I say.

I open the cigarette box, but it's empty. Gabe's smok-ing the last one. I look toward his backpack, hoping he has another pack in there somewhere, but of course he doesn't catch on and I have to ask him. He mumbles something and throws the bag toward me.

"I don't get you, Winnie. I mean, come on! You should be really pissed off with me!"

"I am. I am. I just don't show it the same way, I guess," I say, peeling off the cellophane wrapper.

"Sometimes I think about doing something really bad. Some really fucked up shit." Gabe spits a big hunk of phlegm on the ground.

My mind floods with the thousands of fantasies I've indulged in that were not quite socially acceptable. "Like what?"

"I don't know, like something like…shoot up the school." He flashes a smile at me. "Pull a real Columbine, you know?"

I shake my head and scoff. "Seriously? Shoot up the school? That's dumb. Where would we even get guns from? That just sounds—"

Gabe interrupts me. "My pop kept a bunch of guns back in the day. I wouldn't be surprised if Mom still had a few hidden away somewhere."

"And you think you wouldn't have found them by now?" I say, raising one eyebrow.

"Well, I'm sure I could get some sweet ass guns if I wanted," he says. He stares, almost sneering, but I can see a pleading look behind the hard front.

"Fine, sure, I believe you." I sigh. "You could totally get some awesome guns or whatever, but what would you do? What's the plan, Mr. Psychopath?"

He cracks open a beer and hands it to me before taking one for himself. "I guess I'd start—no, *we'd* start." He grins and shoves my shoulder. "We'd start by dressing hot as hell. All black and spikes and… and as badass as possible."

I laugh, almost spitting out a mouthful of beer. "Okay, so we'd look cool as fuck. Is that the big plan? To walk around looking good and holding guns?"

"Shut up," Gabe says, but he's holding back a laugh too. "There's more. Okay, so we plan it for a day when some of those fuckers are practicing in the gym, and we start there. Bam! Burst through those big doors. Kick 'em open even. We open fire on the whole gym class. Oh, or an assembly! Yeah, that'd be the best! All those arrogant bastards would all be there at once, plus a couple teachers who wrote a few regrettable detention slips." With a laugh, he chugs his beer. I am sipping mine now that the buzz is hitting me.

"Yeah, an assembly, that's actually a pretty good plan, I have to admit. We could mow down all those future Stepford wives who wrote that shit about me in the bathroom," I say. He nods vigorously and loses his balance a little, teetering but catching himself before he falls off the bench.

"Okay, Gabe, I have to give it to you," I say, striking a match. "That does sound like an awesome revenge plan, and indeed, some very fucked up shit." He grins again, stupid drunk and smoke pouring out of his nostrils like a cartoon bull. I resist the urge to mock him.

"Yeah, it'd be so fulfilling. Super satisfying," Gabe says while he opens yet another beer.

I walk myself through his fantasy again in my mind's eye. Gabe tossing a rifle to me as he pulls a hoodie over his quintessential mohawk. I put on a white half-mask, kind of Phantom of the Opera style but more porcelain doll, with my hair teased high and flawless makeup on my good side.

As we barge into the assembly, all eyes dart to us. The fear and uneasiness flood the room with a thick heat. Gabe shouts something and fires away into the crowd, focusing mainly on the teachers, as if it's their fault he's failing. I don't waste my time with the innocent, and instead target that back row with the brainless twats and their boyfriends. The ones who always say those things about me, or don't stop those who do. And that dickhead Patrick who always sits up there too. They deserve it.

I can feel the kick of the rifle as I fire away. Their bodies fall lifeless to the riser below them. Now nothing but bags of meat, oozing blood and staring at the ceiling, stupidly slack-jawed. The sound of sirens and screeching tires comes outside. Gabe points his gun under his chin, smiling just the same as always. I can't do it and cower in the corner as heavy boots stomp into the room. I snap back to reality and feel both excited and nauseated. I take a few sips of my beer to settle my stomach.

"Wanna do it? Come on, we'll be famous, no, infamous forever." Gabe nudges me as he talks. "What's wrong? You look all shook up suddenly." I shake my head and take a few more sips. "Come on, it was just fun to imagine it. You don't have to start freaking out or anything. Anyway, only one of us knows what it's like to kill somebody in *real life.*"

"Ah, Gabe, that's not cool. Stop it," I say, but he's laughing and chugging his drink. "I don't think I want to, you know, kill myself. It's too scary to imagine putting the gun... I don't want that. I'm too much of a wimp."

"Who said anything about killing yourself?" Gabe shouts, and I shush him. He whispers, "Oh yeah, okay, I get it. That's probably how it would have to end. You're definitely right, but you know it was a cathartic exercise to imagine it at least."

"Sure, but I've imagined better," I say, regretting it immediately. Gabe tries to stand, but only manages to stagger a little before falling back to a sitting position.

"Oh, little Miss Murderess, I forgot I was talking to an expert. Tell me. Please, go on. Tell me about your ultimate killing fantasy. This somehow *more* satisfying experience." Gabe says all this while waving his hands about like a conductor. It would be funny if he wasn't so drunk and serious.

"Um, I don't know…" I say, but Gabe tries to grab my beer. "Fine, fine. Remember that girl I told you about?"

"The little girl you think looks like you?"

"Yeah, her. Anyway, you know, I was thinking that maybe killing her would be even better because, well, okay, hear me out." I take a drink of my beer for courage. "First, it'd be much easier. She's not very strong or fast or anything." Gabe nods along and I take another gulp, feeling the excitement build as I say these thoughts aloud.

"Second, we've read so many true crime books and watched all those documentaries, I think we could get away with it, if we managed to do it without witnesses. She's practically a stranger, and we know how much easier it is to get away with killing someone you don't have any connections with. Nobody's ever seen us together. They wouldn't even suspect us. The cops would totally think it was some freak who kidnapped her. I mean, I don't have a record at all. Yours is just shoplifting. If we're careful about prints, they'd never find out. And kids are so light, we could carry a small body like that no problem, wherever we needed."

Gabe is leaning forward, really listening now. The blood pounds in my ears and flushes my face as I continue. "We'd be able to do a real human dissection. That's something only med school students get to do. See how everything looks and works for real. I know you'd love that." I finish my beer and Gabe is staring, silently urging me to go on.

"And, most importantly, there's something incredible about killing that particular girl because she looks so fucking similar to me. It's been driving me crazy. I can't stop thinking about how she's my exact childhood doppelganger. It's poetic or something. Kind of like a suicide, but you get to keep on living.

"I don't know how to explain it. It's like I could kill the me from the past, the me I grew up to be, and just be free. A new person, different, not me anymore, but someone who could do whatever she wanted because her past is dead. Just move on and never look back. I guess that's the part I like the most about the whole thing."

"Wow, that is symbolic and deep and crazy as hell," Gabe cuts in, looking mesmerized. "Okay, you win, you psycho! You came up with the most messed up yet somehow beautiful murder."

"Thank you," I say, grinning ear to ear. "I thought it was pretty lovely myself."

"Jeez Winnie, if I didn't know you better, I'd be absolutely terrified of you, you freak," Gabe says, laughing. "You should make movies or something with a brain like that, you queen of depravity."

He bows deeply, and I giggle. When he comes back up, I hand him another beer, which he happily pops open right away.

"Maybe I *should* be a movie director or something someday." I pull the last beer out of his backpack for myself. "I mean, I do think I have a pretty good imagination."

"Yeah, you totally do. Maybe you're actually destined to be *famous,* not infamous," Gabe says, putting his beer on the ground and leaning against the tree. "I hope you know, you really can just walk away and start over. You can do it whenever you're ready. Maybe that's how you'll eventually end up in Hollywood, writing screenplays and surrounded by a harem of gorgeous men. Ha! That reminds me, let me tell you about this smoking hot guy I saw at the corner store earlier. I pull in to fuel up and there he was, get this, on a lime green crotch rocket."

"That's awesome," I say, but my mind is already wandering. The sky darkens as the sun settles behind a hill. I wonder why it has to get dark so early in the fall. I'll have to head home soon to make dinner. I go over recipes in my head while Gabe talks away.

WINNIE

NOV. 14

"Thank you for being able to babysit on such late notice," Mrs. Carpenter says as she opens the door, immediately pressing a crying baby Allie into my arms. "We'll be back in a few hours, by seven thirty, eight at the latest. There's some lasagna waiting in the oven, you just have to warm it up. And please make sure Julia's in bed by eight. What am I saying? You know the drill." She lets out a piercing laugh. "Thank you again, Winnie! You're the best."

And just like that, she's pushed past me through the door and is already opening in the passenger seat. Mr. Carpenter follows a few seconds later with a mumble and polite nod as he squeezes past me.

As I walk inside and close the door, there's Julia, standing at the end of the hall with a hand on her hip like a sassy teenager. She's wearing star-shaped plastic sunglasses and a pink feather boa. Her favorite "movie star" outfit.

"Hey Julia, you look fabulous," I say over Allie's screams, bouncing her to calm her down.

"I know," Julia says and then bursts into peals of laughter. "Come on. Let's play movie star again. Do you want to be my driver or my makeup artist?"

"You know what your mom said about makeup after last time." Her joy dims slightly as she nods. "So, I guess I'll be your driver. Just let me get Allie calmed down and I'll come play with you."

"Okay! I'll go get everything set up," she says, rushing around the corner into the playroom.

As I continue to bounce Allie, cooing and singing to her, I think of Nikolai. He was so much smaller, more delicate, with a sweeter disposition. A sort of grief rises up in me, but I force it down. Singing louder, I try to drown out both the baby's cries and the voices in my mind. It was a wrong thing you did. Could you do that to Allie too? You know you played that game with her once or twice before, a long time ago. I suddenly realize I'm shaking all over and that Allie has stopped crying. Her big, shiny eyes gaze up at me in absentminded wonder. Then I notice Julia is in the room again, watching me.

"Why are you shaking like that?"

"I'm just cold."

"It's not very cold in here."

"Well, it's a little cold. I'll go put Allie in her playpen and grab my sweater, then I can be your professional chauffeur, Mademoiselle," I say, trying to be playful. I can tell she only half buys it, but that's enough. She stares for a couple more seconds and then skips away. I take a deep breath, pull my sweater out of my backpack, and take the baby to the playroom with me, gently setting her amongst her plethora of toys in the playpen.

Julia has the couch set up to be her pretend limo and hands me a paper plate "steering wheel" as she explains everything.

"This is where you sit and I'm back here. This is the snack machine, and this is the music machine, and this is where all my movie star pets sit," she says, stacking stuffed animals onto the back cushion. "Now drive me to Hollywood. I'm late for a movie!"

"Vroom," I make car noises for a while, until I feel we've driven far enough. Then I squeak my imaginary tires to a halt. "Here we are: Hollywood."

"Thank you, driver. Now I just need your help to find a crown to wear and everything will be perfect."

"A crown? But I thought we were playing movie star, not princess?" I say, turning back towards her. She screws up her face in annoyance.

"Movie stars can't have crowns?"

"Well, I mean, I guess they can. Maybe if they're playing a princess or queen in a movie they're making?"

"Okay, well then that's why I need it. I'm a princess in a movie," she says and crosses her arms. "I wish I was a real princess with a real princess crown."

"Well, I know how to make a flower crown, but there's not many flowers still alive this time of year," I say, and she frowns. "I could try to make a paper one if you want. I think there's even some sequins left in the craft box. We could put those on it."

"Fine," she says, but I can tell it's not what she really wants. As I fetch the craft box, Leigh pops into my mind. She wouldn't have an attitude like this. She'd be appreciative, creative, helpful. I sigh as I lug the container from the closet. Julia perks up a little when she sees all the glitter.

"Oh, we can put so many colors on it," she says as she grabs two glitter shakers from the box and proceeds to open them.

"No, wait," I say, but it's too late. A pile of silver glitter spills onto the carpet. I restrain my sigh and stomp into the kitchen to find the vacuum. When I come back, Julia's already preoccupied with some other game back on the couch. She doesn't even offer to help or apologize at all. Rage floods my mind, but I dutifully clean up like the permanent janitor I seem destined to be.

As the vacuum roars to life, Allie starts to cry in her playpen. I still need to warm up that lasagna. I imagine sprinkling some poison onto it or getting the syrupy antifreeze from the garage and blending up some milkshakes.

Not quite satisfied, the fantasy morphs into a poisoned feast for my own family of gluttons. I imagine Brendan stuffing his mouth. Dad's face glistening from smeared grease. Lilly smiling and licking her fingers clean. All oblivious to the slow, painful death they just ingested. This fantasy works better for me and the rage melts away. Allie shrieks especially loud and I shake my head back to reality to finish cleaning.

After calming Allie down again, I approach Julia and her bevy of dolls. She has them all lined up to watch a fashion show of original designs made from tissues. I'm actually impressed by how creative some of the outfits turned out.

"Do you want me to play with you?" I ask and Julia just shrugs, so I sink down next to her and watch her doll models strut down the catwalk.

"Wow, these outfits are really good. Where'd you learn how to make such fancy tissue dresses?"

"My friend Leigh taught me. If you think these are good, you should see hers," she says and then sighs. "Mine don't look quite right."

At the mention of Leigh, my heartbeat pounds in my ears and my skin rises in goosebumps.

"Oh yeah, Leigh. I think I remember her. You went trick-or-treating together, right?" I ask, trying to conceal the depth of my interest.

"Yeah," she answers, not taking her eyes off her pretend fashion show.

"Is Leigh your best friend?" I ask, but she just nods. "Hmm. Are you two going to have a play date again soon?"

"I'm hungry. Aren't you supposed to make lasagna for me?" she asks, ignoring my question.

"Yeah. I'll go do that," I say, getting up and heading toward the kitchen.

Preheating the oven, my thoughts keep jumping back to Leigh. She's so much better than Julia. I'm glad she's a more talented paper dress designer than that spoiled brat. She deserves to be knocked down a few levels. Leigh is so much worthier of all the praise I constantly hear heaped on Julia. Just because she's outgoing and precocious doesn't mean she's better.

I think of Leigh and her pale face. I can't get over how striking the resemblance is. A prettier, more talented, over-all better version of me as a child. What do I even want with her? The darkness that shrouds the answer makes me backtrack and forces my thoughts elsewhere. Traveling, love, cute boys at school, no matter what I try to think about, the inky darkness of that thought seeps through and voices whisper in the background. For the rest of the night, the thought slithers behind each word and action, intruding into every corner of my mind.

WINNIE

There's a man sitting across the aisle from me and he won't quit staring. I try to ignore him, stare out the bus window, but his eyes burn into me. What a creep. He's a grown man, at least in his thirties, business suit, clean-shaven. You'd think he'd know better. I wonder whether it's the scars or my chest he's staring at. Either one is rude, but I hope it's my cleavage that has inspired this lapse in bus etiquette. Maybe he's just spaced out in my general direction. I've done that before. I pull my hair down over the side of my face and shift in my seat. Almost my stop. Just ignore him.

"Next stop: 8th Street," the recorded voice chimes over the speakers. I pull the cord. Thank god I'm finally there.

As I step off the bus, my phone buzzes, but I wait to make sure that man isn't following me before I let my guard down and check it. It's Krystal: *Wanna come over? :)*

I text back: *No. Downtown*

I take maybe three steps before the phone buzzes again. The entire message is a question mark.

I reply: *Movies with Gabe*

She immediately texts back: *Ok*

I can tell she disapproves, but why does it matter to her who I hang out with now? I pull my sleeves down through my jacket and over my hands. I should've brought gloves, but it didn't seem that cold.

The neon lights of the cinema peek from behind the glassy windows of an office building. As I round the corner, a scowl creeps across my lips. Why am I even mad at her about this? I'm probably reading too much into a two-letter text anyway, but something in my stomach knots when I think of her fake new life. I don't even know if I trust her anymore after all these years. I see Gabe up ahead, leaning against the wall, trying to look cool with a cigarette in his hand, looking down at his phone.

"You smoke too much. You know you're going to regret it in thirty years when you die of lung cancer," I say, surprising him.

He smirks and shrugs. "Pfft, I'll never make it that long anyway."

"Heh, you look like some kind of discount James Dean in this pleather jacket. Where'd you get it?" I reach out, but he yanks his arm away before I can touch it.

"Lay off, jeez. It's an early Christmas present from my mom."

The smile slides off my face as guilt burrows in my stomach.

"Sorry. I didn't know. That was nice of her."

"Yeah, pretty strange, actually. Which reminds me, you started to say something at lunch about your dad acting weird or something?" he asks as he puts out his cigarette. "Well, I mean, weirder than his usual asshole self."

"Yeah, that's what's been strange. He hasn't been an asshole the last couple of days. He hasn't yelled at me, or even at Brendan after he came home last night with a big dent in the car. It's really weird."

"Isn't that a good thing, that he hasn't been beating the shit out of you?"

"Well, yeah, but he's just been acting weird in other ways too. Like he barely says a word to any of us. He just kind of grunts, even when Lilly asks him things. And I'm pretty sure he was drinking before work this morning. He stunk. I'm afraid it's building up into something big. I don't like it."

As we walk toward the ticket booth, some homeless man is throwing up in the street right in front of the cinema. I gag and cover my nose and mouth before pushing the money under the window to the cashier.

"Ugh, that's disgusting," Gabe says, grabbing our tickets and pushing me through the door inside. "Anyway, sounds to me like he's just super depressed or something."

"I don't know. Maybe. I just hope he's not saving up all his rage for when he snaps out of it." We get our ticket stubs and head to Theater 4 for the snooze-fest art film Gabe picked. You'd think the one who pays would get to pick, but I know better than to call out Gabe when he's broke. It's not like he isn't generous when he has money.

"Let's sit up front," he says, but I shake my head. He knows it makes me dizzy. We head toward the middle seats. Then I notice Patrick is sitting in the back row.

"Fuck. Gabe, I have to go," I whisper in his ear, "Look over there." I discreetly point toward the back. Thankfully I don't think he notices us yet.

"Come on. Don't be dumb. He won't bother us."

"No, I just can't."

"Well, whatever, but I'm staying. We already paid and everything," he whispers, and shrugs as I get up to leave.

Squeezing past the seats, I walk out with my head down. At first, I don't think he saw me, but before I'm halfway down the hallway, I hear someone behind me. I'm sure it's Patrick even without looking.

"Hey, Winnie, wait up." I zip up my jacket and keep going. I hear him running, and then he grabs my shoulder.

"Don't touch me. Can't you just leave me alone for once?"

"Yeah. Sorry." He lets go, pushes back his hair. "I just wanted to talk to you."

I consider bolting for the exit, but his posture, the way his shaggy blond hair falls over his eyes, there's something familiar there that oozes anxiety, not the bravado I'm used to seeing from him. This revelation makes me braver, like I could hold the power here. "Why?"

"Listen, I know I've been kind of a dick to you. I guess, I was just thinking, I feel kind of… bad about it." He shrugs and half-laughs, half-coughs. "I don't know why I've been like that. And for so long. I just saw you here and… I guess I wanted to kind of apologize or something."

"What?" I glare at him. He puts his hands in his pockets and looks at the floor. I peer over my shoulder at the exit and think about running again. This feels like a trap.

"Winnie, I— uh, I kind of—" He stumbles over his words, but I'm growing impatient and back away a step. "No, wait! Please just hear me out."

"What?" I ask again, softer than before, trying to anticipate what's coming.

"I guess, I've been embarrassed about it, but I didn't mean all that stuff I said. I actually think you're really pretty." He looks up, flashing a nervous smile.

I frown and take another step back toward the exit. "Huh?"

"No, really. I do. It's just, you know, other people say you're not because of the… you know… scars and all. But I really think you are." He sighs again and rocks on his feet. "I guess I did a really shitty job showing it, huh? I'm sorry, Winnie. I guess I just wanted to tell you that."

I mull over his words, searching his face for sincerity. He seems honest, embarrassed, maybe even ashamed. Up close and vulnerable like this, he's almost cute too, if I could forget everything he ever said or did over the last two years. I try to push down the flutter in my stomach and remind myself flattery is empty.

"Well, thanks. I guess." I turn away and start walking to the exit again.

"Wait! Just wait a second."

"What now?" I run my fingers through my hair, bubbling with uneasiness.

"Now that I've told you how I feel and all, do you think…" His voice lowers so only I can hear it. "Maybe we could go somewhere together and see what happens? I hear you're talented. Maybe that bathroom over there?"

Then he has the audacity to wink.

My face contorts in disgust. I want to slap him, kick him, even kill him, but I find myself running out the exit before I have a chance to think. An usher yells something, but the door shuts behind me.

It's even colder than before, and I hug myself as I storm away. I can't believe I almost fell for that shit. Just another asinine prank. Or maybe he did really want that. As if I'd ever let him near me. I'd gnaw it clean off, spit the blood in his face, and smile.

A man ambles toward me, asking for change and trying to peek down my shirt. I flip him off and keep going. He shouts something, but my ears pound with the thick sound of my blood, drowning out the world, and my jaw clenches so tight my teeth threaten to crack.

Turning the corner, I slow down. Maybe it wasn't that big of a deal. I just hate myself for believing him, even for one second. At least nobody was around to hear it. I bury the shame so I don't have to think about how much some part of me wanted it to be true. Then maybe I could've been the one to laugh in his face for once. Maybe I could've embarrassed him, broken his heart, ruined his life. Instead, he won again and I'm dragging myself home, missing the movie I came out to see.

As I near the bus stop, I change my mind. Best to take advantage of a night out, especially with Dad being lenient lately. The streets are mostly empty. Probably normal for a Wednesday evening. I've never noticed how nice the city is when it's dark and empty. Some of the stores are still open, their bright lights illuminating the sidewalk. The other windows are darkened, intriguing in a way they never could be in the day.

I turn down a side street and even fewer shops are lit up, letting me slide by in shadowed anonymity. I imagine Dad at home, back to his usual ways, waiting for me, but I push the thought away. Maybe I really should run away. Gabe always asks why I don't, but I can't just leave with no money, nowhere to go, and then there's Lilly. Dad loves her, but he doesn't know how to take care of her. She needs me.

Up ahead, a woman stands outside a hotel. She looks around like she's waiting for someone, rubbing her hands over her bare arms, trying to warm herself. In dark jeans and boots, she wouldn't stand out if it weren't for the sleeveless top. I wonder whether she lost her coat. Then I see bruises and sores dotting her arm. I think back to health class and wonder if they're track marks. A few steps closer, I notice deep creases running from her nose to the corners of her mouth and from her eyes across her cheeks. Her face makes me think she must be at least fifty, but her body seems younger. I realize she might be a sex worker and I'm suddenly fascinated by her.

She glances at me, but scoffs and looks away. I walk faster so I can pass her without staring too much, but even two blocks later, I'm still thinking about her. She had one of those faces you're sure was beautiful when she was younger. I catch myself tracing the scars down my face and neck.

I wonder what it's like, being a prostitute. It wouldn't be like the movies with the glamorous high-class call girls and handsome, clean johns. It'd probably be closer to what she's doing. Standing on street corners or at bus stops, waiting for men to approach. It must be nice, in a way. So many men wanting to have you, willing to pay you just so they can be inside you for a moment. Some of them might even be cute or nice or interesting to talk to. Some of them could even be good in bed. I fantasize about trying every kind of man there is, each one showering me with compliments. I wouldn't care if they meant them, just that they told them to me.

Then I remember her bruises. It must be easy to fall into that life. Or worse yet, what if they weren't from drugs? I imagine brutal beatings, rape, and being alone and scared. It wouldn't be any better than I already have it. I could be homeless, or maybe some especially cruel customer would kill me. I shudder at the thought and quicken my pace again.

On the next block, I see another bus stop. It's time to go home. As soon as I walk in the door, Brendan tells me Dad went to his room hours ago and hasn't been out since. Relief washes over me and I don't even mind cleaning up his empty bottles or vomit the next morning. A small price to pay to be left alone.

WINNIE

Arms and legs buried in dead leaves, Gabe and I lie under an oak tree in the park. We take turns drinking from the bottle of Jack he smuggled in his backpack. Sprawled out like a starfish, relishing the satisfying crunch of leaves beneath me, I listen to the wind, to Gabe swallowing, the whiskey splashing in the bottle, then feel its cool glass against my shoulder.

I take it without a word, raising my head a little to prevent spilling as I let the liquid fire fill my mouth and flow down my throat. Lying back down, the warmth washes over. My throat tingles in a comforting way. Far above, a few skeletal leaves cling to their branches as the wind beats against them, working hard to pull them free.

"I love fall. It's the best season," I say, turning my head toward Gabe, leaves crinkling against my ear.

"Yeah, but it's practically winter now." He reaches for the bottle, then takes another swig.

"Let me just enjoy the fall while it lasts. It's so beautiful," I say, and we lay in silence again, listening to the whistle of the wind. The clouds move slowly by, sometimes colliding, forming shapes, gray fluff billowing and bulging. Maybe it'll rain tonight.

I imagine rain falling down in sheets, filling up gutters and creating puddles out of every pothole in town. Maybe Lilly will want to pull on her galoshes and brave the storm with me, twirling and jumping in the puddles, seeing who can create the biggest splash. I smile at the memory of her face beaming last time, but that was more than a year ago. No, I suppose she's outgrown all of that. I push back my hair and wonder why I haven't.

Then I imagine Leigh, even more ecstatic than Lilly ever was, galloping through the oil slick rainbows that collect on the uneven streets. She'll wear a shiny yellow slicker and matching hat with oversized purple rain boots. Her high-pitched laugh, almost a scream, will echo through the woods all the way to my house. Suddenly, I'm overwhelmed by the urge to visit her, as if I could meld with her, take over her picture-perfect life, her loving family, her youth. An unexplainable rage tears my stomach to shreds.

Sitting bolt upright, I turn to Gabe. "What's wrong with me? Why can't I just leave that little girl alone?"

The questions sound ridiculous as soon as they've been spoken, yet there remains this desperate urge I can't explain. I want to cry, to attempt a release of all this frustration and tension whirring in my chest, but find I can't produce even a single tear. Gabe looks at me like I'm some strange specimen, visibly disgusted.

"What *is* wrong with you?"

"I don't know," I say and try to relax, but I can't shake the urge to go see her. "Maybe I've been drinking too much lately. My obsession did kind of start around the same time we started pilfering your mom's good stuff, and you know how nostalgic I get when I'm drunk."

"Well, then I guess you don't need any more of this." He pulls the bottle away from me.

"Oh, come on, I didn't mean it like that," I say, but he opens his eyes again and I lose my train of thought in the cruelty there.

"Then just kill her already. That's what it is, isn't it? Your whole stupid fantasy. God, just get it over with so you can forget about her and move on as your new 'reborn' self or whatever bullshit you said. You're obsessed with pseudo-suicide because you're too much of a pussy to do the real deal." He spits the words like venom, and I'm left wincing.

I lie back down and nestle my limbs into the pile of leaves and sink into shame. Silent tears now come easily, but I don't want them anymore. I don't want him to be right, but maybe he understands me better than I do myself. Maybe I'm stuck in that idea of killing the "past" me before I can grow and leave this state of limbo. Maybe I'm too scared to kill myself and I'm looking for excuses, fabricating fantasies of any other way out.

"Stop being all mopey, for fuck's sake," Gabe says as he turns onto his side and props his head up with his hand. "I'm sorry. I didn't mean any of it. I'm just over all this crazy bullshit. You've been so weird about that girl who looks like you, and yes, you're right, she does look creepily similar. She could be your fucking twin or something, but you've got to let it go already! You have no reason to be this obsessed with some snotty little kid. It's all some melodramatic plot in your twisted little mind and none of that is reality. Reality is the way your family treats you. Reality is the fucked-up things you've been through. Nothing can make that shit go away. But you'll be okay. The sooner you realize that, the better. Now come on and have another swig. I have to go home soon."

I take the bottle from his hand as I sit up and drink a long, slow drink. I don't want to look at him anymore, even when he tugs me to my unsteady feet.

"I really am sorry, okay?" he asks, but it's not really a question so much as an assertion. I just nod.

As we stumble along the dirt path, I think about how Lilly always says the woods are scary in the fall and winter, even during the day. She says the trees look like they have claws and are waiting to scoop us up into their clutches, but I love the way the barren branches reach for the sky and try to tear it open. It's beautiful, not scary, especially when the first snow falls, dusting the gnarled bark with ridges of white, highlighting the intricate patterns we usually never notice. When enough snow falls, it's sometimes hard to tell the sky from the ground except for the dark claws of the trees, reaching upward.

"I wonder when it's going to snow? It usually does around this time of year," I ponder aloud. Gabe stops, and I can tell he hadn't considered it until now.

"You're right, it's been crazy warm for fall. Hasn't even dropped below freezing. I hope it snows soon. It won't feel like Christmas without a little snow," he says.

I'm glad he's not looking at me just then because I'm caught off guard by the way he mentions Christmas. He always hated the holiday and considered it just another brainwashed capitalist reason to spend money. I guess maybe he's changed his mind. Anyone can change their mind, I suppose, and then I steal the thought away and cherish it. Gabe is right. I can always change my mind, too.

WINNIE

"Hi Leigh," I say as I walk into the backyard, "I brought you this." Her face lights up as I extend the crude dandelion crown I wove for her. "Be careful with it. It's kind of fragile."

"Whoa, is this a fairy crown?" she asks as she takes the green and yellow circle of weeds. She doesn't wait for an answer to put it on her head.

"Of course it's a fairy crown! I mean, I did hear from the forest fairies that you are the Princess of the Forest. So, I figured you needed a crown, Your Majesty," I say with a bow, and she giggles.

"You didn't really talk to the fairies," she says and then whispers, cupping her hands around her mouth, "Fairies don't exist." I suppress a laugh when her eyes dart toward the forest, as if she were afraid to insult the nonexistent fae within.

"Sure they do, and you're their leader. Maybe you didn't know until today, but that's the truth," I say, bowing again. She claps her hands and twirls. The crown flies off her golden hair and into the grass, but she quickly grabs and replaces it.

"Do you want a piggyback ride, Your Majesty?" I ask. She nods furiously and so I crouch down and let her climb onto my back. With a neigh and a shake of my long blonde mane, I begin to gallop up and down the side of the yard.

"You're my royal pony of the forest," she announces, and then laughs so hard she almost falls off my back. I set her down gently, and she hugs me in gratitude. Then I hear a man's voice call for her from inside the house.

Shit, that's probably her father. The thought strikes through me like lightning. It's Saturday. Everyone is home. How could I have been so stupid to come on a Saturday? I back away toward the side of the house as these thoughts race through my brain. Leigh follows me until we're both concealed in the shadows and long grass of the side yard.

"I've got to go now, but I'll see you again soon. Okay?" I hastily spit out as I'm backing up, trying to not raise Leigh's suspicions. With relief, I notice the crown had fallen off sometime during the pony ride. I grind my teeth and hope she doesn't go looking for it. It's better it stays lost. Her father is calling again. This time I hear the glass door sliding open.

"Okay, bye!" she says, waving and then prancing back into the yard. I practically run into the front yard and look around to make sure no one is watching. Then I pause. I can hear them in the backyard. Frozen with curiosity and fear, I can't help but listen.

"Were you just talking to someone?" her father asks.

"Yeah, my friend," Leigh's tinny voice replies. My stomach clenches and somersaults.

"Huh? Who?" his voice rings out and I imagine his pensive face looking around the yard.

"The girl! She can talk to fairies, you know? And she made me the Princess of the Forest," I hear Leigh say. I can't help but beam with pride at how happy I made her. I would've loved to be crowned as such at her age too.

"Oh, okay," he laughs, and I exhale with relief. I can tell by the sarcastic, playful tone that he doesn't believe her. "I guess maybe you and your friend should come in for lunch now. It's getting cold out anyway."

"What?"

"Come on. It's lunchtime. I could make another sandwich for your fairy friend if you'd like. Do fairies eat peanut butter and jelly sandwiches?"

"Daaaaad, *she's* not a fairy. She just *talks* to the fairies. And she's not here right now anyway," Leigh replies and then laughs. "Can I have one of the cookies Mom made too?"

I wait to hear the glass door slide shut before I casually stroll the few paces out to the sidewalk and start down the street. I wish I could be her imaginary friend. Then I could spend all my time playing with her and making her childhood perfect. At least she really liked the flower crown. I slow down and consider going back to try to find it. What if her parents see it? Is it believable Leigh made it herself? I shake my head and keep going. Not worth the risk.

I kick a stone and head back home. Lilly said she wanted to bake brownies today, but I know Dad wouldn't approve of our 'making a mess' or 'using up ingredients for other things.' I keep kicking the stone as I try to decide the best way to break it to her. Maybe I can teach her how to make one of those flower crowns. I haven't made her one in so long, and it might distract her enough to forget the brownies.

WINNIE

For the first time in weeks, I wasn't compelled to walk by Leigh's house. Not even a quick glance from around the corner. I cringe thinking of how obsessive I must have seemed. Gabe was right. I was coming across like a total freak. And all because she maybe resembles me a little. Honestly, it's uncanny, but I allowed it to consume me. I don't *have* to go to her house. Going didn't solve anything anyway. Although maybe I didn't go enough or something. It just really felt like I was supposed to see her. Like something special was going to happen, like in the movies. But Gabe was right, it was just a delusion. "Magical thinking" he called it. He's always right about everything.

It's been a day of fresh air and giddiness I haven't felt in years. I've had that strange, excited feeling in my stomach, like before Christmas or going on a rollercoaster. That feeling's been coursing through ever since I got that text from Jeremy. I scrub the plate and think of that breathless excitement I felt when I slid my phone from my pocket and saw it. Laughing a little to myself, I remember Gabe warning me just in time that Mrs. Parson was coming while I was feverishly texting.

It's crazy how things can fall back into that familiar groove after so many months. He even asked me to a movie, like last summer. Granted, this is some cheesy, supposedly scary gore-fest, which will probably suck, but of course I'm going. Anything to get away from this dump, I think as I look around the kitchen that I've scrubbed so many times yet remains a permanent greasy yellow. Plus, I don't have to babysit tomorrow, and it's not until after Dad gets home, so Lilly will be okay. It shouldn't be a big deal at all.

A secret smile graces my lips. It'll be so nice to see Jeremy again.

With my hands soaking in the soapy water, bits of pasta from supper floating through my fingers, I try to work up the nerve to ask Dad. I can see him from the kitchen if I turn my head slightly. His stubby fingers, nails bitten to the quick, packing tobacco into his pipe, then sucking over and over, like an infant, as he begs the pipe to embrace the flame of his match. We only finished dinner half an hour ago, but four and a half empty beer cans already rest on the coffee table by his feet. I wonder whether four and a half beers is that perfect level of intoxication needed to elicit the permission I crave, and truly deserve. Probably not. I swish my fingers in tiny dirty whirlpools as I think.

Too sober and he'll find some hidden insult in the request, some reason for a punishment, and his recent fascination with ropes makes me even more cautious than usual. However, if I wait until he's finished the six-pack, and inevitably the whisky left in the cupboard, he might grant permission but not remember the next day, leading to an argument and punishment. I briefly consider the odds of just planning to sneak out, forgiveness instead of permission, but the movie's too early for that. He'll definitely notice my absence when it's time to put Lilly to bed.

As I scrape away at some burnt cheese on the casserole dish at the bottom of the sink, I knit my brows and know Brendan isn't a reliable option either. Ever since the funeral, he acts like I owe him and he's some sort of saint for even driving me to school. Plus, he'd probably get invited somewhere and rat me out to Dad immediately, just to dump the responsibility.

As the rag fails me, I resort to picking off the last few burnt crusts with my fingernails. I hear the crunching of aluminum followed by heavy footfalls as Dad lumbers into the kitchen behind me. Without a thought, I hold my breath and freeze, willing myself invisible, undetectable, nonexistent. It works as he doesn't notice me at all, stomping his way back to the plaid recliner with his imprint almost visible from years of sitting. Considering his alcohol consumption and slothful ways, it's surprising he's not fat. I tilt my head to the side a little and watch as his form relaxes back into its place in the chair. I wish he was a fat blob instead of this strong, wiry creature. Then he might not be so impossible to overpower.

I turn back to the sink and release the drain. In the living room, a sharp hiss cracks through the air as he pops the lid of his fifth beer and I suddenly decide that's it, after this one it'll be the right time. Plucking the dish towel from the oven handle, I wipe away the lingering droplets from the freshly cleaned casserole dish.

The blaring of the TV combined with the music pumping out of Brendan's bedroom creates such a loud mess, it's almost like white noise: meaningless, empty, and comforting. I let my mind wander back to Jeremy. Putting away the plates and silverware from dinner, I smile and re-read his texts in my mind's eye. I could never ask him what happened, why he disappeared on me. It's not like he'd been the first to do so anyway.

I think back to the day we met. It was early summer, and school had just ended. Lilly was swinging on the rusty metal swings at the park, and I was lying on the bench nearby, listening to music. Eyes closed and sunbeams sending tingles of warmth across me. My hair fell down through the cracks of the bench, leaving my face completely exposed. No one was at the park, despite the beautiful weather, so I wasn't worried about it. Then a shadow fell across me, and I opened my eyes.

Jeremy stood over me, smiling that wide, goofy smile where his nose slightly crinkles up. I almost head-butted him; I sat up so fast, pulling the headphones from my ears. I must have looked absolutely terrified since he immediately returned a surprised look, then started laughing.

"Sorry, didn't mean to scare you," he said, smiling again. My heart pounded as I assessed this stranger. My mouth may have even dropped open a little when I realized he was gorgeous. I remember especially focusing on the snakebite piercings that encircled his plump lower lip. Just the kind of guy I always gravitate toward. He laughed a little again and stepped back awkwardly. Without thinking, I adjusted my hair over my scars, pushing the waves up in a handful then smoothing them down over the side of my face. I swallowed hard and tried to think of something to say.

"I'm really sorry. I just thought you looked really cute lying there like that," he said, drilling a hole in the dirt with the toe of his shoe.

"Oh no, it's fine. You just surprised me." I giggled nervously.

"What are you listening to?"

"Um, just some old shit. Uh, The Cure," I showed him the screen of my phone for several seconds before realizing the screen was blank. He just grinned again and sat next to me.

"Don't call The Cure shit, dude. They're one of my favorites," he said, taking an earbud and putting it in. "Mind if I listen with you?"

"Oh, here," I said, sort of throwing the other earbud in his lap, and instantly wanting to die. He just laughed it off and slid a little closer. We listened to random songs on my phone for almost an hour before Lilly started to complain that she was ready to go home. We exchanged numbers and texted constantly for days. Things escalated quickly, and soon we were a pretty official couple. Out for movie night every Friday. He always held my hand during the scary or romantic parts.

Dad has almost finished his beer in the few minutes that I've been spacing out. Now is the right time, but I still hesitate. I put away the last dishes, taking my time, procrastinating. Finally, there's nothing left to do in the kitchen. I walk to the living room. His eyes are glassy in the blue light.

"Hey Dad, can I go to the movies Friday?" I make sure to stand clear of the TV while I ask, but close enough to get his attention.

"What?" His eyes glide lazily up to me and strain to focus. "What did you say?"

"Can I please go to the movies on Friday?" I try to swallow after I ask, but my mouth is too dry and sticky.

"Sure, I guess," he says. "Do you have money to go? Because we can't afford it—"

"Yes. From babysitting."

He nods, looks back to the TV, and drinks from his beer. "Okay. Who are you going with?"

"Uh, Krystal wants to go see that new scary one."

"I suppose that's fine, as long as you make sure dinner's ready and all that before you go."

I smile and slowly walk back to the kitchen. I want to thank him, but I know if I seem too excited, he'll just take it away. Stay casual, I tell myself, and walk towards Lilly's room. She's playing with her ponies in the big dollhouse Dad gave her a few years back.

"Horses don't live in houses, silly," I say, trying to rile her up, but she ignores me. I tousle her hair a little, but she slaps my hand away.

"I'm playing. Leave me alone."

"Fine."

I walk around the room, picking up the couple of toys she's left abandoned on the floor. I go to her bookshelf and try to decide on a bedtime story for tonight.

"What about starting *The Little Princess* again tonight?"

"I don't care. Can you just leave me alone?"

"Fine, I'll go, but you have to get dressed and be in bed in fifteen minutes, okay? Can you do that?"

"Yeah," she mumbles, immersed in her pony world.

I peer out into the hallway. No one is there, so I'm able to walk to my room and quietly close the door. My phone is charging, partially hidden under the mattress, so Dad wouldn't ask to look at it. I hear its muffled buzzing and pull it out. Jeremy texted: *Hey wanna talk later* then an hour later *Hello?*

Hey! Can't talk now but can call you in a couple hours when the old man falls asleep. K?

Minutes go by as I anxiously wait. I really do have to put Lilly to bed soon. Dad will be pissed if he hears her up this late. The phone buzzes.

Cool :)

It's only been ten minutes, but I tiptoe back to Lilly's room. She doesn't have a clock in there anyway.

"Come on, Lilly. You need to change and get in bed." Her head turns and reveals a nasty scowl. Finally, she puts the ponies down and stomps over to her dresser.

I pull out the pink pajamas, but she refuses to put them on. Supposedly they itch. I replace them and hand her the periwinkle ones with clouds. After she's dressed and under the covers, I get *The Little Princess* and start to read, but she stops me.

"I don't want to hear a story tonight."

"Why not?"

"I just don't."

"Are you sure? I don't want you crawling into my room later and asking for one."

"I'm sure. Stories are for babies. I'm almost seven." She pulls the comforter over her head and turns toward the wall. I laugh and hug her blanket cocoon.

"Seven isn't too old for stories," I say, but she doesn't answer. Listening closely for the deep breaths of sleep, I wait but they don't come. She's not sleeping. She's just waiting for me to leave. I put the book back on the shelf and tiptoe to my room where I'll wait until the house is quiet and I can sneak outside my window for a late-night call.

WINNIE

The steam from the stew rises to my face as I bend over the pot, trying to cleanse my pores. Krystal said it's best with a towel draped over your head, but I'm invisible right now and don't want to draw any unnecessary attention. Chunks of beef bob on the surface, sometimes colliding with pieces of carrot or onion, all floating in the bubbling brown. The steam irritates my eyes, so I close them and try to imagine myself anywhere else, but the yelling from the living room hinders my efforts.

"It was only twenty bucks! Nothing to lose your shit over, Dad." My brother's voice floods the house. I wonder if they shut the window in there, otherwise the neighbors might hear.

My father's guttural voice responds, the house supports shuddering, ready to bow in obedience. "You spoiled brat, you never appreciated how hard I work for you and your sisters. If you don't make enough money at the gas station, then you find a second job, not steal from me!"

I join the house in its trembling. My knees start to buckle, but I hold fast to the oven. Deep breaths. Stir the stew so the bottom doesn't burn. Don't make any rapid movements. Hide in plain sight.

"I didn't steal it. I just borrowed it." Brendan's voice creaks like an old hinge. He's afraid too, but he's stupid. I plead silently for him to stop. He won't. Then he mumbles something, bordering unintelligible, but Dad hears it. My heart leaps and my shoulders fold forward to brace myself. I tuck my head down and crunch my face tightly. Reflexes. I can't help it.

A sickening thunk of flesh and bone. I don't dare look. Surprisingly soft, a body hits the floor. The carpet muffles the groans, and I imagine it soaking up the fresh blood. I can't look, but I know there's blood. I can hear it in his gurgling moan. Dad's heavy breathing is the only other sound.

I squint one eye open, just enough to survey the situation. Dad towers over Brendan. His shoulders heave with each breath, as if it's taking every fiber of his being just to restrain himself. Brendan is facing away. His dark hair curls around the back of his head, resting on the shag carpet. His moans grow quieter and less frequent as the seconds lurch by. I can just make out the dark blood pooling near the top of his head.

Behind me, the floor squeaks a little. I swivel just enough to see the opening to the hall. Lilly's standing there. Her eyes are locked on Dad. Face blank. We're all stuck in this scene for an eternity. All waiting for Dad. Brendan goes completely quiet.

Finally, he moves. Swooping down, Dad yanks the cash from Brendan's hand, lying limply at his side. He doesn't protest. I turn back to the stew, stirring it and trying to disappear, as Dad marches through the house, passing behind me. Lilly's hushed footsteps patter down the hall to her room just in time. The front door slams behind him. I wait a few more minutes, just stirring the stew, almost hypnotized. Tension dissipates from the air and finally it feels safe. I turn down the burner and go to Brendan.

Kneeling on the carpet, I don't take his head in my lap like I want to, since his nose is still trickling blood. It's so hard to get blood out and I don't need any evidence against me. He's conscious but obviously dazed. I turn his head toward me a little and he winces.

"Knock it off," he whispers in a breathless voice. "I'm fine. Go finish dinner."

I nod and return to my task as he pulls himself to his feet. Staggering into the kitchen, he rips a couple of paper towels off the roll and wipes at the nearly dried smears of blood across his face. Then I hear him hobble down the hallway back to his room.

The stew is finished, but I'm not sure what to do since Dad isn't home. I prepare everything for four anyway and call Lilly and Brendan to the table. We need to pretend things are normal, but Brendan doesn't come. Lilly sits in front of her bowl, wide-eyed and looking like a startled deer.

"We should eat," I urge in my sternest voice. Lilly just stares at the wall behind me like she doesn't hear me. I repeat it. "We should eat, Lilly." She continues to ignore me. I take a few sips. The stew turned out better than I'd expected. I continue to urge her with my eyes for a few minutes, then give up and finish my meal. I walk my bowl to the kitchen and clean it, then try taking Brendan's bowl to his room but it's locked, music blaring, so I just pour it back into the pot. Not knowing what else to do, I sit back down at the table across from Lilly. She stares at the wall, hardly blinking.

Dad walks in, slamming the door behind him again. He goes toward the table, and I jump up to fill his bowl. Right as he sits down, and I'm walking back with his dinner, Lilly stands up and knocks her bowl on the ground. Takes her arm, hand hanging limp, and bats it across her placemat. The stew spills all over the floor and her dress.

"Lilly!" I gasp, but she's already running to her room. I rush to the kitchen, wet a dish towel, and immediately start dabbing up the mess. Dad slurps his soup while I frantically clean up. Beads of sweat run together at my temples as I feel Dad watching me.

"Now why would she do that?" he asks behind me. On my hands and knees, I look up helplessly at my father. Sitting in the breaking wooden chair, specks of stew caught in his several days' worth of stubble, he'd be pathetic if it weren't for those eyes. Steel blue, they pierce through me. They accuse me of some secret misconduct. I know he thinks I did something to her. He would never believe otherwise.

"I don't know. I—I—I'm sorry," I stutter, but his expression only intensifies.

"Why are you sorry if you don't know? What did you do?"

"I didn't do anything. I promise," I say, tears filling up my eyes, but I don't let them spill. It wouldn't matter anyway.

He has me by the hair, dragging me toward the hallway. Dragging me to his bedroom, while I crawl and stumble behind. He lets go and locks the door. No matter how many times I've endured it, I'm still terrified every time. I wish I could hide it from him, but he always sees through any weak disguise of bravery or apathy. I must stink of fear. Sweat it out of every pore.

"I know you did something to upset my Lilly," he begins, his face in the flicker of candlelight as he lights each long taper in the beautiful sterling silver holders. I remember when Mom used to put long candles in them and set them on the table around holidays in the years before Lilly. "You might have even convinced Brendan to steal that money. He's too hard-working and slow to think of doing it without someone's malicious whispers in his ear. You did, didn't you?"

I know I can't answer. There is no right answer.

Three hard strikes and my ears are ringing. One more and I feel a trickle of blood from my nose.

"Lie down," he commands, and I whimper, lying back on the bed and putting my arms up over my head. I close my eyes as he slides the straps around my wrists. He doesn't say another word.

Rough hands raise up my shirt. I shiver a little from the cold air on my belly. Goosebumps erupt across my body, but I keep my eyes closed. He gets some kind of sick satisfaction from seeing the pain and fear. It's still there, but I hide it away. I won't relinquish this one iota of control.

The hot wax spills onto my skin and my stomach muscles contract, pulling away from the pain. The burning is intense but fades relatively quickly as the wax cools and hardens. The tender skin under the waxy crust throbs but lacks the immediacy of the first few seconds of singeing nerves. He waits a moment, pulls my shirt all the way over my face, then pours more. I can't help but squirm and gasp. He knows to move to a new spot each time. I breathe into the cotton and remind myself over and over that I am not suffocating. My eyes hurt as I strain to see through the thin fabric, but all I can make out is his shadow. It would be easier to endure if I could predict the drops, the streams, the pain. He won't let me have that. He must know it would lessen the torture. A cycle of agony and relief repeated over and over. I can almost hear each drop sizzle as it hits my pale skin, sliding across, reaching out with amoeba arms, then finally mercifully cooling.

I try to imagine myself somewhere else, but anxiety from the unpredictable pattern of pain stops me every time. Instead, I settle for silently counting away the seconds, then minutes, waiting for it to end. The rhythm of counting, evenly and smoothly, keeping track of each segment of time, is almost soothing. I need it to maintain my stoic aura. How long will this punishment last? Punishments that don't need him present can last hours, but those that require active participation are much shorter. How long has it been? I retrace each drop of wax in my mind and estimate it's been at least five minutes. Almost over. Deep breaths. Drip. Drip. Followed by a stream of wax. I flinch but keep counting.

When he's finally done, he brushes most of the wax off my stomach with his hands. The calluses on his palms tear at my skin, but I don't make a sound. He pulls down my shirt and I suck the cold air down into my lungs. My restraints are loosened, and I slip my hands out, then sit up on the bed. I don't look at him, but I can sense how much he's relaxed.

"Oh Winnie, when will you learn, girl?" he sighs. I'm disgusted at how casual and calm he sounds. "Well, you'd better go get Lilly ready for bed."

I walk out of the room and head straight to the bathroom. In the mirror, I see the red, irritated skin. Carefully, I pull off the last bits of wax and toss them in the bin. The burns are minor. They'll heal in a few days. I comb through the cabinet and find the aloe vera gel for sunburns. The sticky green goop spreads easily across the burns and offers some relief, but it makes my shirt stick to my skin in several damp patches. Hopefully, Lilly won't say anything. A few splashes of cold water on my face from the sink and then I head for Lilly's room. She's already dressed in her nightgown and combing out the tangles from her hair. She looks at me and smiles as if nothing happened at all.

"I'm already ready, so I just need a story and a kiss goodnight," she says, and I try to smile back but my face muscles don't want to cooperate.

"I know you saw what happened to Brendan earlier. He's going to be alright."

"I know."

"Lilly, I could tell you were really scared. It's okay. Dad's not mad anymore."

"I know." The words chirp out as from a songbird, almost mocking me somehow. Then she adds, "Brendan should have followed the rules. It was his own fault."

"What?" I ask, but she just ignores me, setting the comb back on her dresser and snuggling under her comforter. I try to tell myself that it's just a defense mechanism. She needs to understand things in a way that keeps the world simple and safe. She doesn't actually agree with Dad. Then again, Brendan knew he was poking the bear. I heard it all. Plus, it was dumb of him to steal money from Dad.

"I want my story now, please," Lilly says, and I snap back to the present. I pick out *Snow White* from the bookshelf and read it to her as she starts to drift to sleep. After putting the book back, I kiss her forehead and whisper goodnight wishes.

"You should learn to follow the rules too, Winnie. Then Dad wouldn't have to punish you either."

My stomach clenches, and I bite the inside of my cheek as everything flashes red. I nod and force myself out of the room. With each step on her prissy pink carpet, I imagine smacking her head against the wall. With each step on the carpet down the hall, I hear her phlegmy sobs and cries for mercy. Then I'm in my room.

Immediately, I slide open the window and crawl out. I'm running through the forest, a really long way. It must be over a mile. The sun has almost set and the sky's awash with orange. I stop when I'm as far away from everything as I can get. The screams don't sound like me. They don't even sound human. The large stick in my hand is crashing through the bushes and undergrowth. Striking the trees and tearing off their thinner limbs. My shoes are smashing flowers, plants, and then a bird egg I knocked from a branch. The tiny body spills out, revealing itself for a moment, before the shoe is crushing it again. Mashing it into an unrecognizable smear of pink. I see myself doing all of this, but I'm far away. Somewhere nobody else can go. I'm watching my own life through a television screen. All my emotions fade into a haze of gray and I wonder if anything is even real.

Stumbling back home, I get lost several times, but I don't care. I'm a zombie, completely on autopilot. As I crawl back into my bedroom, I carefully shut the window and fall onto my bed, face down on a pillow. I'm asleep in seconds, fully dressed and wearing my mask of thick make-up. I don't hear my phone buzz, but the message waits for me until the morning. It's Jeremy. *Hey gotta cancel the movie. Got a date. Sorry.*

LEIGH

My name is Leigh. You say it like "Lee" but you don't spell it L-E-E. No, no, that would be wrong. I learned it at school. You spell it L-E-I-G-H. I also learned how to write it, big letters and small letters. I used to write only in big letters but now I know better because I'm smarter than I was when I was a little baby. My birthday is soon, and my daddy says that when I'm five, I get to go to kindergarten like a big kid!

I'm growing right up. My daddy sometimes pretends I've gotten so big and heavy that he can't pick me up anymore! It's so funny. I laugh and he always laughs too, and then throws me over his shoulder and pretends he's a monster taking me away. One time, I even laughed so hard I accidentally peed a little, but Daddy didn't get mad.

Don't tell anybody that; it's a secret. I love secrets! There is a big girl with pretty blonde hair and a weird red side of her face that loves to tell me secrets. I'm a good secret keeper, that's why she tells me. I never tell anybody's secrets. Not ever! I didn't tell anyone when Amanda accidentally cut some of her hair at school and I never told about the time my daddy broke my mommy's fancy bowl and had to go to the store to get a new one. I am the best secret keeper in the whole world. I don't even tell when I see the other kids being naughty at school. I'm not a tattle-tell. But you always have to tell if somebody gets hurt, even if you don't want to be a tattle-tell. That's the most important rule at school. Also, to always tell the truth.

I'm playing in the backyard in the sunny part right next to the forest. Mommy says I can play outside until dinner, but that's like a million more hours away. And it's not even too cold with my new puffy jacket.

I have my favorite stuffed animals with me. This is Karina and she's a turtle. I named her that myself. She's my favorite. I give her big hugs, like this, every day! This one is Babar and he's an elephant, but he already had that name. I didn't name him. My mommy said that's his name in the book, but I don't know that book. He's a king! See, he has a beautiful crown, and all the animals bow just like this. He says that today will be the biggest animal wedding this land has ever seen! I need to start preparing. Karina is the bride! Oh, so beautiful! All you need is a flower to carry and you're perfect. I'll line up all the other animals and dolls on either side of the aisle, so the bride will be able to walk down with everyone watching her. Babar, you get to be the guy who says the wedding stuff and tells them to kiss, but who should be the groom? Not just anyone is good enough to marry Karina.

I see the big girl coming to play with me! When she sees me, she gives me a big smile. She's so happy to come play! I love it when she lets me braid her long hair and put flowers in it. She even made me a flower crown one time! It was the prettiest thing I've ever seen. We pretended I was the Princess of the Forest. That's one of my favorite games to play now.

"What are you playing today, Leigh? Oh, I see, you're setting up for a wedding! Who's getting married?" The girl smiles, and I like the way she helps set up the aisle right away.

"Well, that's the problem. I don't know who the groom should be. I don't really have any handsome toys to marry Karina." I point to my stuffed turtle.

"Hmmm, let me think. Let me think." The big girl taps her head with her finger and sticks out her lips in a funny face. I giggle. Then she jumps up, and I almost jump too because she surprised me. "I've got it! I know the perfect groom for Karina and he's at my house. He's a handsome turtle. The perfect match."

"Really? I didn't know that big girls played with toys too. Can you go get him? That would be the best wedding ever!" I say, so excited I can't keep in my laugh.

"Of course!" the big girl says and starts to go back toward the road, but she stops and looks sad. She comes back and sits down crisscross, her head in her hands. I think she might be crying.

"What's wrong? Did you lose your turtle and you just remembered? That would make me sad too," I say and pat her back. I almost hug her but decide not to. She's only come over to play three or four times before and you shouldn't hug strangers.

She shakes her head, and her soft hair covers my hand, tickling my fingers, but I try not to laugh. She looks up at me with really sad eyes but they're not red like when you've been crying. Her eyes are very pretty, and as I look at them so closely, I wish I had eyes like her. A deep in your heart wish, almost like a prayer. But I know my mommy would say that's a selfish prayer.

I think this girl is the prettiest girl I've ever seen, except for the red blotches from her eye to her chin and neck, and some on her arm. I pointed her out to my daddy at the store a long time ago, when I was only two or three. I pointed my finger right at her and asked him why she looked like that. He whispered to me and told me that was a rude thing to do and I felt very sorry, especially after he told me that's what happens to your skin after you get burned really bad. But he wouldn't tell me how she got burned so bad that it never went away. Most burns go away, like when I touched a very hot stove and it hurt so bad. It went red but after holding some ice, it went away.

I was really curious, so at school I asked my friends and both Tiffany and Julia said they knew that girl I had seen. Tiffany told me the girl's own mommy burned her like that! She did it on purpose because she got really *really* mad. She threw hot water on her and it was so bad it never went away. I cried when I heard that. Why would a mommy be so mean? Even though she's kind of a stranger, I still let her play with me because that makes me sad that her mommy hurt her so bad. She's much nicer than the other big girls I see around, like at the mall. She likes to play, and she even gave me a piggyback ride last time she came over. I don't know how she made her mommy so mad when she's so friendly and nice.

"I didn't really lose my turtle, but he's not back at my house. No, I left him in the secret clubhouse in the woods," she says, but then her eyes get really wide, and she smacks both of her hands over her mouth like she said a bad word. I smile because she looks funny and grab her hands, pulling them away from her mouth.

"What? A secret clubhouse! In these woods? No way!" I shout. Then she gently pulls me down to sit next to her on the grass.

"Shhh!" she hushes with her finger over her lips like a librarian. I giggle but stop shouting.

"Is it really a secret? Can we go see it?" I whisper, and she nods.

"I'll take you there, but you have to promise not to tell anyone else where it is because, if everyone knows, then it won't be a secret anymore," she whispers and takes my hand to pull me up, but I take it back and squint up at her. The sun is behind her and she looks all dark, like a shadow.

"Wait. If it's a secret place, then how do *you* know about it? Hmm?" I feel a funny feeling in my stomach like on the first day of school.

"I know all about it because *it's my very own* secret clubhouse. My dad built it for me when I was about your age, and I've kept all my best toys and books there ever since. I don't usually show it to people, but I think you're special. You *are* the Princess of the Forest, right?" she says and does a little bow where she twirls her hand as she leans over. It's funny but I don't laugh this time.

"Yeah, I guess I am," I mumble, looking past her to the forest. It's not dark since the sun is still out, but I can't see very far because the trees all grow together, and their shade turns into one big shadow.

I don't like to go too far into the woods. I'm not scared or anything, but it's a little scary out there. Plus, my mommy doesn't let me go in there very far anyway because there could be snakes waiting to bite you. She said she even saw a snake out there one time and had to scare it away by shouting really loud and clanging things together to make lots of noise. It's very dangerous if a snake bites you. She said it hurts really bad and you can't make it stop. You have to go to the hospital, and sometimes people even die. I don't know if the big girl knows about snakes or knows how to take me to a hospital if I get hurt. She's not a real grown-up.

"What's wrong? Don't you want to see it?" she asks, and I can barely see her because the sun is shining so brightly right behind her head.

"Maybe you should just go and get the turtle by yourself. Then we can have the wedding when you get back," I say, but I see that made her a little sad. I pick up a blade of grass and twirl it in my fingers making a tiny spiral, looking down into the grass away from her.

"I guess I can do that, but then you'd miss out on seeing my secret clubhouse. I've never shown anyone because no one has ever deserved to see it before. Most kids would just ruin it, but I know you wouldn't. Here I had thought I had finally found the perfect friend to show it to, and even give it to since I am getting too big for it anyway." She looks down at me as she says this, and there's something strange about her face. Something that makes me feel kind of like running away into the house and slamming the door behind me, but then it goes away, and I feel sad for the girl again. She must not have any friends and that's why she likes to play with me. I learned at school that part of being a good person is to play with the kids who are lonely and don't have anyone else to play with, not just always play with your best friends.

"Well," I rip the grass into tiny pieces without looking at her, "is it very far away? I'm not supposed to go too far into the woods. Snakes live out there."

She just smiles and laughs in a way that sounds fake, like when my uncle says jokes only babies would laugh at, but I don't want to hurt his feelings, so I pretend it's funny anyway.

"Come on, it's not very far at all. Actually, it's so close, you really would be the perfect kid to give it to because you could go there every day. And I know for a fact that there are no snakes on the way," she says, reaching out her hand. She pulls me up, and I feel fluttering in my stomach again. Her hand feels kind of sweaty, so I tell her I'm too big for holding hands so she'll let go. I wipe it on my pants when she's not looking.

We walk straight back from my backyard, crunching dead leaves all shriveled up everywhere. Usually, I love crunching leaves more than anything, but not this time. My mouth is making too much spit and I keep swallowing.

We step over a few fallen trees and then we have to climb over a really big log with roly-polies crawling all over it. I've never been this far out in the forest before, but I guess it's not that far away from home. I'm getting hungry. My stomach rumbles and I feel like I might be sick.

"You're going to make sure I'm not late for dinner, right? My mommy will be really mad if I am, and not just at me, but at *you* too!" I say in my best teacher voice to make sure she knows I'm serious.

"Of course, of course. Don't worry. We're almost there," she says, but she doesn't even turn to me while she says it. Her voice sounds friendly as usual, but when I look up at her, she looks so serious and I'm a little scared.

"I don't like this anymore. I wanna go home, okay?" I stop walking, and after a few steps, she turns to me. Her face looks scary. Her eyes look darker and her whole face looks sharp and ugly. I gasp, and I want to run right back home, but I can't move.

"No, we're almost there. You're going to keep going," she says in a rough voice I've never heard before, grabbing my arm. Her fingernails pinch my skin through my coat, and I cry out. Suddenly, I unfreeze. Digging my feet into the leaves as hard as I can, I pull away.

"Stop it! Let me go!" I shout and then I start to scream my biggest loudest scream, the one my daddy says makes his "blood run cold."

She's suddenly pushing me to the ground. My leg twists underneath me and it hurts. She grabs at my mouth to cover it, but I turn my head and keep screaming. Mommy will come soon! Daddy will hear it and know it's me and come get me! Hot pain, like a lightning bolt, shoots through my jaw as her fist knocks it open.

My scream stops and turns into a weird, wet noise as blood pours from my mouth. She's on top of me and I can't breathe. I spit out the blood and try to scream again as I claw at her hair and face. She snarls, and her arm raises high in the air before it slams down on my head.

I start to cry, gasping for breath in big sobs. My ears feel full of cotton, something loud and buzzing pressing through, and my head is stuffy, like it's overfilled and could burst. My whole body shakes, but I can't get up. I'm too scared to move. Maybe she'll go away.

She stands up and says something, but I can't hear her through the whirring dizziness. Then she stoops over me, and I turn on my side to hide my face away from her in the leaves. Dirt and leaves stick to my nose and pull up into my mouth with each sob. Her hands are around my throat. Tighter. Tighter. I can't breathe.

I don't want to look at her. My hands frantically reach out for anything. There's nothing but leaves. My head pounds like an explosion. I can't see. My tongue pushes out between my lips. I hear a popping sound. She squeezes even tighter. But then she lets go.

I gasp and spit. I can barely see her now, like she's a shadow. I feel her hand digging in the ground next to me. She hits my head with something heavy. I hear a crack and split apart in pain. I'm spinning. She raises her arm again.

WINNIE

I'm shivering as I stand by the bag. The blue duffle bag I put her in. Really more stuffed her in since her winter coat barely fit. It's zipped up so I don't have to look at her. I don't know what to do.

I pick it up, but it's heavier than I expected and awkward in my arms. Forcing the straps over my shoulder, I stagger through the woods. Head east, toward my house, but deeper in the wilderness. We must be over a mile back. Roots pull at me from under the piles of leaves. I'm weaving between trees. Faster now. I stumble and fall, and the bag slips off my arm, dropping to the ground. My whole body is shaking, and my hands refuse to work, tingling with painful pins and needles. She's too heavy. What do I do? Panic rises up my throat, but I push it down. No, no time to break down. I'll have to come back for her. I leave the bag on the forest floor, pushing some leaves around it, a few on top, but it still stands out bright blue among the earth tones. My blood pumps hotly through my veins and I'm running toward the other neighborhood, the one across the woods. I'm almost there. I can see the sidewalk through the trees. I try to slow down. Don't look too suspicious now.

My hands are trembling so much, I can barely work my phone, nearly dropping it. As I sit on the curb, I focus on slowing my breath while I beg for Gabe to pick up.

"You have to come here. Please. You have to come help me." As soon as he picks up, the words dart out of my mouth. I can't get them out fast enough.

"What?" He's laughing. He thinks I'm joking. "What's going on?"

"I'm serious. Please, please come right now. I need to talk to you."

"Where have you been all day? You don't usually skip without telling me and—"

"Please! I need you right now!" My voice cracks; I swallow the rising panic down again. Focus on my breath. In and out. It's all going to be fine. Don't think about it too hard.

"Whoa, you're for real. Are you okay?"

"No."

"What's going on?"

"I can't tell you now. You have to come here." The words squeeze their way through my gritted teeth. "Please, Gabe. I'm begging you."

"Okay, okay." A pause that lasts a lifetime. "Where are you?"

"I'm on, uh," I look around, the details around me blurring as the adrenaline pumps through my mind. "Pine Street. The street right on the other side of the woods behind my house. I'm sitting on the sidewalk. Please hurry."

"What are you doing way over there?"

"Just come quick. Please, you've gotta help me!"

"Okay, fine. I'm on my way. I'll be there in like ten minutes. Maybe less."

"Please hurry." I hang up the phone.

Calm down. Come on, you've got to calm down. Fuck, they're probably already looking for her. Oh god oh god oh god. I tuck my hands under my thighs to keep them from shaking. It's not even that cold, but I'm shivering violently.

The wait is excruciating. Nobody's outside. Three cars go by. From the house directly in front of me, a man walks out a garbage bag and puts it in the bin. Everyone must think it's just a normal day. It's not. One, two, three, I start to count in my head to push away the fear swallowing me whole.

Gabe's jeep pulls up next to the sidewalk. He parks and gets out, looking simultaneously annoyed and amused.

"What's going on with you? Are you strung out on something?"

"No."

"Okay, 'cause I'd be pissed if you weren't sharing." He laughs, but I can't even force a smile.

"Gabe, I want to tell you something. I need to tell you something. I need your help badly. But I'm scared. I'm scared. I'm scared." The words repeat uncontrollably. I'm rocking back and forth, shaking. Gabe crouches next to me. He cocks his head, puzzled.

"What? What are you even talking about?"

"I need your help. You have to help me. Oh, Gabe. You *have* to help me."

"You're going to need to tell me why you're so upset if you want me to even try to help."

I grab his face and pull his ear right up against my mouth to whisper. "I did the...thing. The thing we talked about."

"What thing?" He's trying to pull away, but I won't let him, clawing at his collar. I can't say it any louder than this. I couldn't if I tried.

"The thing we talked about the other night. The bad thing."

"What? Just tell me. I don't know what thing."

He pulls away enough to look me in the eye, and I want to cry, but no tears come.

"The bad thing."

"Wait, what bad thing? Winnie, just spit it out already!"

"I did it. I killed her."

His face darkens as if a shadow fell across it. I can see his pupils constrict before he scrunches up his nose, squints his eyes.

"What?"

"I killed her. The little girl."

He swallows hard.

"You killed her? That little girl you told me about?"

"Yes."

He shakes his head rapidly.

"No, you didn't." He laughs but his smile melts into a scow.

"Yes, I did."

A shiver runs over him and his breathing speeds up, whistling slightly through his nose. His eyes dart around, avoiding mine. A sheen of anger washes across his face.

"Why did you do that?"

My heart sinks into my stomach. I feel my lip quivering and I can't stop it.

"I don't know. I don't know. I just...did. It's been so horrible, and I just couldn't help it somehow. I can't explain it. I'm horrible. Horrible."

"Are you fucking crazy? You piece of shit! Oh my god, this whole thing is fucking insane. I can't believe this!"

"Please. Please." I plead in a painful whisper, gesturing for him to quiet down as I fight against my throat closing and push down the howling cries building inside me. "You've gotta help me. You just have to! Remember when

I told you about…Nikolai. You said you were there for me. You could help me. I need your help!"

"Are you fucking kidding me? Oh my god, I need a minute." Gabe puts his palm up, and I quietly withdraw into myself. I cradle my head in my hands, bring up my knees, curling my body into a tight ball. At last, tears run down my cheeks. I can't bring myself to wipe them away. I can hardly move at all. Gabe has pulled out a cigarette and is lighting it. He's pacing back and forth, quick, hard steps on the sidewalk behind me.

"Well," he puffs his cigarette and blows the smoke straight into my already teary eyes, "At least tell me what exactly happened."

Everything spills out in a rapid, hushed voice. Everything at home. Everything today. Everything I can't explain. Just everything. His eyes burn into mine as I tell him about the rock I found, and the blood-curdling crack a skull makes as it breaks apart.

"I can't believe *you* did that," he says, and I notice his hands are shaking a little as he lights another cigarette.

"I can't believe it either. It doesn't feel real, you know?" I'm almost ashamed at how much of the nervous tension has faded simply by telling the story.

"You're fucking crazy. You know that, right?" Smoke pours out of his mouth.

"Can I have one too?"

He throws me the pack. "Shit, if anyone needs one, it's you."

We smoke quietly for a moment. Gabe paces again, but slower, sometimes shaking his head and muttering to himself.

"Are you going to help me?"

"Goddammit Winnie. With what exactly?"

"Hiding the body or something… I don't know." As I speak, his face contorts in complete disgust. He puts up his hands, as if to push me away, or surrender, and violently shakes his head. My chest tightens and draws inward. Panic sweeps through me like electricity.

"Please! You have to help me! You have to!" It takes all my strength to stop myself from screaming above this strained whisper.

He stares at me with utter contempt. "Why should I help you? I don't want to get involved in this." Gabe's hot breath hisses in my ear as he puts his face close to mine. "But calm the fuck down. I also don't want you getting fucking arrested, especially with me right here. Jesus Christ, that's the last thing I need."

"I guess—I guess I'll try to do something with her by myself." I hear the words, but it doesn't feel like I said them. Gabe grabs my arm, his grasp digging into my flesh through my clothes.

"Wait a minute. Jesus fucking Christ. Are you telling me that the body is out there, just lying in the woods?"

"Well, kind of. I mean, I moved her away from her house. Just grabbed my duffel bag. Put her in it. Took her out further in the woods. I thought about digging a grave, but I don't think it'd work. They'd find her right away. Right? They're probably already looking..."

"Winnie, look at me." I force myself to look up at him even though his wild eyes scare me. "How long ago exactly was this?"

"I don't know. Maybe half an hour? An hour? I don't know. Maybe longer? I don't remember."

"So, it's just rotting in some duffle bag in your backyard?"

"No. Kind of. Fuck! Oh, Gabe!" My voice raises and my lip quivers as I begin to cry again, but then a car drives by a little too slow, like they're watching us, so I try my hardest to calm myself. My lip still trembling, I push my voice back down to a whisper. "I just don't want to get in trouble."

He sighs, paces a moment, then balls his hand into a fist and punches his leg so hard that I wince.

"Fine. I can't believe I'm doing this, but fine. But you better never tell anyone, even if you get caught. Never fucking ever. Promise," he says, and his grasp on my arm tightens. "Promise!"

"I promise."

"Don't ever say I don't care about you again or any bullshit like that."

I nod and look down at my feet as Gabe punches his own arm and paces a few more steps.

"Okay, okay. Let's take care of this," he says as he stomps his cigarette out. "And I want to at least see the thing before I try to figure out how to get rid of it."

We walk through the woods behind my house, maybe half a mile back. The trees are dense, our heavy coats forcing us to shoulder through sideways. Partially buried under the leaves, the corner of the blue duffel bag peeks out at us. The sun is setting, and I curse myself for being so stupid. I might have never found it again in the dark.

"I wanna see it," Gabe says, unzipping it before I can even mutter an objection. I don't want to see her, so I cover my eyes with my hands like a child. Gabe whistles the way people do when they see something impressive. I lower my hands, allowing just a peek.

I expect to see her stiff, rotting, full of maggots, but, of course, she's not. She looks almost the same as she did before. Her face is pale, somewhat waxy, and relaxed completely into a slack blankness. The mouth hangs open a little, and behind her tiny lips, I can make out the tips of her bottom teeth. Thankfully, her eyes are still closed. She could almost be sleeping. Almost, but not quite. A dark gash, rough with dried blood, rises from an inch above her left eye up into her hairline before it disappears in globs of matted hair. Gabe reaches in and pulls her out a little by her coat.

"Hey! Stop!" I whisper, looking around nervously. There's nobody else though. The body slumps over as he drops it in surprise, and I can see the mottled purple of the back of her neck. I feel queasy.

"What?" he snaps.

"I don't want you to take her out here. It was hard enough to fit her in that bag the first time." Then I quickly add, "We can't get her DNA all over the place in what's practically my freaking backyard."

He nods, stuffs her back into the bag, and pulls the zipper up over her face.

"Where's the rock? Did you put it in there? It probably has your fingerprints all over it."

"Yeah. I'm not stupid. It's in there."

"Yeah, honestly, you're not stupid. That's why I can't believe this shit." He sighs again. "It's a good idea to cross the forest, in case they bring in dogs or something. We don't want them to know we stopped here. Need to put the heat over there instead."

I nod and look away, feeling sheepish.

"Okay, let's get this over with. I'm freezing my ass off," Gabe says and slings the bag over his shoulder. "Where are we taking it?"

"I don't know. Burying her still doesn't seem like a good idea, plus we don't have the right tools to—" We both freeze as a stick cracks nearby.

Gabe whispers so I can barely hear him. "Is that a flashlight? Way over there?"

"Shit! Let's go. Let's just go."

We're squeezing through the trees, trying to be quiet yet quick. We make it to the sidewalk, and I rush around to the passenger door of his car.

"What am I supposed to do with this?" he hisses, but before I can answer, he's tossed her in the back and is starting the car.

"Not too fast," I warn, but he's smirking. That same stupid signature smirk. I slap his arm, and for the first time in hours, let my shoulders relax.

As we drive around, we're brainstorming inconspicuous dumping sites for at least half an hour, factoring in the inevitable search parties and cadaver dogs. I think about how our morbid interests and all the crime documentaries we've seen might actually prove useful for once. Gabe takes random streets, driving slowly but always farther away. The only reasonable place we can come up with is the quarry on the outskirts of town. We agree it's been abandoned for at least a couple of years now and turn onto the highway, leaving city lights behind us.

As we get closer, I beg him to park somewhere discreet and far enough away that no one could place his car there. With a grunt, he slams his head back against the headrest and rolls his eyes but does it anyway.

"You should have to carry it. You did it," he says, but he doesn't even let me try, hoisting the bag over his shoulder. We hike at least two miles before it suddenly opens up in front of us. The steep walls step down like a giant staircase into the massive pool below. The water is jet black, except for the moon's reflection, and as smooth as a mirror.

"Help me find some rocks," he says.

"Not many will fit in there," I say, remembering the frantic struggle in the woods, her arm sticking out, and how I was afraid of breaking it to get it to fit. After everything I had already done.

"Well, we gotta try. Otherwise, what's the point?"

Biting my lip, I dig through a couple of rock piles nearby and find one I think will fit, but Gabe has already stuffed the bag to its maximum capacity by the time I return.

"It's not zipping all the way. See?" I point to where some of her puffy coat and porcelain skin peek through.

"That doesn't matter. It'll be good to get water in. Help it sink faster. Wash away all the fingerprints."

As he's talking, I walk over to the edge and imagine climbing down the sheer white faces, then sliding down, slipping into the milky quarter moon. Disappearing except for a quiet plip followed by a few tiny ripples that travel to the shore, and then everything is still again. Suddenly, desperately, that's all I want: to peacefully slip away, as if I was never here at all. It's what I want for her body and for myself, but Gabe doesn't wait to hear my ideas.

He swings the bag far behind him, then uses the momentum to take it forward, letting go. It somersaults away from us. *Crash.* Colliding with the water, the loud splash echoes throughout the round canyon. I watch it, a frenzy of bubbles escaping as it descends. The bag sinks quicker than I anticipated. It's all over.

Gabe swipes his hands together, as if to indicate a job well done, and looks over at me with one eyebrow raised. "She's sleeping with the fishes now."

My eyes are glued to the spot she was a moment ago. The ripples undulate and become small waves, breaking against the walls. My legs won't move until Gabe smacks me on the back, and I'm forced to catch my balance, scuffling my feet and kicking rocks over the edge. I finally slip on the pebbles and fall backward.

"Knock it out!" I shout at him, but he sticks out his tongue and laughs.

"Race ya," he says with a wink and takes off running. As I scramble to my feet, a genuine laugh bursts from my chest.

"Oh, you're dead!" I shout and break into a run behind him.

WINNIE

I can barely keep from collapsing while I make breakfast. With bleary eyes, I watch the eggs sizzle in the pan. Dad's making jokes at the table. Brendan chuckles but Lilly has almost fallen off her chair, red-faced from laughing. My head wobbles on its unsteady stalk and I bite the inside of my cheek to stay awake.

"Win, can you hurry up with the eggs? I'm starving," Dad shouts from across the room, but it's not his usual menacing voice. He sounds almost happy. I should be thankful. Everything points to a good day, but I can't appreciate it. I want to crawl back in bed. I feel like I could finally sleep. The sun streams through the kitchen window and I wonder how a little light burns away those anxious thoughts that keep me up every night. I'll have to sleep eventually. My mind wanders back to an article I read about people dying from lack of sleep, but I push it away. The eggs are ready.

Dad eats quickly and mechanically, only allowing a gasped breath when absolutely necessary. Brendan and Lilly push the eggs around their plate and nibble toast. I'm content with a glass of orange juice. Nothing makes me more tired than a full stomach anyway.

I've just finished scrubbing the cast iron when there's a pounding on the door. My blood quickens in my veins, my whole body tense and alive. Wide awake, I stand, but Dad is already getting it.

"Who the hell could it be this early in the morning?" he asks, but his hearty laugh doesn't reassure me at all. I'm sure it's the police. It must be. There's nobody else it could possibly be. My heart leaps into my throat and chokes me. I dart halfway across the kitchen, toward my room, but I don't know what I can do. There's no escape. They probably have the place surrounded.

"Good morning Mr. Campbell. Can I talk to Winnie?" Gabe asks from the front door.

"What? Why are you here, Gabe? It's Gabe, isn't it?"

"Yes sir. I really need to talk to Winnie about our biology project. It's due today but I'm still working on my half, and I thought I could drive her to school so we could go over it on the way." My eyes roll back as I snort a laugh. God, he's good.

"Well, she has to finish getting her sister ready—"

"Oh, that's fine. I don't mind waiting a bit. I could drive them both to school if you'd like." I know exactly his smile and posture without seeing him.

Brendan unfreezes from his confused stare toward the door and shouts, "Yeah, Dad, let him!" He grins at me and takes another sip of coffee.

"Okay. I guess that's fine. Um, just come in and wait in the living room."

"Thank you, Mr. Campbell," Gabe says, strolling past Dad into the living room. Dad looks back at me and I flinch. As I frantically finish cleaning up from breakfast, I hear Brendan creep to his room and his muffled voice through the walls, probably chattering on the phone. Dad disappears, but

I figure he's in his room getting dressed. I pull clothes over Lilly as she protests and whines about being a "big girl" before she proceeds to put her shoes on the wrong feet. I don't bother to fix them, instead roughly running a comb through her hair and pushing a headband into its shiny black.

"Come on, we've got to hurry," I tell her, but she grins and pushes her tongue through the hole in her front teeth.

"Is that your boyfriend?" she asks, swaying back and forth.

"No."

"Are you sure?" Her face beams. "He's handsome."

"Come on," I say, shoving her homework notebook in her backpack and pushing her in front of me out to the living room. Gabe smiles and gets up as soon as we enter.

"Hi Gabe," I say, my voice straining, "What a surprise seeing you here. How random."

"Well, you know, I'm still confused about the whole DNA/RNA thing, and I thought you could explain it again on the way to school. Then I can finish my half of the project," he says, looking at Lilly since she's staring at him. He winks. She giggles.

"Yeah. Okay. Let's go."

He nods and ushers a starry-eyed Lilly out the door. I shout down the hall, "Dad, we're leaving!" before following.

Driving to the elementary school, I space out, gazing out the window while Gabe talks to Lilly. I snap out of it when I notice we're almost there.

"There's no reason in my mind a girl as pretty and smart as you couldn't be both a cheerleader and an astronaut someday," Gabe says in his velvet voice. Lilly erupts in nervous giggles behind me. We pull into the driveway. Lilly unbuckles and starts to get out, but Gabe stretches back across the center console and stops her.

"Wait, would you do me a favor before you go?" he asks. "What?"

"Could you give me your autograph?" He flashes a smile as he asks, and Lilly explodes in giggles again.

"Seriously?" she asks, but he nods, so she pulls out her homework notebook and a pencil. Looking back at him twice, checking his sincerity, she finally scribbles her name across the page and rips it out, handing it to him.

"Thank you, Lilly. I'm going to keep this somewhere safe for the next ten, fifteen years. Then, when you're a superstar, I'll sell it for a million dollars." As he says this, she blushes a deep red and smiles so hard her eyes almost squint closed.

"You're funny. I hope you come over again," she says as she opens the car door. "Have a good day!"

"Bye Lilly," he says, and she slams the door, an obvious accident based on the wide-eyed look she gives us before scurrying away.

I twist in my seat to fully face Gabe as we leave the school drop-off. My eyelid twitches uncontrollably, even though I'm able to keep the rest of my face in its composed mask. He's smirking and watching me from the corner of his eye.

"Why'd you come over?" I ask. "You're lucky Dad was in an unusually good mood today."

"Yeah, sorry about that but," he pulls into an almost empty parking lot, "We really need to talk." I see him consider shutting off the engine but deciding against it with the cold front blowing through. The old clunker might have a hard time starting again.

"What do we need to talk about? I feel like we've been doing great. Totally free of suspicion." I even attempt a smile while I say the words, but my lips won't cooperate. Maybe it's sleep deprivation and that's all, I try to comfort myself, but I'm still disturbed by the way my muscles won't listen to me.

"First of all, I don't think that's completely true. For god's sake, Winnie, you look like you haven't slept in a year. That look really doesn't go well with your absence the day she went missing and all."

"Come on. Maybe I'm sick with worry," I joke but I can tell he doesn't find it amusing. "I'm absent all the time. There's no way they're checking attendance records trying to find a kidnapper. Seriously, there's no connection between me and her. I didn't babysit her. Nobody even thinks we knew each other."

"How are you so sure nobody ever saw you hanging around, acting like a total creep?" He sneers as he asks it, and a twinge of guilt pulses through me.

"I'm sure because if they did, don't you think somebody would have come to question me by now?" He looks away, out the car window, and sucks at his lip rings. He knows I'm right.

"I still just don't get it," he says, turning back to me. "I just don't."

I nod and shrug since I don't know what to say. There's no good explanation, at least not one that can be put in words, logically spelled out. The mixture of anger, envy, and excruciating depression that just seeing her face brought up, like a boiling brine threatening to spill over. Her existence taunted me, reminded me of what had waited for me if things had gone the happy fairytale way they were supposed to, and the delicious power, intoxicating and strong, when I took it away from her. Watching the life drain from her face, and knowing it was because of me, was a cathartic release, unlike anything I'd ever felt before. These thoughts sound so sick, they disgust me, and I know I won't ever be able to adequately explain them. It's beyond the realm of words.

I don't know what to say, so I rub his hand and tell him, "It's going to be okay." It doesn't soothe him in any visible way. He just stares at me like I'm some strange specimen to figure out. My heart flutters and I want to explain it all, but I know Gabe well enough to know he won't understand, and I don't have the right words anyway. He punctures my thoughts with a stern look.

"I'm worried it's going to surface again, or really, I'm worried about *when* it's going to surface since that's the inevitable conclusion to this whole thing," he says. I once again lose control of my face and feel my brow furrow in confusion and anxiety.

"What are you talking about? We weighed her down. You made sure we did. She won't float up with all those rocks in the bag."

He waves away my words as if I'd said something child-ish. "No, I've looked it up. It won't work. I mean, it'll work for a while, sure, but not long-term. Even if we'd done a better job, it'd still pop up eventually. It's just a matter of time. Time and other factors like water temperature, current, aquatic life, body composition, and a million other things."

"You've researched this?" My eyes squint as rage hard-ens in my stomach. "Please tell me you didn't do it on your own phone or computer, like an idiot."

"No, I used the private browsing. Nobody would find it if they searched my computer," he scoffs.

"Why are you so obsessed with this? There were no witnesses, fingerprints were washed away, and they wouldn't ever be able to come up with a motive or connection if they tried. We're home free."

"Don't say 'we' as if I'm a part of this. I just helped you get rid of the body. That's all."

"Then why are you so worried?" I try to touch his hand again, but he pulls it away. "Come on, they'll never know. It's the perfect crime, just like we'd talked about."

He laughs and rolls his head against the headrest. "It's going to come up. You didn't do something stupid like leave something in that bag, did you? Even a single hair could be traced to you through DNA, you know," he says, his cadence just as condescending as the way he'd spoken to Lilly. She might not have noticed, but I do, and it makes me hate him. How could he think so little of me after I've shown him the things I can do? The things others couldn't even allow themselves to think of that I've lived through and forced to fruition.

"There's nothing in the bag."

"Are you sure?"

I cross my arms against my chest. "I'm sure."

"I think I'm going to go back. I need to see whether it's surfaced."

"Why? What are you going to do if it did? You can't climb down there and try to weigh it down again or anything. Come on, be realistic, Gabe. Just leave it alone."

"I need to know," he says, refusing to look me in the eye again as he puts the car in drive and takes us to school. The silence weighs on me like a heavy fog, filling my lungs with tension. As we finally park again, I have to break it.

"All that going there will accomplish is drawing attention to you and, through you, me."

"I know I shouldn't go. I just need to know."

"Please don't. Let's just act like everything's fine," I say, but he gets out and leaves me alone in the car.

He doesn't talk to me again all day. He doesn't sit next to me in class or at lunch. As I watch him get in his car to leave, I wonder if he's going there, but I already know the answer.

He texts me later: *Didn't see it.* I know he's too smart to have let himself be seen, but I still have trouble falling asleep, a knot in the pit of my stomach.

WINNIE

The vibration of his text against my wooden nightstand wakes me up: *Did some more research. She's def gonna pop up and soon.* I roll my eyes, then glance at the alarm clock. 3 a.m.

Head on the pillow, I close my eyes and try to fall back asleep. Maybe I do, but it's hard to tell where my paranoid thoughts shift into nightmares. All I know for sure is soon it's 5 a.m. and I'm up doing the usual morning routine. All morning I pretend to ignore the message, refuse to respond, even though it's all I've thought about since I saw it.

At school, I see him trotting toward me across the parking lot. As nonchalantly as I can, I turn away and relax my body language. I won't let him know it's bothering me. As he comes closer, I notice from the corner of my eye that he doesn't look tired. He probably sent me that text to torture me. Then he smiles, a genuine one, not that usual smirk, and I let the idea flutter away. I smile back. I'll never understand him.

"I know you read my text," he says right away.

"Yeah, well, I haven't had time to answer. Doesn't matter anyway. You're totally wrong."

"No, I'm not," he says, confident as always.

"Yeah, you are." I close the distance between us, looking around to confirm no one is close enough to listen. "I saw a documentary the other day where a body wasn't found for like twenty years and it was just like this. They weighed down their body, and we did too. I was there. Remember? That bag was heavy as fuck. There's no way she's popping back up."

"She will. I'm telling you. It won't be that long from now either, unless we get a good freeze. God, that would be a miracle," he says, and I detect the faintest worry in his voice. Standing much closer, I can see the telltale lines of concealer under his eyes, and I know he's hiding bags like mine. It somehow brings me relief to know he didn't sleep well either.

"How could she come up? I mean, sure, they might find her if they dredge the thing, but she won't just pop up."

"Didn't you ever even pay attention to any of those true crime shows we watched? It's the bloating. The chemical reactions during decomposition. She's gonna come up. Soon. We didn't weigh her down anywhere near enough."

"You don't know that," I hiss.

"But you don't know that I'm wrong either," he says.

I back up the slightest bit, and he relaxes. He's probably right. When he says he's researched something, it usually means like scientific peer-reviewed journals, not just some stupid TV show or documentary. A putrid taste fills my mouth as my anxiety rises.

"Well then. Okay. What are we supposed to do?"

He takes a deep breath and looks away before he answers. "I really don't know."

"Then why are you telling me this?" I fight to control the volume of my voice.

"Well, I mean, I guess...we need to know these things. Don't you want to know?"

"Not if there's nothing I can do about it," I say.

He just shrugs. "Maybe we should leave town. Let's run away together."

I roll my eyes. He's suggested the same thing a million times and I always excitedly make plans, only for us both to make excuses before following through. Lilly needs me and his mom needs him. It's the same cycle every time.

"No, for real this time," he says. "We can be truck stop hookers and hitch our way across the country to like California or, really anywhere better than here."

I briefly entertain this fantasy of us at a truck stop, dressed up like movie prostitutes with feather boas and sequin tops, making more cash than we know what to do with, but then I remember what truckers look like. And smell like. I remember the real sex worker I saw downtown with her rundown face.

"I don't think it'd be like you think," I say, but I'm not sure he heard me since he doesn't even acknowledge it. He just gazes off into the distance behind me, like I'm not even there. I wait in his silence until he's ready to break it.

"Maybe I'll go without you."

"You wouldn't. Would you?" I ask, but I know the answer. I've always known this town, our friendship, it's all just a liminal stepping stone in his life. He'll move on eventually, without me.

"I'm just messing around. Calm down," he says, waving me away.

The bell rings and everyone staggers inside except us. I'm waiting for Gabe to somehow dismiss me and end this tension. The question of what happens next hangs in the air between us, but we answer with steaming breaths in the winter air. I wonder if he's waiting for me as much as I'm waiting for him, but then he suddenly comes to life again.

"I promise I won't leave, but this whole thing is bull-shit, Winnie. You know that, right?"

His words are sharp, and I can't look at him while he's talking, but he grabs my chin and pulls my face up to see his rage.

"I didn't ask for this. Sure, we talked a lot of shit, but I didn't even believe in my own crazy ass plans. That was all just drunken shit talk. But you went and did this thing and now I'm a part of it. I didn't ask for that. Say it." He grabs my ponytail from behind while his other hand squeezes my lips into a fishy pout. "Say: You didn't ask for this."

He forces my lips to move and strengthens his grip on my hair as I mumble, "You didn't ask for this."

"This is my own crazy, stupid mistake, and you had nothing to do with it."

Once again, he squeezes my lips mockingly as I repeat, "This is my own stupid mistake and you had nothing to do with it, Gabe." I pull backward and break free from his fingers, shaking my head to try to loosen his grip on my hair.

"Gabe, stop it! I know you had nothing to do with this. I won't forget. Just stop, okay?" I plead. He lets go of my hair.

"Fine." Then he turns and goes inside. His face back to his usual icy mask. Guilt knots my intestines as I watch him through the glass doors. I shouldn't have gotten him involved, but then again, I couldn't have done it without him.

I wait around outside for a while, kicking rocks and trying to decide if it's worth going in. I don't feel like being at school today. Honestly, deep down, I feel compelled to go somewhere I haven't been in years: my mother's grave.

Eventually, I give up and walk across the parking lot and down the road. Cars whiz by and the wind pulls at my clothes, knots my hair, but I don't care. I just focus on walking. After a few miles, my feet go numb, maybe from the cold. It's probably a good thing since I'm sure they're developing pretty nasty blisters by now. My boots are not good shoes for long-distance walking, but I didn't think I'd be doing this when I got dressed.

Finally, I turn down the short dirt road that cuts across the vacant fields towards the graveyard. Its entrance is marked with a useless gate since it's connected to a fence knocked down in parts by wind and neglect. Not many people come out here to visit. It's the oldest cemetery in town but looks only half full. Maybe that's because of the desolate feeling out here, far from the bustle of town. It's a place to be buried and forgotten. I've often wondered why Dad didn't pick one of the nicer, newer places. The only thing I can conclude is Mom actually wanted to be out here. She knew it was like this and still chose it. Maybe she didn't want anyone to visit. I know it wouldn't be me she'd want to see crying on her grave.

It's not hard to find her. Dad spent a lot of money on a decorative marker with a fat cherub statue draping flowers across the lettering. Among the modest headstones, it sticks out in preposterous glamor. A tinge of green grows across the baby angel's face, and I gently trace my fingers along its lips. It's almost jovial look and the blooming stone flowers seem completely inappropriate at such a somber place. I move my fingers down to trace my mother's name. *Theresa Campbell*.

A strange urge overcomes me, and I find myself lying face down on the overgrown patch of grass that covers the earth between my body and hers. My hands claw into the green blades, and I pull at them like a woman pulls her hair in grief. I realize I'm crying. Wailing into the ground with my face buried in the green. My mouth is full of grass, and I breathe in dirt with each gasp that precedes my stifled wails.

I can feel her beneath me, through the packed earth and even through the shiny wooden coffin, pressing her hands upward as I press my own down towards her. She is whispering to me, but I can't make out the words over my wails. Behind my eyelids, I see a vision of her, as she is now. Withered away, her skin hangs like a deflated sack against her skull and bones. Her black hair no longer glossy but broken and stringy with only a loose hold on what remains of her scalp. Once plump lips have thinned and pulled away from her teeth to reveal their long roots. She's turned all black and brown and yellow, nothing like the soft colors of life. Empty eye sockets burn into me and she whispers louder.

She tells me secret things I never wanted her to admit: She never loved me. I was an accident. I am nothing compared to my sister because she is beauty and life. I am nothing but the personification of destruction. She whispers about my fate and how it must happen. I'm following along the destined path like the good girl I long to be, but my path is only one of hurt and pain. I've hurt those children, and I will hurt more. She hates me and wishes she'd killed me when she had a chance. Killed me before I was even born. I beg her to stop, but she whispers on and on.

A rage grows within me as her whispers intensify to a deafening frenzy. I scream into the ground, begging her to stop.

"That's enough! You're wrong!" I shriek into the earth. "You think you hated me then, but you'll see."

Beneath the still surface, settled among the rocks, Leigh's body swells in preparation for its debut. Her stomach extends under the heavy coat, pushed out by the gasses of decomposition. Every tissue in her body bloats, distorting her into some creature unrecognizable from her former self. Her skin has morphed to a bluish-green and threatens to slough off, but there's no current to provoke it. Her childish features have swollen to disturbing proportions and her eyelids have been forced open to blindly take in her watery grave. Bodily fluids seep upwards in small streams from her face through the unzipped hole in the bag. She can wait no longer.

Little by little, the body wriggles in her blue vinyl coffin. Her head pushes up against the zipper, trying to escape, but instead, they rise together. Faster and faster, the remains expel gasses, propelling her upward, until she splashes past the surface. Like a champagne cork, her body pops from the water, creating waves that hurry to the stony walls and crash violently, announcing her arrival. First bobbing in the sunlight, then floating calmly, she spends hours waiting, but the body knows nothing but patience now.

A thirteen-year-old meanders toward the cliff edge, spray paint canister in hand. He thinks about how his friends will show up later and be impressed when they see the rock face bearing his name. At the edge, carefully examining the treacherous paths down the wall, a blue shape in the water catches his eye. It's likely just trash, yet he can't help but to focus on it, trying to make sense of the floating heap. Then the sun catches the golden strands of hair floating along the edge and he feels sick.

He doesn't want to believe it could be what he thinks it is, but the unsettled feeling in his stomach forces him to back away. The picture he'd seen on the television the night before flashes in his mind. A blonde little girl in a purple dress, smiling at the camera. No. Could it be? Don't look at it. Get away from here. As he runs down the graveled path, back toward his grandfather's house, he notices every breath, each heartbeat, and forces down the knowledge that one day they both will cease.

WINNIE

I can't bring myself to go to school today. I spend the day
not doing much of anything, sitting in my room, switching
between the bed and the desk chair every couple hours. I
take a hot bath in the middle of the day to try to clear my
mind. Stare at the walls, out the window, at my knees poking out of the water, I spend the day staring. Staring and
thinking. Half-dreaming, half-dying.

Hours of time are spent reliving my childhood in as
much detail as I can remember, almost conjuring up the
smell of Mom's signature perfume and Lilly's baby powder
fragrance from her diaper years. Blurred visions of beach
vacations and sunsets. I can practically taste the chocolate
orange in my stocking from my favorite Christmas of all
time, back when I was eight and carefree.

My tenth birthday with the Lion King theme including matching cake, banners, balloons, paper cups, and even
a t-shirt featuring Simba. It wasn't what I'd wanted, and
was honestly a little embarrassing, but it made Mom so
happy, I didn't say anything and feigned awe at the way
even the tablecloth was patterned with characters from
some old movie I loved when I was a baby. She was already

starting to lose it then, could often be found muttering to herself in the kitchen if she didn't know you were watching.

I let that one fade away and, in its place, the fair from two years ago surrounds me with flashing lights and sticky fingers from cotton candy. Brendan isn't being a jerk and Dad hasn't punished me in three weeks—a new record. Lilly bounces with every step as her body tries to fidget away the sugar rush. Somehow everything has been better recently. I wish I'd known how temporary it would be, so I could have savored it more.

A tiny, warm hand guides me through the games buzzing and clinking, a zigzagging pull towards the rides. As we wait for Lilly's favorite (I can't remember its name, just that Brendan calls it the "barf-o-rama" because it spins so fast and erratically), she hums and twirls in tiny circles of absolute bliss. I try to tie back her hair with a pink scrunchie, but it won't stay. The long black hair is too thick and silky. I remember an irrational worry plaguing me about her hair getting caught in the machinery, but when I mentioned it aloud, Brendan smacked my arm for even considering such a horrific accident. As if imagining the tragedy could cause it to become reality. Even then, when things were as good as they ever could be again after Mom, it was still always my fault.

By the end of the night, we stop up at the top of the Ferris wheel and Brendan is rocking it because I told him I didn't like it. Lilly screams with fake fear and exhilaration, and my knuckles turn white from their death grasp on the flimsy safety bar. Finally, we come back down, and then Brendan drives us home to a quiet empty house. Dad didn't come home until late the next evening. In my memory, I breathe in the peace of the dark house, the last time I felt truly relaxed.

Eventually, my thoughts drift away from memories and into fantasies. Not the typical fantasies of Jeremy or terrible violence, but new elaborate experiences I've never dreamed before, completely overtaking me as clear as reality.

I become an empress lounging in my private garden, sparkling in jewels and finery, a white tiger yawning in a cage near a bubbling fountain. Servants come and go, bringing chocolate strawberries and petit fours on golden plates. My slender fingers pick the best-looking ones and delicately place them in my mouth. Sapphires and emeralds glitter on my rings, and rubies spill across my dress and onto the lawn. A servant brings a mirror with golden glass so I can admire every inch of flawless porcelain skin, each golden curl, and the flower crown weaved into my hair. There are only faceless servants and yet love seems to radiate from all around, warming and caressing me. It is a vision of paradise, but over time it transforms into something else.

I become aware of a small bright light rising from the fountain in the middle of the grounds. Like a firefly or a stray ember, it drifts through the air, growing larger and brighter with each inch. The servants and garden fall away around me, but I hardly notice, mesmerized by the light. My neck extends and my head leans back to follow it higher and higher until the light bursts above me, taking the form of a brilliant star.

Golden rays strike out from its core and blind me. All is white for a second, then completely dark. The warmth collapses into itself as the star implodes, and all that remains is a feeling of startling cold and slowly sinking into nothingness.

Out of the void, far in the distance, a figure appears. I wait for what seems like hours as my vision returns and the figure advances, but I can't make out any features until it is quite close. Suddenly, I recognize her. It's Leigh.

She's smiling and walking toward me, holding a flimsy circle of weeds out: the crown I made for her to wear as "Princess of the Forest." She isn't mad or hurt. Her skin glows golden and alive, and her face beams, happy to see me.

Standing in front of me, she looks up with her blue eyes and blushing cheeks. She pushes the crown out to me, tapping my stomach with it. Finally, as if emerging from a trance, I realize what she wants and take the crown. She giggles and mimes for me to put it on. I obey and she pulls my arm, stronger than the real Leigh had ever been. I almost topple onto her, but she stops me right when my ear is against her lips and whispers, "There is still time for redemption."

As I pull away to look at her, she isn't Leigh anymore. A grizzled, old man stares at me, inches from my face. His lip pulls up into a snarl and his dark eyes burn into me painfully, but I can't look away. A long gray beard, full of tangles and thorns, grows from his face and, paired with the cloak draped over his hunched body and gnarled walking stick, he reminds me of a wizard from some forgotten folktale. We stare at each other for several moments before he smiles and spits in my face. I groan and wipe the mucus away with the back of my hand. His rusty voice mutters, "Too late. Too late indeed."

I burst from the vision like waking from a dream, but I haven't been asleep. Dread falls over me like a shadow. Lilly is home. I can hear her playing in her room. I realize I'm in the living room, in Dad's chair, which is definitely not where I had been when I first started daydreaming. My hands slide down my body and I'm mercifully somehow wearing my robe. Embarrassed, I head back to my room, but then I hear Dad's voice from the kitchen. I almost break my neck with how quickly I turn to him. The color drains from my face, down my neck, seeping into the rug under my feet and leaving me blank.

"So, you're finally awake then," Dad says in a scruffy voice, but he actually doesn't sound that angry. I can't respond. I'm frozen. I look at him, begging for mercy with my eyes when I notice he's cooking dinner, but he won't give me the relief of eye contact.

He doesn't say anything else to me all evening, even when Brendan starts asking about why I was sitting in his chair, with wet hair and in a bathrobe, staring off into space. I almost want to laugh, but I haven't fully thawed even after all that time. I can't bring myself to help clear the table and do the dishes. Instead, I sit there, paralyzed, helplessly watching and waiting. Watching Dad do all of my chores after shooing away my siblings. Waiting for Dad to punish me. It's inevitable.

Eventually, he finishes a half-hearted cleanup of the kitchen and gets Lilly ready for bed. The sound of their muffled voices down the hall coincides with my limbs finally following my commands again, tingling but unfrozen.

Brendan disappears soon after dinner. Sometimes I think he does feel a little bad for me. He never wants to be around for it. Dad calls me into his room, I hobble on unsteady legs down the hall, and the punishment begins without a word spoken by either of us.

The straps around my ankles are too tight and my feet pulse with pain. I'm glad for the pain. It means at least my circulation isn't obstructed. My shoulders ache from having my arms stretched awkwardly above my head, but at least those bindings are comfortable. The beating isn't as bad as I'd expected after everything that happened. My only worry is the burning pain in my lower left stomach. It feels like an exceptionally deep bruise. Hopefully nothing more. That was the first punch. That one's always the worst.

The crusty rag in my mouth tastes disgusting, like dust and oil. I consider pushing it out with my tongue, but it's too risky. Next time I come in this room to clean, I'll make sure to swipe this rag, so I can throw it in the laundry. It's bad enough to feel dry-mouthed and partially suffocated. Chewing the rag a little, I bite down hard on it to see if it helps lessen the pain, but like always, it's useless. I wish I could loosen those straps just a little. Enough that the pounding stops. I can feel my heartbeat in my feet.

This headphone treatment is a relatively new punishment, but it's been easier to adjust to than any of the others. Sure, excruciatingly loud music being pumped into your ears is horrible. It's painful, you can't sleep, and after a while, you feel like your head is filling up like a water balloon, bound to explode any second, but it's also easier to ignore than the outright physical pain. At first, it worked exactly how he intended, and I couldn't focus on anything but the sounds drilling into my eardrums, reverberating in my skull, but a few punishments later, I'm able to accept and transcend it. Dad obviously must not be aware yet, or else he'd have moved on to something new.

My little secret makes me smile slightly before the pulsing in my feet brings me back to reality. I focus once more on my breathing. Deeply inhale, filling up every cubic inch of lung, then slowly exhale through the nose until every last molecule is gone. Repeat. Repeat. Repeat. I let myself float away from my body. I hover directly above it. I stay safe and weightless right where my breath reaches. The music fades into the background of my mind. The pounding is the only thing I can't shake. God, I just need those straps loosened a bit. Relax. Focus. Breathe. It'd be much easier without the rag, but when I focus on this calm, deep breathing, I don't feel so strangled. I can do this.

I let my mind rewind the visions from today and play them again against the red darkness of my eyelids. There was meaning there. Some kind of sign. It must be or else how could my unconscious set me up for this? I basically begged for this punishment when I froze up and abandoned my responsibilities. I rewind it again and again. I wonder if I'm just this fucked up over Leigh, but something about it feels like more than that. I can't figure it out.

The door opens. Dad slips in and shakes his head like he's disappointed with me before untying the straps around my feet. He just keeps shaking his head and clicking his tongue, the way dads do on family sitcoms when one of their kids is being a rascal. As he unties my wrists and turns off the blaring noise, my ears ring and I wonder whether any of those TV kids could endure even ten minutes with a dad like mine. I want to laugh, but I keep my face blank. They're not nearly strong enough, but I am.

WINNIE

"Come on," Gabe says, and grabs my arm, pulling me toward the door. It's the first thing he's said to me all day. He still sat next to me in class but refused to acknowledge my presence. I stumble behind him into the parking lot. We're headed toward his car. I shiver and wish I'd worn a thicker sweater. Only seniors are allowed to leave for lunch. I glance around, biting at my thumb while I search for teachers, but the coast is clear. One less thing to worry about at least.

I know what he wants to talk about. I heard it on the morning news, blaring in the other room, while I got Lilly ready for school. I've ignored it so far. I wonder if it's somehow easier for me since I'm the one who actually did it.

As soon as we're safely enclosed in the car, his words burst out in breathless worry. "They found it. The body. They found it."

"I know." I rub my arms and he finally turns the key. The heater is on full blast, but it isn't warm yet, so I turn it down and cradle myself. Gabe keeps looking at me and away, again and again, drumming his hands against the steering wheel. "If we're going to go somewhere, we should do it before anyone sees us out here," I say, but he ignores me.

"They found the body." He slams his fists against the steering wheel and repeats it again. I pull my knees up against my chest in a hug, burrowing my face between them.

"Don't you get it?" he asks, but I stay hidden.

With a growl, he throws the car in reverse, and we jerk backward. The tires squeal and my head hits the chair, but I quickly hide myself away again. The engine groans as we peel out of the parking lot and down the road, but he soon spies a parked cop and eases up. I feel his demeanor calm as the car slows to the legal limit. I peek out from my cocoon and see the usual relaxed expression painted across his face. It's the same Gabe as always, yet I find it more unnerving than the angry, frightened version from moments ago.

A few minutes pass and we pull into a fast-food parking lot. Without a word, he parks and gets out. I stay inside and wait for him. Holding two drinks and a paper bag, he's back in no time.

"Thank you," I murmur as he hands me one of the sodas and a burger. He nods and smiles. We eat in peace, and I hate myself for enjoying each salty bite as much as I do. Somehow, I feel I should have negotiated and not blindly accepted this truce. Part of me feels like I should be fasting, starving myself in a sort of penance.

As we finish and toss the crinkled wrappers in the bag, Gabe says it again, "They found the body."

"Yes," I say. I start to curl into myself again, but he stops me with an outstretched arm.

"They identified her. They said they had to use her dental records."

"Yes." Worry floods my mind. Stomach acid burns its way up my throat, but I force it down.

"She was probably too bloated to identify the normal way."

"Yeah," I say, trying to block out the mental image.

"I need to know," he says, "Are you sure there wasn't anything in there? In the bag? Not an old receipt, a hair tie, even a gum wrapper?"

I nod furiously. "I'm sure. I really did check."

He clicks his tongue ring against his teeth and nods back to me. "Okay. Okay," he says but I get the feeling he's saying it more as a reassurance to himself than me.

"Thank you for lunch," I say, but he just shrugs. I slurp the last sips of Coke from my straw and pull it up and down to hear it squeak against the lid.

"Why did you do it?" He asks so bluntly, I'm taken aback.

"We've talked about it before," I say, but his eyes plead for more, so I add, "I don't know. I just did it."

"That's not it."

"I told you. She looked just like me. It was a weird compulsion." I struggle with the words. "It just happened."

"But that doesn't make sense," he says, but there's nothing else I can give.

"What do you expect me to say?" I ask. "What do you want to hear?"

He bristles. It's not the response he was looking for.

We drive the short road to school and are back in time for class, but Gabe's still on edge. He doesn't speak to me the rest of the day, or reply to any texts after school, but I know he won't do anything. Not because of fear, but pride. I know, deep down, he's hoping they never discover the truth as much as I do, but more for his own private gloating than any other reason.

Back at home, I play with Lilly for a couple hours before Brendan shows up and demands I start dinner because he's starving. I sigh and set the dolls down. Lilly knows better than to say anything, but her eyes reveal her disappointment. It was the best we've gotten along in weeks.

As I walk into the kitchen, Brendan pulls me to the corner and starts whispering, his eyes darting around to make sure Lilly isn't listening. "Have you gotten the Christmas presents yet?"

"Shit. No. I haven't even thought about it," I say, my heart sinking.

"Well, you'd better do it soon. Dad will be pissed if not. Remember the year before last?"

"Yeah. Of course," I say, "But, come on, there hasn't really been a good time to go begging Dad for Christmas money either."

He nods and rubs his chin thoughtfully. "I get that. But why can't you use some of your babysitting money? I know you've got a ton stashed away somewhere."

"What? No way! I don't have enough for all the expensive shit you and Lilly want, let alone something nice for Dad. No, I'll have to ask him."

Brendan shrugs, grabs an apple, and walks away as he bites into it. I work on dinner and mentally plan out different approaches to asking for the money and the many possible reactions they could elicit. Eventually, I give up on it. At least for today. I know I hardly have the strength to keep going as it is and the last-minute Christmas scramble will be better if I have a little more time to build myself up again.

Dad comes home as I'm putting the chicken in the oven. He already stinks of booze.

"How long 'til dinner?" he asks, his glassy eyes obviously not noticing the tray I just inserted in front of him.

"About an hour. But I can make you something to tide you over until then if you're hungry." He waves me off as he lumbers toward the living room to collapse into his armchair and absorb his typical diet of crappy TV dramas and random sporting events. He only waits a minute or two before yelling out for me to bring him a drink, which I do immediately.

I watch the chicken through the oven window and curse myself for picking something that takes so long to cook, or for not at least starting it earlier. Lilly tries to creep up from behind to scare me, shouting "Boo!" and tickling my ribs, but I push her away and sit down at the kitchen table.

"I'm hungry. Is dinner almost ready?" she asks but stops whining when I shoot her one of my meanest glares. She must've heard Dad complaining. There's no way she's hungry already when she ate all those graham crackers as her after-school snack.

"No, it's going to be an hour or so," I say through gritted teeth. She frowns and sulks away. I hear Brendan call something about leaving as the front door shuts. Why would he give me such a hard time about dinner, then leave anyway? I twirl my hair around my finger as I wait, revisiting my usual daydream of some disgusting meal eaten greedily by my family before its real contents are revealed. It's always a relaxing activity.

When the chicken is finally done, I take it out and finish preparing the salad and setting the table as it rests. Lilly's already sitting at her usual chair, waiting with her face squished between her palms.

"Finally," she snorts. I ignore her and grab the salad dressing from the fridge.

"Dinner's ready!" I yell to Dad, listening to his chair squeak as he lifts his ancient body from its warm embrace. I also hear the front door open followed by Brendan stomping through the house. I turn back to the kitchen as they come in, making the excuse that I forgot the tea pitcher, but really to hide the slight smile. Secretly, I'm proud he came back in time for dinner. He knows I'm a better cook than his girlfriend's mom.

I chew slowly to the symphony of silverware clinking and lips smacking. I focus on being present. When everyone is busy eating, it's almost nice to be with my family. Then Lilly ruins it all.

"Winnie, this chicken is really dry. It's gross. Why did you make it like that?" She pulls apart the breast on her plate into white strings.

"It's fine, Lilly. Jeez," Brendan mumbles under his breath, but Dad is already laughing.

"Maybe you're destined to be a food critic or something, honey," he laughs and slaps Lilly's back. "You must be almost grown now that you've finally noticed Winnie's lack of culinary skills."

I know it doesn't matter. I know I shouldn't let these things get to me, but I'm turning bright red, seething beneath the surface.

"Good thing you're book-smart, Winnie, since you'll never catch a husband with that face and this cooking," he jokes then laughs so hard it morphs into a breathless wheeze.

I don't ask to be excused. I get up, as slow and calm as I can muster, and walk out onto the back patio. I'm so mad I can't feel the icy wind biting at my exposed skin. There's no way I'm going back in there right now, even for a coat. It turns out I don't have to, since Brendan soon follows me, my coat in hand.

"That was pretty messed up, dude. I just wanted to say," he whispers as I pull the coat on. I nod, not looking at him.

Standing together on the back patio, we watch as it begins to snow.

"Finally, some snow," Brendan says, "Maybe we'll end up with our usual white Christmas after all."

I shake my head as I pull out my phone to show him the weekly forecast. "No way, it's going to be too warm to stay more than a day."

He shrugs but stays standing next to me for a long time, even putting his arm around my shoulders and pulling me toward him. My legs are shaking from the cold, but the brisk air is better than the thick, suffocating heat awaiting us inside. Leaning against my brother, watching the snow fall across the lawn and nestle into the crooks of the tree limbs, I almost feel like everything will be okay and normal again someday.

COLE CAMPBELL

POLICE INTERVIEW TRANSCRIPT
PART 2

DEC. 17

Det. Wilson: Okay, Mr. Campbell. I know this is difficult, but it's time. I need you to go over what happened this morning.

Campbell: I woke up. I don't know what time. Don't bother asking.

Det. Wilson: Okay, then what?

Campbell: I noticed right away that Winnie was missing because nobody was making breakfast. Winnie always makes breakfast.

Det. Wilson: Did you look for Winnie right away?

Campbell: Yeah. I was kind of mad she wasn't getting everything ready, so I went to her room straight away, but she wasn't there. It didn't look like anybody had slept in her bed, it was so nicely made. And the room was really cold with the window open, like she left it open all night.

Det. Wilson: Then what did you do?

Campbell: Well, I texted Winnie, but that's when I noticed her phone was still there, plugged in on her nightstand. That was weird. She's always on her phone. So, I got this bad feeling in my gut, and then I checked in Lilly's room, and she wasn't there either. Her bed was all messy though, like she'd been there, and her dresser drawers were all pulled out, half open. I really didn't like the look of that.

Det. Wilson: Did you check on your son?

Campbell: I knew he wasn't home. He'd told me he'd be spending the night elsewhere, but the girls should've been home. I did text him though, and when he didn't answer right away, I called until he picked up. He was groggy but swore he didn't know where the girls were. He must've heard the nervousness in my voice because he said he'd be home right away. I thought I might be overreacting at first, but you don't know these girls. They would never leave without telling me.

Det. Wilson: Okay, so what did you do after you called Brendan?

Campbell: I searched the whole house at least twice. I felt like I was losing my mind and they must be there somewhere. I tried to wait a little while for Brendan, made some coffee, but I was going crazy just sitting around, waiting. I walked around the block, looking into everyone's yards as much as I could from the street. I know that doesn't make sense, but I was panicking. I tried to tell myself that Winnie just took her to the store. That they had to run there real quick for something for breakfast and that's why she didn't take her phone, but it didn't feel right. She's never done anything like that before.

When I got back home, I called Lilly's friend's house. Her mom picked up and said she hadn't seen her. She sounded worried, so I tried to calm down and laugh it off. I told her the girls probably went to the store and I'd go check it out. I sped over to our usual grocery store, but nobody'd seen them. I tried a couple other stores and drove all the way to the mall, but it wasn't even open yet. I just didn't know where to look.

Det. Wilson: You really looked all over for them?

Campbell: Of course I did! I gotta admit, I was almost crying when I left the mall. I was so worried about little Lilly. Oh Lilly...

Det. Wilson: So, you went back home, and then?

Campbell: When I got back home, Brendan was there. I could tell he was worried too, and I knew something was wrong. I knew it in my heart. I almost called the police then, but Brendan said to wait. He said maybe Winnie was playing a trick on me, trying to get me back for last night. I knew she was really pissed about that whole thing, so I tried to calm down and just wait, but as I was waiting, I started looking out at the backyard, and then I got the idea to check the woods. At the time, I was thinking that Brendan was right and that would be just the place she could convince Lilly to go hide with her, you know, play a little trick on Daddy. So, I made Brendan come out there with me and we started looking around and then, and then—

Det. Wilson: And then you found her out there.

Campbell: My baby girl! Oh, Lilly was just a broken mess. We didn't have to go that far to find her. I don't know how that could have happened so close to home and I didn't hear her! I didn't hear anything!

There was blood everywhere, and she had gotten sick all over the front of her sweater. I just collapsed, and I couldn't stop crying and rocking her. Holding her. Trying to wake her up. Brendan was yelling at me to stop touching her, for evidence, but I told him to shut the fuck up! This was my baby girl, and I needed to hold her. She was already cold by the time I found her. So cold.

I hope I didn't mess up the evidence, but I couldn't help it. I was just crying all over her tiny little face. My baby.

Det. Wilson: Then Brendan says he ran back to the house and called the police, and you stayed back with Lilly. Is that right?

Campbell: Yeah. I couldn't leave her. They had to restrain me when they came to get her.

Det. Wilson: I am so sorry for your loss, Mr. Campbell. I assure you we are doing all we can to locate Winnie. I know you have your own ideas, but at this point, we aren't sure if Winnie is involved in this, or if we could possibly be dealing with a serial killer. I don't want to frighten you, but there are some similarities between your daughter's death and another case and we're hoping we won't find Winnie in a similar condition.

Campbell: What would it matter, anyway? I've already lost my baby girl.

WINNIE

The stone spins in the air as it falls. It barely misses the red sedan racing underneath us. I pick up another and roll it in my palm. I love the sensation, so smooth and cold. I bring it close to my face then suddenly hurl it as far as I can. Rotating through the air, it flies over the concrete then arcs downward. It falls to the ground with an audible clink then bounces up violently under the semi that roars over it.

"Winnie, I don't know if I can do this. I can't keep this up."

I don't acknowledge his words. Maybe if I don't say anything, he'll calm down and forget about it. I breathe in and then push all the air out, completely emptying my lungs.

"I'm getting really freaked out," he says. I toss another stone as far as I can. "Stop throwing rocks and listen to me for a goddamn minute! I'm scared."

I look at Gabe. He's shuffling his feet, looking down at the highway. There are bags under his eyes and he's licking his chapped lips. But I can sense he's not really scared. There's none of that feeling I've worked for years to control. I would know. I'd be able to feel it oozing from his pores.

"What is it really?" I ask as I chuck another rock. "What are you afraid of?"

His face darkens, and he picks up a sizable rock and toss-es it toward the grassy median where it disappears into one of the remaining patches of snow. He stares after it. Another truck rumbles under us and the overpass shakes slightly.

"Maybe you should turn yourself in." He says the words so nonchalantly, as if they didn't hold my entire fu-ture in their meaning. Then he throws another rock, never looking at me.

"Maybe I should what? Are you serious?" I grab his shoulder and force him to face me, but he turns his eyes toward the highway again.

"I think it's for the best. It would be best for everyone."

"What do you mean? That would be the worst possible thing I can imagine. Why are you saying this now? After we've gotten away with everything."

"You mean you've gotten away with everything. Don't drag me into this."

"How the hell can you say that? You're part of it now. Don't try to pretend you're not," I'm shouting, but he still doesn't look at me. He just drops his shoulders and taps his tongue ring against his teeth with an annoying *click click click*.

Finally, he looks me in the eye. "Honestly, this whole thing is out of control. You don't even seem like yourself lately. Don't kid yourself. Everyone notices how suspicious you're acting, and it's only a matter of time before they fig-ure it out. I mean, they have the goddamn body now." My jaw clenches and my teeth grind so hard they threaten to fracture. "They'll find the dog in the woods behind your yard. Then it'll turn out somebody saw you playing with her. I just know it. They'll figure it out. You've seen enough true crime shit to know how it all goes down."

"Some crimes do go unsolved, Gabe. Lots of them. Cold cases. There's nothing connecting me to her. It was the perfect crime. We said that." My voice cracks despite my efforts to appear calm.

"Come on now," he says as he puts his hand on my shoulder. "I know you well enough to know that you can't keep up this charade forever. It's the right thing to do."

"How? How can you be saying this?"

I'm starting to hyperventilate, pulling my hair, eyes wild. Gabe stares down at me with his hand still on my shoulder in faux compassion. I feel like a child, and it makes me hate him. A fantasy flashes in my head of pushing him over the railing into oncoming traffic, but then it dawns on me.

"You're not scared or concerned or anything like that. You're just worried about your own sorry ass. You think—" I interrupt myself with a laugh. "You think I'm going to take you down with me. You think they'll find some reason to question me, and I'll implicate you as an accessory immediately. Break under pressure. Hell, maybe even blame the whole thing on you! I mean, which one of us is the one with the criminal record again? I forget."

His arm drops limply back to his side. "Shut up, that's not it at all."

"Oh, that's not it? So that's not it at all. Then why, tell me Gabe, did you suddenly grow a goddamn conscience and want me to turn myself in? Whatever happened to living a life of doing whatever the hell we wanted? What happened to all your bullshit about power and control and freedom?"

He sighs and turns away from me again, leaning against the railing and staring far away. I'm panting with rage, waiting for an answer.

"Why? Tell me why, if that's not it. If I'm so wrong, then tell me the truth, but don't you dare try any more of that fake shit. Be honest with me. You made me promise to always be honest with you. It's the least you can do before you throw me to the fucking wolves."

A cloud of steam accompanies his sigh as he cranes his neck back, his face to the sky. When he turns back to me, all the darkness and worry have left his face. It's almost a look of pity.

"Okay, the truth. You're partially right. I actually am worried about all of those things. I sure as hell don't want to go to jail, especially for your weird psychotic kid shit, but that's not all." He tries to hold my hand, but I pull it away. "Winnie, really listen to me. You are seriously losing it. I'm not just saying this to be a jerk. It's true. You're not in control anymore. You think you are, but you're not. I don't know if this could be somehow tied to your mom's whole thing or if it's guilt tearing you apart or who knows, but this is not going to end like we want it to. I know you and now I realize, you are not going to be able to let it go and move on. I mean, maybe you'll prove me wrong, and that'd be great, but you're right, I don't want to go down with you. You're one of my best friends. Hell, I love you more than my own family, but I'm not giving up my life for you. If you're not going to turn yourself in, then fine. Don't. But if you don't, I'm not hanging around here waiting for you to slip up and ruin my life. You get it now?"

My breath slows as he tells me all of this, and I close my eyes to fully process it. As he finishes speaking, I feel his hand pushing my hair behind my ear and then combing it down with his fingers. I don't want to believe him, but I do. Maybe he even truly cares about me.

"What are you going to do?" I ask.

The silence between us is broken by a car blaring some Tejano song with its windows down. It's gone in a moment, but I can't help but roll my eyes at how these important moments in one's life are never as sacred and serious as you see in the movies.

"Well, I guess I'm going to leave town. I've been thinking about dropping out anyway. School's just not for me."

"I wish you wouldn't, but I can't stop you… Are you going to turn me in?"

"Never. I won't tell anyone ever."

"I know you don't trust me, you've told me as much, but I promise I'll never tell them about you helping if they catch me. But they won't! You really don't have to leave. Yeah, it sucks they found her, but they can't prove anything. Just stay and things can go back to normal. We can forget about all this shit." Tears are running down my face and I wipe them away with my coat sleeve, smearing my makeup and hating myself more with each passing second.

"Okay," he says, and we wait in a heavy silence for a few moments that crawl as slowly as hours. He means it. He's going to leave me all alone.

"When are you going to leave?"

"I'm thinking this weekend."

"Won't your mom miss you? She'll probably call the cops."

"No. She won't."

"She loves you in her own way. She'll miss you. Cry. Drink even more than usual."

He glares at me, and I drop the guilt trip.

"Fine. But what will you do? You don't have much money."

"I don't know, but I'll figure it out."

"You really won't tell me where you're going?"

"No. I just can't. Not now. You understand?"

"I guess." I attempt to say the words, but it explodes into a sob instead. Gabe pulls me against his chest and rocks me back and forth.

"Don't cry. Maybe I'll come back. Maybe I really am just all weirded out about this whole thing and everything will go back to normal, like you said, but if that's going to happen, you have to pull it together. I can feel you're on the edge. Don't jump off."

"God, Gabe, you sure know how to make things fucking dramatic," I half-laugh, half-cry. He chuckles.

"Here," he says and slips something into my pocket. "I don't want to leave you thinking I'm a total ass." I reach in and feel the glossy box. It must be his new tarot deck.

"Thanks."

"I don't know. Maybe I'm all wrong. I just feel something weird. Like a bad feeling. Maybe I need to leave for a few days and get my head together. Maybe I'm being all intense for no reason." We laugh, and he strokes my hair. "Just try to, well, stay normal. Let this blow over. This was all crazy shit, but it's over now. Here, let me drive you home."

"Thanks. I think I left my bus money in my other coat, so I really appreciate it."

"No problem."

We get into his jeep, and he drives me home with the top off, even though the cold air bites our faces red.

"I'll see you tomorrow at school, right?" I ask as I slide out of the car.

"Yeah, of course." He smiles and drives away as soon as I've shut the door.

WITNESS STATEMENT

I, Stephanie Jackson, of [address redacted] am the Claimant in this claim. The facts in this statement come from my personal knowledge.

On the date of December 16th, at approximately 11:30 pm, I heard voices arguing from behind the Campbell residence. I was walking my dog at the time and stopped momentarily to listen to the argument. I know the Campbells as casual acquaintances and could recognize the two voices as the eldest daughter, Winnie Campbell, and her younger sister, Lilly Campbell. Lilly said: "I don't want to. Please stop pushing me." Then Winnie said something to the effect of: "I don't care if you want to." At that point, Lilly started to cry and whimper. I decided to keep walking my dog since I felt this was a private matter and not any of my business. I walked an alternate route home and did not pass the Campbell residence again that night and did not hear any other unusual conversations or noises.

I believe that the facts stated in this witness statement are true.

Signed
Stephanie Jackson
Dated Dec. 19th

WINNIE

All day, my heart's been throbbing in my ears, deafeningly loud. Gabe's gone. At least, he's ignoring me. Just like he said, he won't answer my texts. I knew he meant it, but I can't help but feel lonely. It's probably better he's gone anyway. He might try to stop me.

The front door slams and Lilly drops her backpack on the floor, stomping toward her room. Another door slams, this time to her bedroom. I think to myself that I must not be the only one having a shitty day, although this quickly turns to resentment. Of course, everyone will feel bad for her and try to cheer her up while I won't get an ounce of sympathy, at most just an acknowledging shrug from Brendan. What kind of bad day could a child her age even have? Sneaking down the hall, I lightly press my ear against her door and listen for sobs but hear none. Back to the kitchen to slave away on a casserole that Lilly will most likely refuse to eat. At least Dad usually loves my casseroles, I think as I slice tomatoes for the side salad.

Lilly doesn't come out of her room until dinner, not to say hi to Brendan, and not when Dad makes his own door-slamming entrance. Despite his loud arrival, I see he's in a better mood than usual from the way he jokes around and rough-houses Brendan, grinning and probably smelling a little of liquor, although I don't want to get close enough to find out.

My blood still throbs in my ears as I think about another day without a punishment and smile. It's been three already. The record is forty-four, but I would never let my hopes rise that high. Plus, there's no hope at all, because I'm sure there will be one today. It will happen because I'm putting my foot down finally. My heart feels like it might burst from the nerves as I peek into the oven.

Sliding on the floors in her socks, Lilly slips into the kitchen and tries to sneak a couple grapes from the fridge, but I catch her.

"It's almost time for dinner. How about you help out and set the table?" I ask it as casually as possible, and it seems she doesn't really notice at first. I watch as comprehension furrows her brow.

"What? That's your job," she says and tries to walk away, but I put out my wooden spoon to block her path.

"Not today it's not. Today you're setting the table."

"I don't know how," she starts to whine, but I'm already prepared. I shove a stack of plates and a fistful of forks toward her.

"There's not much to put out today since it's just a casserole with salad. I'm pretty sure you're smart enough to figure out what to do," I say, winking, knowing that comment won't let her turn me down. With a scowl, she takes everything and stomps to the dining table, making sure to slam each plate down and drop each fork from shoulder height. Dad doesn't notice at first, but he comes to investigate the sound and sees the last fork drop.

"What are you doing, honey?" he asks. "Playing restaurant with your sister?"

"No," she snorts. "Winnie made me set the table even though that's her job."

"Hmmm," Dad says, but that's it. I don't see his face because it'd be too dangerous to look. Instead, I focus on taking out the casserole and checking it's done. After a few minutes, I finally decide it's safe and call everyone to dinner. Neither Dad nor Lilly look upset, and my heart slows for the first time today. I force the hopeful feeling back down my esophagus and drown it in food. There's no way things are changing. It's too late now. Unless it's not. A tentative look up to their happily slurping faces almost regurgitates the optimistic feeling onto the table.

Brendan finishes first and starts to get up, but Dad puts out an arm and stops him. Any trace of hope washes down my body and through the floor.

"Hold on, you're not excused yet. We're having a family dinner and you'll be excused when I say so," Dad says. Brendan sits back down, resting his head in his hand and occasionally biting at his fingernails as he waits for everyone to finish eating.

Dad finishes but sits there, not saying anything or even seeming to look at anything in particular. Lilly is done next, but she knows better than to try to be excused. No matter how tender and casual Dad's voice was, his message was clear. There will be a family matter to attend to when all is done. Even though I know it won't make any difference, I eat very slowly and savor the taste. The food has even started to get cold by the time I take my last bite. The end was inevitable, and I put down my fork in finality.

"Everybody's done. Can I go now?" Brendan asks, but Dad slams his hand down flat on the table, hushing him.

"Now, before dinner here, I witnessed a little altercation between you two sisters. Lilly, I'm gonna ask you first.

Tell me what happened." His voice booms and I can see Lilly is shaking a little, but there's no way her blood has run as cold as mine. Of course, she's too cowardly to look at me before she tells her ridiculous story.

"Well, uh, Winnie, she made me...she made me, uh, set the table. Even though it's her job..." Her voice trails off to a whisper.

"Did you want to help set the table?" Dad asks.

Lilly pulls her shoulders close to her ears, sinking inside herself, before answering, "No. I didn't want to do it."

"Why not?"

"Well... it's not my job. It's Winnie's job," Lilly answers and I chance a quick peek at Dad. He's nodding thoughtfully, his hand still planted on the table. I knew this rebellion would lead to a punishment, but as it comes closer to actualization, I find myself paralyzed with fear.

Dad takes a long drink from his beer can and slowly shakes his head. "And what do you have to say for yourself?"

"I-I-I just... it was j-just," I stammer along before stopping myself to take a deep breath. My heart pounds in my ears as I turn the rest of me to ice. "I thought it was about time Lilly had some responsibilities too."

There's not the fiery explosion I expected, just a wry smile crossing his face. Lilly stares. Brendan is obviously spaced out and not paying attention to the 'family meeting' at all, probably ever since he realized it doesn't directly involve him. Dad leans back in his chair and chuckles a little to himself.

"Daddy! You can't be serious. That's Winnie's job! I'm not supposed to have to help with all the house stuff. I'm just a kid," Lilly whines then begins to cry. I want to laugh but I don't trust that Dad is finished yet.

"Hmmm, some responsibilities, huh?" Dad asks and then chuckles again. Lilly's pleas have risen to that irritating falsetto that is closer to a dog whistle than human speech.

I know I shouldn't, but I can't help but release the whisper I'm dying to say, "Don't be such a crybaby, Lilly."

The words hiss out and at first, I think maybe no one heard, but Lilly turns to me, her eyes wide with shock, and she somehow manages to raise her cries up two or three more octaves. I roll my eyes and look away only to be hit by something slimy from her direction. I peel it off my face to reveal it's a chunk of caramelized onion from the chicken casserole.

"Why, you spoiled brat!" I shout and immediately clamp my hands over my mouth. My eyes dart to Dad but he looks exactly the same. Back to Lilly, her jaw dropped in startled silence.

"Come over here, Winnie," the low, calm voice calls to me from across the table. My jaw clenches and I stand up slowly. Any resistance would just make it worse. Mechanical steps around the table, nearing my father, his face a mask without emotion. When I'm standing right next to him, he turns to me.

His mouth pulls itself up in a friendly grin, cheekbones rosy, as he says, "Pull down your pants."

My face crumples like a wadded paper and tears I didn't know were waiting flow down my face at the audacity of his command. I take a micro-step backwards and ball my fists without meaning to as I look back and forth between the surprised faces of my siblings.

"Drop your goddamn pants, girl. Now!" he says.

I can't. I can't do that. I'm shaking my head frantically and backing away a few more steps.

"I'm sixteen, Dad. I'm not going to do that," I say, but he's up from his chair in a flash. He grabs me by my hair, yanks at my belt, and pulls down both my pants and underwear. I see Brendan avert his eyes from my nakedness and I'm grateful. Lilly pushes back her chair from the table to gain distance from us but stares anyway.

Dad pulls me over his lap. At first, he spanks me like a little child, with quick sharp slaps, but his rage is building and culminates in punches so deep they seem to bruise my bones.

Crying, snot pouring down my face, I wriggle but can't get free. I look to Brendan and he's watching now, but when our eyes meet, he looks away again. Waves of shame pulse through me. I can't see Lilly, she's behind me, but at least I don't hear her laughing. That bitch, she's the devil. She wanted this to happen. Each strike ignites a raging flame in my belly. The flame grows until I am nothing but a conflagration of shame and anger. By the time he's finished, I am no longer. I've burned away and there's nothing left but hate.

"Get up," his gruff voice commands, and I obey. I stumble from his lap, wiping tears and mucus from my wet face with shaking hands. As I pull up my underwear and pants together, I wince as they pass over the places he savaged. I can just imagine the black and purple bruises already forming and how difficult it will be to hide my pain when sitting. All part of the punishment, all intended side effects, I'm sure. As I begin to walk away, Dad slaps me, and I almost fall to my knees. I wasn't expecting it.

"Now I think you've learned who's the one who needs to take responsibility here. Responsibility for treating your sister so bad," he tells me through gritted teeth, and I nod, feigning complete submission with my downcast eyes. It pleases him, and I'm released.

I walk, never run, to my bedroom and shut the door as gently as possible. Alone, I bare my teeth and snarl. Seething with anger, I pace back and forth, back and forth. I'm planning. I'm planning it all. Tonight, it'll happen. I need to be free. This is the only way.

It's only been a few minutes when a knock at the door startles me. I collapse back into my weak disguise.

"Wh-who is it?" I ask in my meekest voice.

"Go clean up from dinner already. I don't want us getting roaches or any shit like that. And put your sister to bed," Dad yells through the door.

"Yes, sir," I say, and play my part as the good little slave for the last time.

LILLY

Winnie is waking me up, shaking and shaking me. I try to pull the covers tight over my body and bury my face in the pillow, but she pulls both away. She's whispering, and at first, I can't understand her. I look out the window and see it's still night. I don't understand. My head is groggy and dream-like.

"Get dressed, quick," she whispers at me, but I shake my head. I start to cry a little. I want to go back to sleep. I can tell it is very, very late. Even the TV is off, and Dad is snoring down the hall. She repeats it, but I ignore her, turning away from her and scooting myself toward the wall. Maybe she'll go away. She's shaking me again and I'm crying louder until *smack*. She slaps my cheek and it's burning with pain. I shush my cries and sit up to look at her.

Winnie's eyes are wild, both scared and scary at the same time. I've never seen anyone look this way before. I know it must be serious since she hit me. She's never hit me.

She thrusts some daytime clothes toward me, and I take them, dressing as quickly as I can. My hands are shaking, and I can't stop myself from looking around the room, looking for anything to explain this. Something scary must be waiting for us and we have to get away.

Winnie's behind me, pulling my arms through my coat. Forcing myself to look over my shoulder, I can see her face is softer and I relax a tiny bit. I can breathe a little better as she shoves my shoes on, but I don't dare to point out that they're on the wrong feet. I can fix that later. Now is a time to hurry. Why are we dressed to go out? I look out the window again, but the dark night is still waiting there.

"What's happening? I don't understand," I whisper, but she doesn't answer right away, just looks out the window with me. I can feel the tension and I wonder, is this an emergency? I always wondered what an emergency felt like. I force out the words, "Are we in danger?"

She turns toward me with a frown. I feel myself shrinking as I stare into her big eyes. The pupils grow so large that the light blue surrounding them is barely visible.

"Just keep quiet. We're going outside," she says, and I nod, but can't move. She gently tries to push me toward the door, but my feet have grown roots into the carpet, completely stuck.

"Why are we going outside? Where are we going?" I ask.

She sighs but doesn't look at me, just pushes harder. I still don't move. My whole body is shaking, but I'm more confused than afraid. If she would just tell me, I could move my feet, go with her.

She refuses, opting instead to pick me up and swing me onto her back, like the piggyback rides from when I was smaller. I can't help but melt into her shoulders.

With a grunt and some huffing, she carries me through the quiet house. I've never seen the house this late at night and I'm awed by the way the shadows of furniture stretch across the floor in disturbing shapes. Turning my head slowly, I scan each room, taking in the strange scenery, until we slip through the backdoor into the yard.

It's very cold, even with my coat, and I'm shivering as Winnie puts me down. The grass crunches under my feet, frosted blue-green across the yard. We're walking toward the forest. I keep looking back at the house. The icy air stabs inside my lungs and I finally emerge completely from my sleepy daze and really look at my sister.

She's dressed different from normal, more layers, that puffy coat she always says she hates, her P.E. shoes. I've never seen her dressed like this. She's wearing her school backpack and not her usual black purse. There's no makeup on her face and its broad, white blankness makes my stomach lurch, yet I'm still walking beside her.

I trip over a rock, and she catches my arm, yanking me along, not letting go. We're almost at the forest and I look back to the house only to receive another rough tug. I stop and grind my heels into the dirt. She almost loses her balance before she lets go and turns to face me.

My mind buzzes as I try to decide what's happening. She looks angry. Is it because of what happened at dinner? I didn't mean to get her in trouble. Not big trouble like that. She must know that. We all have to save ourselves however we can, and she's the strongest. I could never be that strong. I hope I grow up to be more like her.

But today, that was too much. We all know that. I was angry at Dad with her. I tried to turn away, but he made us watch. But she knows I'd never tell anyone about it. I love her too much. She protects me.

We must be in danger to be leaving in the middle of the night, but then, why does she look so angry? Does Dad have something worse planned and we're escaping? What about Brendan? Or is this to teach Dad a lesson, disappear for a couple days and show him how much he needs us? I don't think he'll learn anything from that. Poor Dad can't help it. He wants to be a good dad, but he can't.

Winnie shakes my shoulders, bending slightly with her face close to mine. "Come on," she hisses, but I stay still and build up the courage to talk.

"No, Winnie, stop. What's happening?" My voice creaks in my parched throat. "Dad is sleeping. I heard him. We don't have to hide."

"We have to go in the woods now. Okay?" she asks but I can tell there's really no choice. Still, I stay anchored to the ground.

She's pushing my back and I cry out, "I don't want to! Please stop pushing me, Winnie!"

"I don't care if you want to," she says, but I won't let her push me. I drop to the ground.

Her face softens and she kneels, now looking into my eyes with kindness. She starts to speak but suddenly stops herself and pulls me against her, bowing her head into my coat and holding me tight in her arms. I smile, hug her back, and then I hear her muffled sobbing and feel the vibrations echo in my ribcage. I play with her hair, just like she does when I'm sad, and hum a little song I learned at school, but she cries harder. I've never seen Winnie cry like this, but sometimes it's good to cry.

I'm glad I'm not wearing gloves as I pull my fingers through her blonde waves and I think about how beautiful she is, even if she does have a few burn scars. She can be mean sometimes, but she's my sister and I love her forever. I whisper this last part and she finally stops. Slowly, she takes my arms in her hands and pushes me just far enough away that we are eye to eye again.

"We have to go in the woods now. We just have to, okay?" she asks, but I bite my lip and shake my head a little.

"Don't you trust me?" she asks, and I nod. She stands up, takes out a flashlight, and walks into the woods. I hesitate only a moment longer before I follow.

Branches catch on my hair and jacket as we stumble through the brush. The flashlight bobs with our steps and my eyes have mostly adjusted, but it's still hard to see. I almost trip on a root but catch myself only to feel a bramble scrape across my face. Hot tears run down my cheeks, but I keep my crying quiet. This must be a really bad emergency, I have to stay strong.

"I want to go back home. It's scary out here," I tell her, but maybe she doesn't hear me. We go on. We walk maybe ten minutes, then come into a tiny clearing. I remember being here before. A long time ago, Dad tore down all the branches and even cut up a big tree to build a playhouse out here, but all he managed to do was lug over a couple boards before the project was forgotten. Two-by-fours are leaned up against an old log, and I smile a little at the thought.

"I remember this place. Those were happy days, before Dad got mad all the time," I say, and I think I see Winnie smile a little. "I wish things were like they used to be."

"Me too," she says.

"But Winnie, what are we doing out here? Are we hiding?" I ask as I look around the clearing. Winnie doesn't answer, instead dropping to her knees and rummaging through her backpack. Suddenly, she turns off the flashlight and the dark surrounds us except for the bit of moonlight peeping through the branches overhead. I gasp my breath into my lungs and hold it there for a moment, trying to keep out the darkness.

"Turn on the light! Turn on the light! It's too dark!" I shout, but then she's on me, pushing me backward so hard that I fall flat on my back and hit my head on the dirt and roots. I'm crying and she's scrambling on top of me, shushing me like a mother to a baby. I try to scream, but she pushes her hand over my mouth, and I just moan against the palm instead. I can't control my eyes, I'm looking everywhere in the darkness, trying to understand, yet I can't look at her, my sister, because I know then something bad will happen. I don't understand, and I just want to understand.

"Lilly, listen. Lilly," she whispers, her breath warm against my face. I try to bite at her hand, but she smacks me with the other and I stop. I'm whimpering, shaking, begging her to stop with my wide-open eyes. She smiles like it's all an innocent game. My heart beats painfully in my chest. Shushing me again, her free hand strokes my cheek.

"I just can't take it anymore, understand? God, of course you don't. Everything has always been perfect for you, there's no way you could understand. Well, it doesn't matter anyway," she says and reaches behind her.

Then I see it. A knife. The big knife from the kitchen. It glints in the moonlight and my bladder lets go, warmth gushing down my legs. I have to go home.

I'm up. I'm running. I'm pushing through branches, but they're caught on me, holding me back. My arms flail in all directions, trying to get through. As I break free of the branches, I hear her. She's right behind me.

She grabs me. I scream, and she pulls my hair back hard. I'm scratching at her. Red lines trickle blood from her face and neck. I'm hurting her. I keep scratching. Then I feel a sharp punch in my gut and another. I look down and see the blood pouring out. Lots and lots of it, all over me. I'm instantly dizzy, but I know I can't let myself pass out. I reach down, try to hold it in, but it flows hot through my fingers.

I scream as loud as I can and turn to run again, but I feel it ripping through my back, tearing me open. Heat floods me in pulsing waves of nausea, but I push on. I'm vomiting and stumbling, and she's still hurting me. The knife is coming down again and again, tearing gashes in my back. I can't stop now. Crawling, getting back up, stumbling again. I have to keep going. She's still there, hurting me over and over. The cold air is filling voids deep inside and I see wet, secret pieces of myself on the ground below. I know I can't keep going anymore.

I fall down, and my arms are so heavy, I can't get back up. My fingers reach out for anything, but there's nothing but dirt. My body is so heavy now. I twist and focus on breathing. I'm trying but it's so hard to get any air in. I just want one more breath!

I know she's standing over me. I don't want to look at her, but I understand. I try to say her name, but just a gurgling noise comes out. The sharp pain fades in and out with each small breath I manage to take. I'm so sleepy. A coldness creeps through me, dulling the throbbing pain. I think I hear her say "I'm sorry," but maybe I don't. I close my eyes and let the heavy sleepy feeling pull me under.

GABRIEL WALSH

POLICE INTERVIEW TRANSCRIPT
PART 2

DEC. **19**

Det. Garcia: Thank you for coming back in to talk with us again.

Walsh: Of course. I hope everything from yesterday helped at least a little, but honestly, I don't know what else I can tell you.

Det. Garcia: Everything you've told us has been very helpful, but we uh... we need to talk about some phone records now.

Walsh: Phone records?

Det. Garcia: Hold on, I'm going to get Wilson in here to talk to you about it. He's got the records. Let me go get him.

Det. Wilson: Hey Gabe, thanks for coming back.

Walsh: Yeah, uh, Detective Garcia said you want to talk to me about some phone records?

Det. Wilson: Yeah, yeah. That's why we called you to come back in. We need to talk about these texts between you and Winnie. They're, well, a little disconcerting, Gabe.

Walsh: What texts?

Det. Wilson: Well, we have Winnie's phone, and based on a couple things we saw there, we also got a warrant for some of your phone records. We have all the times and dates of both of your phone calls and texts, as well as the content of the text messages. Doesn't matter that you deleted them. We were able to get them anyway. It seems there are some of these texts, well some entire conversations actually, that we're a little confused about. Maybe you can clear this up a bit?

Walsh: I don't know what you're talking about.

Det. Wilson: Come on now, don't play dumb. I know you're a smart kid. If you just tell me about these texts, I'm sure we can work this all out.

Walsh: I seriously don't know what the fuck you're talking about!

Det. Wilson: Now calm down there, Gabe—

Walsh: Is this about—about—uh, those detective shows we watched? Oh man, is that what this is? Because we would watch all these murder shows and text about them and after everything that's happened, I could see how that could look bad but—

Det. Wilson: Slow down. Take a deep breath. I can tell you're really on edge, but I just want to know the truth. I'm sure this is all a misunderstanding, but we are definitely not talking about some show. We are talking about several text conversations that seem to be linked to—

Walsh: No, stop it! You're wrong. I don't know what you think you know, but it's not true! I'm telling you the truth. We texted about murder and dark shit all the time. Sometimes maybe we even pretended we were involved or something, and that must be what you're talking about. I'm not going to prison for some stupid texts because you can't find Winnie!

Det. Wilson: Gabe, stop it and listen. Really listen to me. We have some texts that indicate you might have something to do with another missing person. Not Winnie, but a little girl named Leigh Bennings. She went missing back in November and, well, there's some very bad news about her...

Walsh: What?

Det. Wilson: We found her body a few weeks ago. There's no way you haven't heard about it by now. It's been all over the news. Don't try to pretend you didn't know that. Now, what I need to talk to you about are these texts because some of them have us wondering if maybe you know something about this girl.

Walsh: What? What the hell are you talking about? I have no idea who that girl is or what could possibly be going through your head to make you think I know anything about any of this!

Det. Wilson: It's all right here. Wait. Here, take a look for yourself. She uses Leigh's name right here and... here. And then this whole conversation here, it's plain to see that you're concerned. I know you know something about this, but you're gonna have to tell me the truth, or else it's just gonna be worse for you. If you don't tell me, well, then we're going to have to assume some bad things about you, Gabe. And I know you're not a monster, right?

Walsh: I already told you, I don't have any fucking idea what you're talking about!

Det. Wilson: Stop cussing at me, I'm trying to help you out. Look right here, at this conversation. It sounds like you wanted to get help, but Winnie wouldn't let you. Was it an accident, Gabe? Did things just get out of hand?

Walsh: What?

Det. Wilson: You say here that Winnie was "obsessed" with her. What did you mean by that?

Walsh: I don't know, I don't even remember any of this. These don't look like my texts. You're just trying to pin this on me!

Det. Wilson: Tell me what happened that day with Leigh. What did Winnie and you want with her? She was such a pretty little girl, was that it? Was it—

Walsh: Don't you even, you disgusting pig!

Det. Wilson: Okay, okay. Calm down, I told you already to stop disrespecting me. I'm trying to help you out. I need to know the truth from you or else we have to go with what the evidence is telling us, and that's not a story that ends well for you.

Walsh: I don't know what Winnie did, but I have no idea what any of this is about.

Det. Wilson: Oh Gabe. I know. We know. It's okay. You can talk to me about this. Tell me what happened, and I can help you. I promise.

Walsh: No, I don't know what you're talking about!

Det. Wilson: I'm trying to help you out, but if you don't want to talk about this, then we're going to have to arrest you. Is that what you want? We have some very compelling evidence that you were a part of this. DNA evidence, and you watch enough true crime shows to know how juries feel about DNA.

Walsh: That's not true. You're lying.

Det. Wilson: Hey, Garcia! Can you bring me that DNA profile we got from the duffle bag?

Walsh: No. No. That's not true.

Det. Wilson: What's not true, Gabe?

Walsh: I didn't do anything to that girl! I don't know what you're talking about with these texts and duffle bags and all this bullshit!

Det. Wilson: Stop it, stop it! Sit down. You need to calm down right now and listen. This is important. Oh, thanks Garcia. Okay, here we have the DNA analysis.

Walsh: You don't have my DNA; how can you know it's a match?

Det. Wilson: Are you so sure about that?

Walsh: Let me out of here. You can't keep me in here.

Det. Wilson: Gabe, take a deep breath and tell me the truth. That's the only way you're ever getting out of here.

Walsh: I want to call my mom.

Det. Wilson: We can't let you do that right now.

Walsh: Then I want a lawyer. I'm not talking to you anymore.

EVIDENCE: HANDWRITTEN LETTER BY MR. COLE CAMPBELL TO MS. EDWINA CAMPBELL.

NOT MAILED
DATED APPROX. JANUARY 1ST.
FOUND IN MR. CAMPBELL'S VEHICLE
NEAR BODY.

Dear Winnie,

I've been sober for the past week and I'm finally ready to do it. Say it all. As I write this, knowing you probably won't ever read it, I honestly want to cry. I want to cry for you, but I can't get myself to do it. It's been bottled up way too long by now. Okay, I'll just say it. I was a shit dad. I always was, from the very beginning, even with Brendan. I'll admit, especially with you. You and I both know why, but I suppose it wasn't really your fault. I think I've always known it wasn't, but I just couldn't let it go. That's not an excuse. It's just the truth.

I loved her so much, even with all her flaws. You can't imagine the kind of love we shared. Those years, before you kids came along, were the happiest years of my life. I don't think anyone has ever been as fucking happy as we were. Then it all had to change.

She wasn't the best mother, but at least she tried. I gave up trying after she died. I guess you know that. Except with Lilly. I really tried to be good to Lilly. She looked so much like Theresa. The same dark hair and sly smile. I never noticed those things until she was gone. They even had the same laugh, only Lilly's was like the little girl version.

I couldn't help but see Theresa every time I looked at Lilly. I didn't mean to favor her, but I know I did. It was obvious I did. I did even worse than that. There's no need to get into all of it, but I think I was trying to kill your spirit. Maybe I was even trying to kill you. I don't remember anymore. It just kind of became the way things were after Theresa. I didn't mean for any of this to happen.

What about forgiveness? That's what Brendan asked me the other day, God help him. Forgiveness was never an option. I couldn't forgive you for pushing her past her limit. The hammering, the late-night rants, and the sleepless nights. We all suffered, Winnie. It wasn't just you. But the rest of us knew to let her be. She would calm down eventually. Things were going to get better. I swear to God, we were so fucking close to the end of all that shit! You didn't know this, but she had agreed to see a doctor again. She was going to start taking a new medication. She had an appointment all set up with the psychiatrist for the next week. I was with her when she set it. But no, you couldn't just let her have a couple more nights, could you?

We were all suffering. She was suffering too. I think you didn't see it. You didn't see your own mother was suffering. The mother that loved you more than anything was fighting her own demons, and you didn't care that she was in agony? I know, I know. You were just a kid. I have to keep reminding myself, even now.

She never meant to hurt you. She wasn't herself. It was the illness. There were voices in her head. It wasn't that she wanted to hurt you; she was confused. It was like she was someone else entirely. You must know, that wasn't your mother that did that to you.

She loved you like you wouldn't believe. I can remember the day you were born like it was yesterday. Theresa couldn't stop smiling, even as exhausted as she was. She was so happy to finally have a little girl to dress up. She'd been wishing for you her entire life. All those little pink dresses she made for you, with little fabric roses and lace around the edges. All those dolls and bunnies and the stupid wooden rocking horse with painted-on eyelashes and braided rope hair. All that shit for a daughter that wouldn't give her a chance to change things.

She never meant to hurt you, but I sure as hell did. That's not easy for me to write, even knowing you won't read it. It feels strange to admit it like that. I know deep down it was wrong, but I can't bring myself to feel too bad about it, even when I try. Everything gets all mixed up and I feel angry again. I feel like beating your ass all over again, just like you deserve.

I know I brought all this ruin on our family myself. I wish you could know how truly sorry I am. Sorry that I let you do that to my Theresa. Sorry that I couldn't save her. Sorry I didn't lock you in some room and throw away the key. Sorry that I didn't send you off to live with my mother. I never told you, but she offered to take you girls when Theresa died. Said they needed a woman's influence. But I couldn't let Lilly go. She was so pissed, that's why she hardly ever called or came by. Maybe you didn't notice. It turns out, that might have been the best choice I ever could've made, but I was too stubborn to see it. I've thought about that every day since you took my Lilly and left. You'll be happy to hear that the guilt has burrowed holes throughout my entire soul thinking about that. You'd smile to see me now, and a small part of me doesn't blame you.

I'm a damned bastard with a leather heart and I treated all three of you kids wrong. It's the truth, and I'm a horrible man who will probably rot in hell for all I've done. I'm hoping not, even though I probably deserve it. All I want is to be with my family again, behind those pearly gates. Maybe God'll let me look through and catch a glimpse of my Theresa, my Lilly. Maybe you're there too since they still haven't found you. Brendan goes on and on about God's mercy, so maybe he can do what I can't. Or maybe you'll be waiting for me by Satan's side.

Where'd you go that night? I wish I could know the answer to so many things. Did you kill that dog they found in the woods? Did you hurt that other little girl? Why would you do that? Some random little girl you didn't even know. You always seemed to love children. But then again, I thought you loved my little Lilly too.

You called her your little Lillian-Lemon-Pie. That was before Theresa went away and everything fell apart. You used to hold her in your arms and sing to her. I loved you most back then. There was a time when you were precious to me. Maybe I will feel that way again when we meet on the other side. Maybe heaven is a fresh start, all a family again.

Fuck this letter. It's pointless after all. You'll probably never read it, only maybe Brendan will, and if he reads it, I want him to know I love him and I'm sorry I wasn't a better dad. I'm also sorry about this goodbye. I was always shitty at goodbyes. There was probably a better way than this, but I don't have any energy to try anymore.

I guess it's time to go. I have everything ready. The rubber hose and everything all set up. I'm a selfish bastard for hoping it's painless when I know what my Lilly went through, but I can't help it. If you're already gone, I wonder, was it painful for you too? Slow and excruciating? I don't know if I want that. Or are you out there somewhere? I hope you're dead and gone so I can have another shot at everything. Maybe God will have mercy and take us all back to the beginning and let us live it again, the right way. I could love you again. I could stop us from ruining everything and we could all be happy like it used to be. I'm gonna go hoping for that. That's the only solace I've got left in this empty heart of mine.

See you on the other side,
Dad

WINNIE

Everything was ready before I went to wake her up. My bed made, the backpack full of necessary items, and a final text each to my only friends. Of course, I had to leave the phone there on my nightstand. I couldn't take it with me. I didn't bother to put on makeup except for a slight rub of foundation over my scars, just to minimize them a bit. I hate it when that's all people can see. I had a real plan this time. A better plan than before.

I was the hairy worm, for months nestled in its cozy cocoon, and now finally emerging as something wonderful.

After it was over, I dropped the knife. No need to bother about fingerprints or DNA or anything like that. I had become a new person right then and there. My metamorphosis complete through her blood.

I did make sure to check for a pulse before I left her though. Even though I hated her, I also loved her. She was still my sister. Fingers pressed to her clammy, pale neck; I could rest assured that I didn't leave her to die alone. She had moved on to the nothingness that awaits us all, and a surge of power coursed through my veins when I fully grasped that I had sent her there. Neither of us would have to worry about anything anymore. I stood reborn and she could waste away into dirt and bones. We weren't very deep in the woods, but I knew nobody would find her until daylight. I had time.

Feeling my cheek, I ran my fingers over the already scabbing scratches from her fingernails. She put up more of a fight than I expected. Maybe she was a little like me deep down after all. I whispered a goodbye before I left her and walked into the woods, my backpack heavy and the straps digging into my shoulders. I whispered a goodbye and good riddance to Mom too. It could all be over now. I had everything I needed, and they would never find Winnie: the life-taker, the murderer. She didn't exist anymore. I've become like a moth, finally transformed and bursting free from my cocoon. I knew what I needed to do.

Walking without panic, slow and methodical, I was a new girl. No, not a girl, but something different altogether. Nameless, powerful, and finally almost free.

ACKNOWLEDGEMENTS

I cannot express how thankful I am to all the people who helped make this book a reality. My husband Martin has always been my biggest supporter, held my hand through all the emotional rollercoasters, gave me time and space to write, worked through plot holes while we chain-smoked on a balcony in Amsterdam, and allowed me to follow my dreams to become a writer. My sisters Tara and Hannah also offered endless support and helped with each draft of this fucked up story. I can't thank all three of you enough. I love you so much.

My agent, Clara Chuiton, has been my champion, fighting for this and all the other sad, disturbing stories I dream up. Thank you for believing in me. Also, thank you to both Clara and Evelyn for helping to edit and polish this novel.

Thank you to all my family and friends who have supported my journey to become a published writer and encouraged me to never give up. Thank you especially to my dad for teaching me to read and write at a young age, nurturing my creativity, and "publishing" my first books about Bunny and Bear in Emma Land. It's because of you I fell in love with storytelling.

Finally, thank you to everyone who picked up this book. All I've ever wanted was to share my writing with the world and you have made that possible.

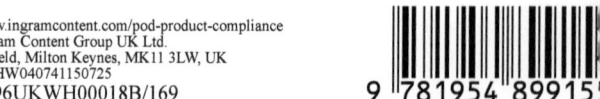